HOWE·LIBRARY

HANOVER
NEW HAMPSHIRE

Also by Christopher Tilghman

The Way People Run: Stories
Mason's Retreat
In a Father's Place

ROADS OF THE HEART

ROADS OF THE HEART

A NOVEL

Christopher Tilghman

 RANDOM HOUSE — NEW YORK

Copyright © 2004 by Christopher Tilghman

Library of Congress Cataloging-in-Publication Data
Tilghman, Christopher.
Roads of the heart : a novel / Christopher Tilghman.
p.   cm.
ISBN 0-679-45780-1
1. Middle-aged men—Fiction.   2. Conflict of generations—Fiction.
3. Parent and adult child—Fiction.   4. Fathers and sons—Fiction.
5. Divorced people—Fiction.   6. Married people—Fiction.   7. Aging
parents—Fiction.   8. Adultery—Fiction.   I. Title.
PS3570.I348A49 2004
813'.54—dc22
2003060311

Printed in the United States of America on acid-free paper

Random House website address: www.atrandom.com

2 4 6 8 9 7 5 3 1

FIRST EDITION

DESIGN BY MERCEDES EVERETT

To my brothers,
Ben, Bill, and James

All the true fragments are here.

—John Ashbery

Roads of the Heart

ONE

The sound his father had made was "mop-jeck," or perhaps "mott-seck."

"I'm sorry?" Eric leaned forward. He was sitting on the edge of a hospital bed, a wood-grained model that the man from the rental company had suggested for a "gentleman's décor"; his left buttock was asleep. They were speaking over the insistent tinny hum of an electric space heater. They were sitting in his father's bookish study. Outside the door, the grandfather clock ticked. His father was installed in his wingback chair, which was where he always spent most of these Sunday afternoons, resting after the exertions of church. He had a steel hospital bed table drawn tight in front of him, as if to keep him from pitching forward. He had been listening quietly as Eric did the usual: emptied his mind of news, whatever stray bits, factoids, and epiphanies he could conjure out of the gray background of his suburban life. It was like chanting, this largely one-way form of conversing, an exercise in the free-ranging self-examination one might engage in while praying, or on an analyst's couch. Unless his father grabbed the bait on a certain subject, Eric would just keep tossing out the line.

It was a dreary March day, casting the kind of spiritual light that seems to illuminate one's vague fears and concealed regrets.

That was the sort of thing Eric had been speaking about, whether he and Gail had made the right choices; whether their son, Tom, blamed him for his uncertain start in life; whether happiness is something you earn and whether unhappiness is a punishment for your sins. It was an odd, rather Calvinistic line for Eric to take: he had erred enough in life not to seek that sort of scorekeeping.

"Mottsecks," his father said again, working his mouth around its hurried emptiness.

Eric's father, Frank Alwin, had been a handsome man with a thin and craggy face, a serious nose and strong chin. He was tall and, though quite slender, had always given the impression of power: a gangly welterweight who might still deliver a brutal punch. He had been a dairy farmer of sorts, enough to give him troublesome skin and a penetrating, sun-narrowed scowl, but his real career had been as a state senator in his native Maryland, a career that he conspired to the level of majority leader before his enemies' plots and his own deep character flaws brought him to his knees. Since then, age and physical calamities had ravaged his body: it was hard to think of any major medical event he had not been through, even if the Big One still seemed well in the future. But because he had lost so much of the use of his body, his eyes could seem almost magical in their ability to communicate, as if his soul had moved from his damaged heart and scrambled brain and taken up residence on those surfaces; the eyes, moist and youthful, quick as cats. Still, when a word is needed, even magic cannot replace it. It mattered to Frank, this ragged verbal fragment, and he looked at Eric desperately but not hopelessly, as if by trying once more, he could make the air in his voicebox behave itself and produce the sounds he imagined so precisely. He pointed his thumb back at his chest and said it again. "Mottsecks. Me."

Eric had long ago devised an expression for times like this, when the word mattered. It was what one does with a friend who stutters, a look of support and patience, a calming and confident arching of the eyebrows, a face frozen, ready to reanimate as soon as the battle in the mouth's soft tissue was done.

"Shit," Frank said. Some years ago he had "plateaued," as the speech therapists put it, but short words beginning with sibilants had always been easy. "Help."

"Was it something I said?"

Frank sighed, deep with the frustration that would never be lifted. His blue eyes became moister. This state was actually not so new for him: his emotions had always been too big for him to contain: passions had led him astray; his softheartedness had caused him to hurt people. Tough on the outside; putty in the middle. That's what had taken Eric most of his fifty-plus years to figure out about this man, a man who never admitted his faults, never apologized, seemed never to feel an ounce of guilt. "Don't explain; don't apologize": that had been his unofficial creed in his political life. A typical postwar man, not one of a "greatest generation" but a human being deformed by history: that's what Eric had initially concluded back when he used it as a reason for damnation. He had since rediscovered this explanation as a reason to forgive. But it all, the deformation and the subsequent charade, had to have taken a toll; none of it was natural. Eric had been assuming that for years now, inside, his father was bleeding from the wounds.

For a moment it seemed Frank would try the word again, his face tensing for the effort, but then he gave up. "Shit," he said again. "Skip it."

"No. Let's get it. I've got time." Eric tried not to wince as a sudsy mid-Atlantic storm began to splatter against the windows. The drive back up the New Jersey Turnpike in this slush would be hell; he imagined a wreck somewhere near the Cherry Hill water tower that would back up traffic all the way to the Delaware Memorial Bridge. It was Sunday. He always made these trips on Sunday, the day one finally has to make good on everything procrastinated on through the week and weekend.

Frank shook his head but mouthed the damnable word again; his lips were loose and rubbery. Two syllables, soft at the beginning. Sometimes these clues meant something; sometimes they didn't. "Grammy," Eric said, an impulse. It didn't sound anything like the word, but earlier they had been looking at a picture of his grandmother, who had been dead for forty years. Frank had been organizing old photographs, his latest project. "Garden," said Eric, momentarily caught on words that began with "G." It was probably time to order seeds, not that the vegetable and flower gardens on the place had ever been of interest to Frank. Gardens were something imposed on the place, and on Frank, by Alice, his elder daughter.

"No, no, no." Frank pounded his hospital table in frustration, but the attempt came out this time as a plea. "Mottsecks. Help."

Eric tried to recall exactly what he had been saying when his father interrupted, an impossible task since he was only rarely aware of what was coming out of his mouth in these conversations. From visit to visit he could rattle on at length about almost nothing: who would have thought to tell his elderly father about his neighbor's new dog, how the housebreaking was going, the installation of an invisible fence? This could be an effective kind of torture, like riding coast to coast in an airplane with one of those people who like people. It reminded Eric of the patient-sitting jobs he used to get at the Mary Hitchcock Memorial Hospital in Hanover, New Hampshire, back during Gail and his fling as rural hippies. Companionship during the long deep hours of the night was the point, but the patients were mostly cancer-ridden old farmers, and Eric was a hippie with long hair and a beard, and he believed that fertilizer was poison, that mechanized farming was evil, that the world was running out of oil anyway.

Off in the house, he could hear Adam Miller making tea. It was an odd arrangement, by Eastern Shore standards, a man as a nurse and a housekeeper for a gentleman; not quite right. What sort of man would do that work, Eric himself asked when Alice proposed Adam almost two years ago.

"What is that supposed to mean," she snapped back. "Are you asking if he's gay?" Alice liked to get to the heart of things, although the real person she was defending was their younger sister, Poppy, who was gay and lived in Houston.

Eric wasn't asking that and he had never done anything in his life but support Poppy. She was the lost baby, the one they all loved best. "I'm just making sure you checked him out," he said to Alice.

Alice didn't answer. Of course she had done everything but hire a private detective.

"What does Dad think of him?" asked Eric.

"I don't think Dad has that much of a choice."

"Still."

"I think he likes him."

And so he did. It was Adam who helped Frank get started in the morning, tied his neckties, faced the daily task of giving him speech, filling in the blanks, writing the letters, making the telephone calls. Frank seemed to accept from the beginning that a man who had been married twice, divorced bitterly by the first—the mother of his children—and widowed by his second, and who had behaved wretchedly to both, probably should end up largely in the company of men. Ever since Marjorie, his second wife, had died of cancer, that's the way his life had been anyway.

Eric gave his father what he hoped was a sympathetic smile and was met by a shrug. "What a bummer," Eric said. The wind rattled the windows; the chill seeped into the room.

"Don't know." It came out "Du-now." He meant, as he had previously been able to make clear, that after more than ten years of this he'd come to believe that an inability to speak was an affliction only his God could have served up as a test, a punishment, a preparation for the eternal fire. He did not like others, especially his son, dismissing his own private destiny—brutal as it was—as merely bad luck, simply a weak fitting in his brain plumbing.

"Sure," Eric said. "Sorry."

A shrug again, this one delivered with forgiveness, a gentle narrowing of the eyes.

"Want to try to write it?" Eric leaned forward to move the pad on the table under his father's good hand. Sometimes this worked, but the letters and sounds were just as likely to become scrambled; his hand had deserted him as much as his tongue. Language was now a befuddlement to his whole body.

Frank picked up the pencil, fixed it against his thumb with three fingers as people writing with the wrong hand will do, but then put it down. He raised his bushy eyebrows as a joke. It meant he had given up.

This angered Eric, this luxury of powerlessness. Frank had made this precise gesture long before his strokes, back when he had made a good mess of something, let his children or his wives down, broken his public trust. Powerless in the face of what? His own character? Seeing it, Eric was suddenly back in the heat of older battles with his father, battles not so much won or lost as abandoned in a decisive draw and years of silence. And he was back in his private battles against his own repetition of these faults, his own weaknesses, his own willingness to leave important things undone in the name of what . . . peace? He could see his own eyebrows arching like that: an iterative curse. More and more, these days, as he looked into the mirror, unshaven in the morning, he saw his father's face staring back.

This is the nature of family, after all, a certain compression of time, a simultaneity: all family joys in a single flutter of the heart; every woe dripping through a single unhealed wound, a fear that to fix any one piece of it, you have to fix it all.

"Is it Maryland? Are you talking about the state?"

"No. No. No."

Eric drew the letters "M-O-T-T-S-E-C-K" on the pad and circled the "M." "Is this right? Does it start with M?"

"Yes."

Normally, one might think they were getting somewhere. The problem was that "yes" could sometimes mean "no." "No" was more reliable—that made its own sense: so much easier to express what he didn't want than what he did; so much easier to send a dish back to the kitchen than to make it clear what he really wanted. But "no" was not unfailingly accurate.

"Mike? Mike Greer?" Mike was the plumber in town. It wasn't right, but Eric was strangely unable to think of relevant or likely words that started with "M." Mirage. Marriage. Million. Makeshift. Masterpiece. Montana. He didn't even offer one of those, even though the thought of being on a two days' hike into Glacier National Park was attractive. Frank was tired out by now, anyway. But the truth was, Frank never really gave up on a word even if others had. In a day or two, or in a few weeks, he might find a picture to point to, or Adam would draw one, or the word itself would emerge from those damaged lips, perfect as a newborn unscarred from its tortured birth. But lately Eric had begun to doubt that everything his father wanted to express was getting out. If the word were a thing, the thing would be found; if it were an errand or a deed, one of them would figure out what it was, all of it being fairly predictable. But what of his father's thoughts, what of the existential? As Eric had tried to suggest to his sister Alice, even if she did not share Eric's taste for literature, what of Wallace Stevens's pressure on the heart of the inexpressible? "Sure. Sure," said Alice, wary of poetry. But what late-life wisdom or reflection might his father have to share but be unable to express? He was eighty-two now, and despite his apparent indestructibility, he wasn't going to live forever. It could be like this "mottseck" at the end, the small gathering at the bedside, the various families leaning forward to record the last utterance, only to dissolve into grotesque slapstick: "Did he say 'glyfith'?" "No, I heard 'glowforth,' you know, 'Go forth.' " "You're all wrong. It was 'Glaswirst.' I heard it plain as day. He was asking for a glass of water."

The door opened and Adam burst in with his tea tray. He was a big man, tall as Frank but much broader, with the sloping shoulders, heavy neck, and round close-cropped head of an athlete. His powerful physique made his talent and commitment to caregiving all the more appealing. On his time off he might well have been a weightlifter or a bruising attackman in the adult lacrosse leagues, but Eric knew nothing of Adam's private life.

When Adam started working for Frank he had worn white nursing clothes, but within days had understood that this wasn't necessary or even desired. Now he wore his own uniform, jeans and a sweatshirt, with a fanny pack full of Frank's necessities: spare reading glasses, medications, pens, and a small steno pad for jotting down notes, or making pictures, or writing words. He had filled and saved many dozens of these pads, and Eric often wondered what a stranger or distant family member would make of these recorded transactions, the last years of a stroke victim's life told in a rebus. Eric could read them perfectly. Upon arriving for his visits he always asked Adam if he could glance through the latest, and Adam would hand them over; but first, he rifled through them and ripped out a page or two here and there, sometimes several pages—a complete conversation—and placed these excisions from the record on a feathery pile he kept at one corner of his desk.

"It's showtime," said Adam. As always, he had brought along a Coke in a can for himself. He served them the tea and pulled up a Victorian stool, one of those monstrosities with claws and heads.

Frank took a long, very loud sip through the good corner of his mouth. "Perfect," he said to Adam, fingers circled in the OK sign.

"Mr. Frank, he's always trying to butter me up," said Adam, popping the tab on his Coke. When Adam smiled his whole face became merry.

The aroma and steam of tea brought cheer into this crowded

room, built as a library in those heady nineteenth-century days when an Eastern Shore farm, even one as modest as this one, deserved the high Victorian treatment. There were bookshelves on three sides of the room, running around the doors and fireplace. Frank had retained his ability to read, but only a few pages at a time; he often had a book out, something he had loved from his studious teenage years: Kipling, Jane Austen, Rider Haggard, Edna St. Vincent Millay, but the mildew in these volumes made him sneeze. "Dust catchers," Adam called all the books and gewgaws: an unhealthful environment. "Call for a Dumpster," he said the day he arrived, to the dismay of Alice, guardian of the family past.

The window in front of Eric looked out the lane and into the dark flat landscape beyond. Dusk was coming in and the wet flakes flattened into large splotches as they hit the black glass.

"I told you you shouldn't have come," said Adam. "It's right nasty out there."

"This was supposed to be rain."

"Home," said Frank. The word was round in his mouth, the "O" coming from deep in his throat; to someone untutored, it would have sounded like a groan. He raised his flat palm up and pushed the air toward the door. "Go home."

This was an expression of love and concern, and Eric knew he didn't need to respond. "Dad's trying to get a word," he said to Adam.

"Animal, mineral, or vegetable?"

"Vegetable," said Frank. It came out "Jetable."

"Dad. Come on."

"What did it sound like?" asked Adam.

Eric kept his eyes on his father during this, because he hated to have conversations about Frank when he was in the room without pretending that he was part of the dialogue, the peculiar etiquette of caring for someone who could barely speak. "Dad, do you want to try again?"

"No."

Eric was tired, too. He and Gail had been out late the night before. "A classic Summit evening," she had said sourly on the way home, but Eric had enjoyed himself. He was in one of those moods when all the women, women he'd known for years, seemed especially sexy; no harm in that. What else would brighten the day quite as much? He had fawned a bit over Rebecca Walsh, especially when she asked if anyone—"anyone," she had said, a private viewing—wanted to see her thong underpants. Eric didn't really want to see them, but he would have loved to know if she was actually wearing them. By the time he and Gail pulled in to their short driveway they were both staring ahead into the wash of the headlights, as if they hoped something unexpected would pop out of the dark: children in Halloween costumes, a film crew making a movie, a moose. He had hoped they would put the mood aside for lovemaking, but she was still angry at him, so he went back downstairs and listened to all the longest and dreariest CDs in their music library—Bruckner, then Mahler, then Gorecki's Third—and was at it late enough for Gail to come looking for him in her nightgown. "Is this *necessary*," she bellowed over the screeching of the soprano.

"We'll try later in the week," said Adam. He ripped off the sheet from the pad.

"Fine," said Eric. He stood up to go to the bathroom.

"Gail called," said Adam as he brushed by. "She said to stay over." There were no telephones in this end of the house; Frank hated now to hear phones ring, but he once had been a master on the phone, scheming with his cronies, mollifying constituents. When he was still quite little, Eric used to love to sit silently in the wingback chair and listen to his father talk, strings of syntax, the rhythms not of conversation and consensus, but of cajolery. Every once in a while, Frank would glance over at the small boy and wag his eyebrows. See? he was saying, see how much fun you can have with words? If Eric faulted his father for any of that now, it was that he had not warned him against being sucked in: if your words have the power to fool anyone, the biggest fool is usually yourself.

Eric went out into the hallway and closed the door behind him. The wind was picking up from the water and was driving billowy drafts down the center of the house; away from the space heater he felt the Chesapeake chill ebbing and flowing. He walked to the doors on the land side and cupped his hands around the sidelights, looked out onto the lane and into the gray fingers of bare beech boughs. Not much snow was sticking on the ground; Adam was correct about this being nasty, but it was no blizzard, a slushy inconvenience at worst. Winter in the landscape had always seemed benign to Eric, even as a child. Later, when he was sent off to prep school in New Hampshire in order to be removed from the family fray, he felt the first sharp warnings of a true freeze in November, and he learned that cold was nothing to be trifled with, that real winter could kill him in a hour or two, freeze the layers of his body until it stopped his heart. Not on the Eastern Shore. The heart was safe from the cold there; spend a winter night outside and you'd get wet, wet as a camper, but if there were danger to the heart, it would come from the inside.

He walked into the lavatory off the kitchen. This convenience, carved out of a pantry, had always given Eric the creeps, with a ceiling much too tall for such a small space, and an old-fashioned toilet tank mounted halfway up the wall. When he was eight or nine he was sitting on the toilet and glanced up at the tank to see the tail of a blacksnake. He had grown up with blacksnakes. Often they slithered their way into his solitary games, and they paid for the mistake with an ax chop or a .22-caliber slug to the head. But this snake curled overhead was something out of a jungle movie, a primal image, and it was years before he entered the room again.

He reflected on this memory for a moment or two before he remembered why he had come in, and then went back out into the kitchen. It had been renovated by his mother in the late fifties, done up in the optimism and appetite of those years. The yellow Formica of the counters, seared with brown circles, still looked as if it would last centuries, but his parents' marriage had not survived the next decade. His mother had gone home to Birmingham, Alabama, in 1968 and remarried happily, had gotten on with her life as if there had never been this wartime wedding to a skinny Navy lieutenant in Norfolk and over twenty years imprisoned on an Eastern Shore backwater pining after her husband, who was across the bay in Annapolis having affairs with senatorial secretaries in the shadow of the statehouse dome.

Eric reached for the phone and called Gail; she answered after several rings, breathless from her NordicTrack. Eric could imagine the tiny jewels of sweat across her upper lip.

"I'm sorry," she said.

"For what?"

"Oh . . ." She paused, as if trying to pick out any one thing to apologize for. "I was crabby last night. It's not really your fault."

" 'Not really.' In other words, my fault."

"Not your fault. It's just those people."

"No kidding."

"They just make me feel so hopeless. There's nothing in their lives. All they're doing is temporizing. They don't even deny it."

She was right, maybe, but the truth was, Eric had very little to do with these old fellow suburbanites. He'd never felt the pressure to join them as Gail had during her years as a largely stay-at-home mother. "Okay. But I really don't need 'hopeless' right now. I'm in the Inferno already."

Her tone brightened, a change of topic. "A tough visit? Is anything up?"

"No. Not really. Just more of the same. Maybe it's the weather."

"It's snowing here. Did Adam give you my message?"

Eric said that he had, but that he needed to get to work early tomorrow. Besides, he added, in his current mood, spending the night at the farm wouldn't be a lot of fun. It was the nights that were hardest, anyway, with the night nurses, and with his father wandering the house, bellowing his late-night lamentations in his private tongue.

"He's trying to get a word."

"What does it sound like?"

He fiddled with the telephone cord, picked up one of Adam's cigarette packs. The Surgeon General has warned . . . "It's nothing. Hard to explain."

Adam and his father were conversing when he returned, sitting comfortably in the ionic heat of the space heater. "Gail says to give you her love."

Frank smiled. "Good girl," he said perfectly. "Lucky boy." Often, when his mind and thoughts were unclouded by contrary emotions, Frank could speak almost normally. His thoughts about almost every younger woman were like this, uncomplicated, full of warmth, a joy to yearn for the female.

Eric considered this equation, GG = LB, and wondered whether it shouldn't in fact mean more than it did. He had never for one second since he married Gail thirty years ago questioned the fact that he was a "lucky boy," but that didn't seem to stop him from screwing it up. Maybe even gave him license to fail, because what he had was undeserved. But Eric was feeling better for the conversation, as cryptic and married as it was; he knew the one thing he could not bear was to live without her.

"So beautiful," said Frank.

In fact, Frank had thought so from the moment he met Gail. It was when, freshly graduated from Middlebury, Eric and Gail paid a call in Maryland. Gail had never met her boyfriend's father; over the year and a half of their courtship, Eric had told her little: a state senator, majority leader, kind of self-involved, why do you ask? But here they were, driving across the bridge from what Eric still called Friendship Airport, and she was nervous. "Don't worry," said Eric. "He might not even show up."

But he did, greeting them from the top step of the back porch— khakis, white shirt, red bow tie—solicitous as an innkeeper. He stretched out his hand to take Gail's and held it, in the Southern manner, longer than necessary, and his slightly crooked smile held a touch of gentle irony. "At last," he said, as if he had been unfairly denied this pleasure previously. "Just as beautiful as Eric said. Don't you agree, Mike?" His longest-lasting and most sacrificially loyal toady, Mike Billings, stuffed briefcase in hand, had followed Frank out onto the landing.

"That's right, Frank. Pretty as a picture."

"Hi, Dad."

"Come in. Come in. Mike was just leaving," Frank answered, and then led Gail into the house, leaving Eric to unload their suitcases and to endure an extended leave-taking with Mike. Eric disliked him, had, at some time during his teens, ceased to be flattered that his father's cronies thought it worthwhile to suck up to the Senator's children.

Eric found them on the porch, drinks in hand, and Gail was sitting on a low wicker ottoman directly in front of Frank, practically at his feet. She was holding a tattered copy of *The Lord's Oysters*.

"Get a drink, Eric," said Frank.

"No. That's okay. I'm fine."

"I'm telling Gail y'all can't possibly leave in two days. I've cleared the deck. No calls. I promise."

Eric looked at Gail; he wanted to tell her not to be fooled by that "y'all"—Frank only used a Southern accent when he wanted someone's vote. Perhaps she wasn't snowed yet, but she was entranced by this outpouring of slightly reckless charm. He was perhaps nothing more in those days than a *type,* but he was a type of man that she had never experienced. So Southern in manner, so facile in conversation. Gail's father was a loan officer in a bank in Reading, Massachusetts; her mother taught second grade.

"I've planned a dinner party for tomorrow evening. Mrs. Swenson has already started to cook. Alice and Alden are coming."

"My sister and her husband," said Eric.

"Well, she knows who they are, don't you, Gail? Eric forgets about us when he's up north, but down here we're *family,* are we not?" He was acting positively Johnson-esque.

"Sure, Lyndon," Eric answered, although the question had not been directed to him but to Gail, and Frank waited for her to answer, to assent, to accept this proposal, to crawl under his wing.

"If that's what it takes to get supper," said Gail.

Frank treated them to a round of full laughter. He took her hand and patted it. "Good. Good," he said.

Frank had recently bought a boat, a clinker-built Chris-Craft with an eighty-horse Evinrude, which, for a lifelong and devoted sailor, signaled something, and in fact, Eric learned later that this was a time in his life when Frank was at his most reckless: he'd already passed the high-water mark of his congressional ambitions, and now he was intent on making as much hay as he could in his more local arena. He was moving fast everywhere, on land and on the water. After they had sat on the porch for a few more minutes, he told them he wanted to take them out for a spin to "clear your brains of airplane air," as he put it. Gail and Eric went up to change, and after he had pulled on his bathing suit Eric tiptoed into Gail's room and found her in her underwear, leaning over her suitcase. He came up behind her and put both hands on her waist, and then dropped them into her underpants. "Eric. No," she said. "He's waiting."

"He is not. He's already forgotten about us. When we come down I'll have to remind him that he said he'd take us out."

"But really."

She turned her back to him as she put on her bikini, such a

lovely body. When she faced him he said, "Don't you have something a little fuller? I'll have to bring along a bucket of cold water and douse him."

"Oh, stop. He's funny. You didn't tell me that."

In those days Eric was still trying to win her. That spring she'd been keeping him in a suspended state between delight and despair, going out on a date or two with other boys, and telling him he was uptight to complain. It was agony; maybe she'd actually slept with one of them. So here his father was, forcing her practically to accept a marriage proposal Eric had not yet made, charming her for him, a Cyrano in the wings. Eric knew it might help, but it made him sick, his father flirting with his date. Maybe they'd have to fight over her. The truth was, if it came to it, to a choice of some sort, a competition, Eric wasn't sure who would win.

They took a six-pack of beer along for their boat ride, a full-throttle drag race across a bumpy chop, with Frank at the wheel chortling as the spray soaked them all to the skin. Eric drank two of the beers on the way to the crab shacks, cutting his lip once when his head was jammed into the can by the heaving of the boat, and when they came back, a bushel of crabs lashed to the transom, he drank two more. He was drunk and already nauseated by the time they hit cocktails on the porch, and threw up before the crabs hit the pot. Gail helped him to his bed and pulled off his pants, and he passed out. Later—God, it seemed like two in the morning—he was conscious for long enough to hear his father's voice deep in the house blasting out a joke, and Gail laughing. When he woke in the morning, hung over, they were already in town buying supplies for the party. Mrs. Taylor, the housekeeper in Frank's intermarriage years, said what Eric least wanted to hear. "If I were you, Eric, I'd sober up and keep an eye on that lady."

On the last night of the visit, after Gail had gone to bed, Eric found Frank in his study—right here in this room. Eric tried to thank him for the visit, for making such an effort. Eric meant it; for the first time that he could remember, his father had been true to his word, had given the party, had let three days pass with no drop-ins from cronies, no trips to Annapolis. Perhaps exhausted from the effort, Frank was sitting glumly in his chair, in the dark of a single small lamp on his desk.

"We'll be leaving at six in the morning," said Eric.

"Fine. Safe trip."

"You've been great to Gail. She likes you." He was being grateful here; he owed his father this dangerous truth.

Frank sighed; he took a drink from his highball glass. "A lovely girl. You should marry her."

"We haven't quite gotten to that, but yes, I should. If she'll have me."

"She'll have you, but—" He stopped himself, spent a moment stifling what he had a moment ago been raring to say, and then gave Eric a genuine but hopeless smile.

"But what?"

"You'll probably just screw it up."

Eric didn't know how to react to this—was he commenting on Eric's character, or on life in general?—and he still didn't know what he felt about it. "Why?" he asked finally.

"Because you're my son," Frank answered.

That had been thirty years ago, and Eric was still in love with Gail, and Frank was still in love with her, and though Eric had screwed plenty up, the marriage had survived; from a distance, and perhaps even at the core of it, little had changed.

Adam had been talking to him as this long memory flashed its delicate and brief illumination. "I'm sorry?" said Eric.

"Mr. Frank wants you to call Mike Billings."

"Mike Billings? Is that it?" Mike Billings. Mott Seck? Billings had been working, for reasons that were both obscure and suspect, on a "narrative," as he called it, of Frank's career in the Maryland Senate. He had taken pains to indicate that he was not interested in the "denouement"—in other words, and pronounced correctly, Frank's expulsion for padding his payroll—but neither Alice nor Eric believed that for a second. "Mike?" he said again hopefully, accenting and drawing out the "M" as if to force it into his father's mouth as a replacement for the lost word.

"I don't think so," said Adam, rifling back through his pad. "We talked about that on Tuesday." He held up the pad for Eric to see, and under the Tuesday heading was a perfect caricature of this very fat, balding old politico; Eric could hear Billings wheezing just by looking at the drawing. In his two years on the job, Adam had discovered a completely untapped and unexpected genius for cartooning.

Eric turned to Frank. "What do you want me to talk to *him* for?"

"Be nicer. Nice to Mike. A hard life."

"He'd sell you out in a heartbeat."

"Sizely," said Frank, full of cheer. Whatever his final thoughts about his ruined career as a public servant, he still took great pleasure in the unvarnished duplicity and nastiness of politics.

"What's he want?"

Frank put out a long, spiky finger and traced a question mark in the air, and then pointed his fingernail at Eric.

"He wants to ask me questions? About your career? I don't know anything about your career." This caused a slight dip in Frank's mood. For a number of years, including the last desperate months when his father was being expelled from office for maintaining a phantom typist, Eric had been almost completely out of contact with him. That was past now, but not forgotten by either of them. "Don't worry," said Eric. "Whatever I don't know I'll just make up."

"Fiction," said Frank. "Good at it."

In fact Eric had once believed he would write fiction for a living, a few years of apprenticeship and then *Wham!* That was one of the reasons he and Gail had moved to New Hampshire after college, safe with a high draft lottery number. But during the one long winter that he took a serious stab at it, all he did was read Jung and Schopenhauer and—perhaps a measure of how desperate he was to avoid his own blank page—Kant. When he did put paper into his typewriter, all he did was write letters. They were good letters, many of them to classmates and former objects of affection whom he did not know all that well and did not much care about. The only real result was the beginning of a lifelong friendship with a man named Sheldon Levine, who began his first reply with "Gee, Eric, I didn't think you even liked me."

"Okay," he said. "I'll call him. Any other scut work you want me to do?"

"No. Go home. Be careful."

He glanced at his watch; four-thirty on a nasty day and he had waited too long. In his visits during the summer, when all this unrelieved gray, gray land and gray water was abloom with color, they often took a shuffling walk at this hour, always the same route down to the water, back up to the barns, and then home. They kept this path mowed like a golf course. The walk would take Eric no more than a few minutes, but with his father it was an hour-long foray, with stops at the same points as he observed whatever minute evolutions might be occurring in this all-but-unchanging scene. One year, Alice and Eric pooled their money and bought him a golf cart, which sat today in an old chicken coop accumulating pigeon droppings and mud-dauber nests. It had been Alice's idea. She believed their father was "stagnating" and needed only to be "more mobile" to regain some of his energies. Eric would never forget the look on his father's face the day they presented it to him; so angry, offended, completely devastated that two of his children would get together and buy him something so obscene. Besides, all this walking, this peering longingly at the water, was a statement of what he truly wished he could do: go for one last sail. Eric did not know exactly who did this, but every year someone pulled Frank's daysailer out of the shed next to the golf cart, rigged it, and placed it on the mooring ball just off the dock. It was always there, bobbing its innocent invitations, the taut halyard pinging against the aluminum mast like a school bell calling the children. Frank had loved the water, the motions of sailing, but had long since made it clear that in his new state it would terrify him, that he would never do it again. Two things he would never do again unless his God still had miracles in mind for him: talk without impediment and sail out onto the bay.

Eric stood up, remembering to lay hold of the envelope of old family photographs that Frank wanted him to have reproduced. "Do you want to try with that word one more time?"

"Go home. Forget it. Sorry."

Eric leaned down to kiss Frank's dry, papery forehead; the warmth of the skin always surprised him. "I love you, you old fart. I'll see you in a few weeks."

"No. Don't come. Forget me. Live your life." This was as always. He reached up to caress Eric's cheek, and left his hand there for a moment, enjoying his flesh, and then gave him a little slap. He pursed his lips into a kiss and said, "Love Gail."

"She'll come next time."

"No."

Adam followed him out into the hall and watched him put on

his coat. He held the envelope and then handed it back. "Something's on his mind. I'll see what I can do."

"There usually is. 'Mottseck,' " Eric said. "Beats me."

Eric's beloved Alfa Milano was covered with a thin bumpy coat of snow, but at least here on the farm, nothing much was sticking to the ground. Years ago he wouldn't have paid any attention to the dangers of driving in this stuff—the old paradox: heedless youth, cautious maturity. The will to be alive, that's what these visits to his father taught him as much as anything, that however diminished, it's good to breathe. Whatever his father believed of the afterlife—churchgoing had always seemed to be, like so much else his father had done in life, a political calculation—he didn't want to let go of his senses just yet. Lots of Eric's friends' parents were dying these days, some of them stripped of dignity and joy, wanting to get it over with. However it would play for Frank at the end, he wasn't there yet, this busy self-absorbed man with inexpressible things on his mind, sifting and organizing the ephemera of his past, preserving his photographs, his house, his barns, his two hundred acres of farmland.

Eric slopped off the car as well as he could and headed down the lane and over to Route 301. He had done this drive hundreds of times in his life, and it had never been a burden, returning to or departing from his native ground. The fact was that he still found this landscape exotic, a secret, a private store of strength. Eric was a flatlander through and through. He liked feeling small, so free in this immense space, under the purple dome of the night sky.

In the slop he kept to the right, letting the tractor-trailers whoosh past him, but this four-lane stretch was not heavily traveled; even with its dangerous grade crossings, it was a stretch where one could easily lapse into meditation. The snow was still falling, large flakes smack out of the darkness, clumps of brilliant froth. When he reached the Delaware line, and the road narrowed to two lanes, he had to concentrate more fully on his driving, and he passed an accident scene on the strip of fast-food joints in New Castle, but once over the bridge and onto a New Jersey Turnpike that was clearly less crowded because of the weather, he could fall again into his thoughts.

He had been speaking of his life to his father, about the conventional choices he and Gail had made even as they both believed they were destined to spend a life a little more on the fringes. They were children of the sixties, after all. They had started with flair, raising pigs and smoking dope and practicing an extreme form of survivalism. But when the gratuitous hardship of that life began to seem unnecessary, they headed to Manhattan, a way station, they thought, where Gail had a job with some friends in an art gallery, and Eric would put his energy into applying for graduate school in philosophy as a fresh start on career path #2. But he took a job in the meantime at an ad agency, liked it, and had never left. They moved to Bronxville when Tom was born, and finally to Summit. There was nothing so wrong with any of it; it was the kind of progression that makes a life, good or bad, and they could follow it with the belief that their principles were intact. They loved their reading; they loved their music; Gail had her theology, her Harvey Cox and Elaine Pagels and Hans Jonas, and Eric had his philosophy and poetry; as Eric would put it in his best bachelor-of-arts manner, they believed like Schopenhauer that these arts and reflections offered them a purchase on the sublime world of idea, another world out there, a promised land or simply the promise of such a land. But their forties and fifties now seemed peculiarly full of blockages, doors to joy that would no longer open all the way; pleasure had become habit.

The point, as he was beginning to make to his father, was that they had been given a good deal and probably not taken it as far as they could have. He still wondered why. He wanted to do something about it, make some sort of fresh start, but they had put some of their own roadblocks in the way. He had not been a faithful husband, which he had admitted to Gail in due course, and in partial payment a few years ago, Gail had slept with one of Eric's old friends, and then told some friend, who then spread the word. Perhaps this was her real problem with Summit, that the women did not trust her, that she threatened them with her honesty, that they were envious of her freedom as they imagined it. Who knew? Eric and Gail were always more interesting—to themselves, anyway—than their friends, but Gail was not exactly right or kind about them; their friends weren't boring, Gail and Eric were simply bored by them.

It was the fight, or nonfight, with Gail the night before that had started this mood, and so it was as he sat with his father that he was asking whether he should have done any of it differently. Frank had been listening carefully, and when Eric's words came to him, he set his mouth into a disbelieving frown and shook his head and he said he didn't know. Frank had never been one to engage in such reflections. He didn't know if Eric should have done anything differently: who was to know? But as the air turned gray outside, they leafed through the old photographs of people who, on the browning and fading surface of the thing, had never failed at their duty, or at their marriages, or at remembering their mercies. Eric had seen many of those photographs before, but he was enjoying looking at them through the lens of this mood, wondered aloud whether they had ever made bad mistakes, and he did not notice that a silence descended over his father, his crippled hand folded into the one still-powerful palm, this person trapped in a ruined body. Eric looked up, startled by a sudden presence in the room. His father was being visited in this stillness, and Eric immediately looked into those eyes for the meaning of it. He didn't find an answer then, but it was happening now as he drove through the snow on the Turnpike of all places, drawn right in, through those gates of light, clutched and pulled, and there he was in his father's soul.

Mottsecks.

Mistakes.

The word hit him so hard he was suddenly panicked, as if a truck had rammed into him from behind, and he was now swerving toward the shoulder and into the trees. He slammed on the brakes and he was in a skid and was trying to steer into it as he had learned so long ago in New Hampshire to do, and he was glancing from the invisible road ahead to the black rearview mirrors. He heard the clatter of the warning strip on the shoulder, and he still wasn't sure he had control of the car, but he was slowing down and the road behind was clear, and a few moments later everything was still.

Sweat was pouring from every pore, and his skin seemed cold. A truck speeding by almost panicked him again, and he pulled a little farther off before he put on the emergency brake and the flashers, and then slumped back into his seat, completely spent.

Mistakes. Help.

TWO

What a mess we can make of things, the advantages we can piss away, the love we can refuse from people who want to give it, the good advice we can fail to hear or ignore. What does it take to make us stop making mistakes, or doing all these things? Why do we seem so uncorrectable?

When Eric got home that night Gail was asleep, and they did not talk in the morning; by the time he was up she was out for her run. Miles and miles through these streets, three, four times a week, and now she was talking of entering a marathon, even a triathlon. Occasionally Eric went out with her, but neither of them expected him to keep up. When she ran, she motored. She'd jogged like a train down every street and through every crosswalk of their neighborhood a hundred times, and had observed at house after house and at garage after garage the suburban rituals of the new day. Wouldn't that be enough to make one come to loathe, or to fear, the repetitive patterns of the average life?

On Monday night he hoped when he got home there would be the cheery ambiance of a roast chicken in the oven, of Prokofiev on the stereo: but no. She was in the kitchen on the phone to Tom. She was wearing tight black leggings and a short purple sweater, a style that always turned him on, at least on a woman like Gail, with a body like a teenager's but with an experienced soul. Eric listened for a few moments. "Everyone feels that way," she said. She gave him a distracted wave. "Okay. Go on." She was clearly listening to a lengthy tale, hands fiddling with the cord, and then caught Eric's eye. "What?" she mouthed, slightly irritated at his dark form lurking at the door.

As far as Eric could tell, Tom had chosen Colorado with a dart thrown at a map, though he was a good skier and had tolerated well enough the backpacking trips they took him on in his younger days. Tom had never seemed to his father to be a person motivated by what he liked but rather seemed pushed by what he didn't like. Apparently, he didn't like New Jersey, which was not a view Eric would debate. Tom had been in Denver for a year and a half, since his graduation from Wesleyan, and though he could certainly have found much more meaningful work, he had settled on temping; he was fluent in Spanish and Russian, which meant his gigs were often to one side of conventional office work. That was the appeal, but his roommates, computer types in college, had been wooed and hired from one venture to another. For the past year he had been blaming his father for encouraging him to major in comparative literature, as if that had limited his options. Eric knew a major in literature did precisely the reverse, and Tom's complaint was a peculiar injustice anyway; Tom had never been willing to take guidance from his father on anything; even at age four, trying to learn how to swim, he did exactly the opposite of what Eric suggested.

When Eric came back downstairs, changed into his jeans, the conversation was over, and Gail suggested they go out to dinner. "It's called Shaba, that new Japanese place up at the Garden Mall."

Eric could not keep track of all the new Asian eateries opening throughout this American heartland in New Jersey; he liked these cuisines well enough, but not as much as Gail did, not as much as every other woman he knew. Asian food was women's food, small bits of things, salads by any other name.

When they got there, nosed the car into a space right by the front door like a motel room, there was a small line of people outside. Most of these people seemed to be on dates, but restaurants in New Jersey malls are not where one goes to court someone; this was a place for young couples, when love and banter and sex were still easy, when friends were fun, when they still think they're some of the lucky ones, the ones who won't be burned. Eric stood there feeling slightly out of place, not because he and Gail had not been graced with years of pleasure in their adolescence of marriage, but because in maturity one seems to have little to say in those transitional moments of the day, breakfast, shopping in the supermarket, waiting in line. Their banter wouldn't be about the latest movie, or that wild night last Saturday, but about their son, or about themselves, which wouldn't have been banter in any case, but work, often dangerous work. She gave him a pat and then one of her appraising looks. It was clear that she wasn't entirely satisfied by what she saw, her faithfulness mingled with the belief that there should still be, at this late date, some modifications here, as if he were a soup or a stew that for all its natural ingredients still lacked . . . what? This was all accomplished and communicated in a slight narrowing of the eyes. Eric didn't think he ever looked at her like that. He believed he processed his love for Gail more in the high contrast of his moods: anger, affection, desire.

They did not have to wait too long. The room was sparsely furnished; the few crepe paper decorations didn't strike him as Japanese; they seemed like something generically Oriental ordered from a restaurant supply catalog, probably left over from the Korean restaurant that had recently outgrown the space. As they sat down, Eric began to study the menu, but she seemed to be staring out into the room, at all those happy and confident couples.

"Hello?" he said.

"Sorry. I'm just looking at those people across the room."

He twisted around slightly; the room was filled with people. "What people?" he asked.

"The two over in the corner. She's crying."

"Then let her be. Don't stare."

"He's breaking up with her. He's trying to be kind, but he's telling her it's over."

"You can tell all this?" The room was almost deafeningly noisy; he had to work just to hear Gail.

She shook her head, as if he might never understand what she understood. "It's sad."

"Of course it is. Ninety-nine percent of the time it's for the better, for both of them. The man who calls it off takes the shit, and the woman is free to get on in life, without guilt." He picked up her menu and handed it to her. "What's up with you? This was supposed to fun. This was your choice."

She flashed him another hopeful smile, all brightness for him; it was a gift, something packaged. "What do you mean?"

"You invite me out and then spend the whole time staring at some poor bastards across the room. This isn't fun."

"Well," she said. "This is us."

"It isn't. It's what we've been recently. You could try harder, you know."

She fixed her mouth into an immobile grimace somewhere between apology and blame. Eric scanned the menu for a few seconds, and even the translations made no sense to him. What were they doing here, in a mall on Monday night? "Okay," he said finally. "We can still go."

"Don't be mean."

"Why did you want to do this?"

"So we could talk."

"About what. Saturday night? Was I really acting so awful?"

"Just talk."

The waiter came over, Japanese, maybe; he could tell that this was not a happy table, and he gave Eric a corrosive look: *a butt-hole like you with a great chick like her, and you're dumping on her?* Gail ordered, but Eric didn't have a clue. He never did, anyway, in restaurants. He felt slightly ill, thick in the gut: food, any kind of food, didn't seem an option.

"So how was the visit?" she asked when he had finally made a selection, the kind of deliberate change in topic that could make one nervous.

"Dad's busy with those family photographs. I'm having them copied for him," he said without any real interest.

"You sounded troubled when we talked."

"Well, yeah," he said. "I was mad at you."

She nodded, but did not pursue the topic. "You said he was trying to say something. Did you figure it out?"

He wasn't ready to share the true answer, because he still could not make sense of it. His father admitting to mistakes? He told her that it had something to do with Mike Billings, one of the relatively innocent casualties of his father's infractions.

Gail wasn't interested in Mike, and didn't believe the lie anyway. "Really?" she said.

"Let's not talk about my father."

"Well, sure." She gave him a peeved look and then kept her eyes on him, challenging him to produce a more interesting topic.

"Actually, it wasn't about Mike."

"I didn't think so."

"It was 'mistakes.' He kept saying 'mottsecks' and it wasn't until I was driving home that I figured it out."

"Whose mistakes?"

"Well, his, I guess. Who else's?"

Gail knew Frank as well as anyone did, perhaps could understand him more broadly than Eric, as children-in-law can sometimes do. "Not a chance," she said.

Eric took a sip of beer; it was warm and he drained the glass before it got any worse. "Well, I'm not sure."

She shook her head. "I'm not saying that he's not aware of what he has done in his life—"

Eric interrupted. "Of course he's aware. How could he not be?"

She glared at him: of all people among Frank's small number of loyalists, Gail would be perhaps the only one who believed that in his own imperfect way, Frank acknowledged his weaknesses. "I'm saying that expressing something like remorse is off his chart. He's built his whole life on denial. That's what politicians do."

"Maybe he's growing up."

"A little late in the game. He's got a lot of ground to cover, if that's really what it means. But I still don't believe it." The waiter came with their dinners. Eric had ordered a number that he liked—27—and it turned out to be a sort of beef dish in a spicy sauce, which was just what he would have ordered if he had been paying attention. They ate for a few moments.

"What were you talking about when this came up?"

"I was talking to him about us. Nothing deep. Just our choices." He waved around the room to indicate what choices he was referring to: their suburban life. "That's really what you were saying on Saturday night."

"Whatever I was talking about, I wasn't talking about mistakes."

"Then what were you talking about? Did you really want to talk about Dad?"

Again, a long pause, during which Eric's stomach heaved anew; the spicy sauce burned.

"Well," she said, "it's this: Are we making each other really happy?"

"What do you mean?" he said.

"Do I have to define the word?"

"No. But maybe you have to define 'really happy.' It sounds like a setup. It sounds like that couple over there." He repeated what she had said about them: he's being kind, but he's dumping her all the same.

At last, she blurted it out. "Maybe we should separate for a bit. What if I moved out? In my own place somewhere close by. I've been thinking. Maybe we should."

Eric felt he had known this was coming from the moment she suggested they go out, maybe even before, from the moment he walked in the kitchen and she looked at him so impatiently and dismissively as she was talking to Tom on the phone, maybe even last year when she threw a book at him, a big hardcover biography of Emerson, of all things to turn into a weapon. Maybe things really were as bad as all that, but it didn't seem so to him. This just sounded like something from the seventies, a room of one's own and all that nonsense. "Why?" he said at last. "What would that accomplish?"

"I'm trying to think what would make you happy."

"Me?" He tried not to raise his voice, especially as the waiter was removing their plates and all but throwing the menus at them for dessert. Eric wanted to ask for a brownie fudge nut sundae. "What you're talking about doesn't have anything to do with me. I mean, are you seeing someone or something like that? Am I being ditched?"

"No," she said, but her eyes darted off into the room, back onto all those couples, who would probably be going home to make love and then lie together, naked and heedless, in front of the *Late Show*.

"Is this something you have been planning?"

"No. Not at all. It just came out. I'm sorry."

"I don't want to lose you," he said.

"You're not losing me. But I think we have to do something. Learn how to take pleasure in small things again. Maybe—" She interrupted herself, but not quite quickly enough: "I mean, I know I'm as much at fault as you are. But I'd like to know what you want from me. Tell me things I can do that can give you pleasure. Don't you see? That's the love I want, the love of people who have been married for thirty years. It's not just fucking. What I would love from you is a list, a list of things I could do to give you real pleasure. It would break my heart if you couldn't think of a single thing you wanted me to do for you. Because that's the way it feels with you these days."

Gail's speech, so profoundly, brilliantly true, left him wordless and defenseless. It was such a female form of love she wanted; it was what she deserved. She deserved to live with a woman, as Poppy did, who would buy nice things for her on impulse: flowers, a pretty scarf that was just right for her coloring, the new Barbara Kingsolver novel. He would live with a man; they would behave carelessly to each other, and at the end of the evening, without preamble, without soft music and back rubs, go upstairs and have efficient and effective sex. But, alas, he was not gay and neither was she, and they were condemned to trying to make the best of it.

"Well," he said, "I've been trying to think. I've been trying to do better. You don't know how much I love you," he added. "I haven't made you know, have I?"

"No. You haven't. It's because you don't know yourself."

"I do."

"You don't. You mull but you never examine. Sometimes you give off a burned odor, as if you're rubbing two stones against each other, over and over. Sometimes I think that everything you know about yourself I've told you. Really. I mean it. Hello? Doesn't anything get through?"

They rode home mostly silently, though without any more talk of separating, and when they walked into their house he had the sudden idea that maybe fucking wasn't everything, but if they could make love tonight, it would be a place to start. After he walked their old Labrador, Maisie, he came upstairs to find her already in bed, and he felt like the freshman that had fallen in love with her, desire conveniently eliminating all other concerns. She was willing to please, but he knew she felt no comparable desire, and wouldn't force her. Instead, they snuggled warmly naked, Eric at her back, and it was okay, almost enough, because he loved that back, those shoulders, those buttocks, for the person inside.

But after she fell asleep there he was, unreleased from his tensions by orgasm, his lovely wife at his side maybe not for too much longer, and a world of mistakes settling onto his pillow, and people all over the globe searching for something better, or tolerable, humanity's savage landscapes; and his father, who was now beginning his hopeless nightly prowls; and himself, whose mistakes had come because he was simply a fool and had sought love and joy and sex in greater measure than Gail would give him. He could only wonder whether, in the face of this abridged catalog of ills, anything would stand up. Could really withstand. It was faith that he lacked. Faith in any of its manifestations. He had stopped going to church as soon as he was confirmed and released from Sunday school, not because he didn't believe there were higher dimensions in our little struggles, but because these dimensions seemed to be something one searched for alone, in books, in reflections, in being more ardent than the next person. Over the years his life had seemed seeded with promises of wisdom—three or four times in his life he felt he was almost there, in trivial incidents that against all reason seemed to offer a moment's purchase on the sublime or evidence of a tantalizing grace; he could list those moments, just as he could list the three or four times in his youth when he came closest to killing himself in traffic accidents, which in their own way gave evidence of fortune's hand. But he had not added to either of these lists in so long. Had ceased to believe in them, a practical man, a sober driver, the here and now. It was a loss, perhaps the true self-inflicted indignity of age that he was now actively colluding with his own mortality. Do you know what I mean, he wanted to ask someone at that moment, wake Gail up and ask her, do you feel like this too, or am I crazy?

The next morning he woke up as usual to Maisie's chin on the edge of the bed next to him, and in an hour he was dressed, fed, informed by *The New York Times,* advised on traffic by NPR, coffee'd thanks to the retrofitted cup holder that he had ordered from one of those catalogs full of insane devices of convenience, and on the way to catch the 6:49. That was what he did with his mornings, like everyone else in Summit. Years ago, when they had first moved to New York and were living on the Upper West Side and

Gail was working in her art gallery and he was awaiting his admission to or rejection from graduate school, he took a job as the most junior gopher in an advertising agency. It was still a fairly sleepy trade back then, and no one made many claims about their powers or their creative genius, but he liked the casual atmosphere, the irreverence about clients, and he liked having a job, a paycheck, a regular thing. In New Hampshire he had spent three years scrounging for money and telling himself that he was living to the fullest on his own terms. Perhaps. The week the two acceptances and one rejection came from graduate schools, he was also offered a copywriting job at the agency; he compared his failures at a solitary desk with the collaborative, collegial bustle of the agency, and he chose the agency. He learned quickly that he had a nice facility for the hundred-word burst, mostly because Mrs. Ellsworth in sixth grade had so drummed into him the notion of a perfectly constructed paragraph. He had a good amount of early success, he and his collaborator, Livingston Warren, devising clever campaigns for life insurance companies, for cookies, for a line of pots and pans—those were the early successes. Well, what they were doing did no harm. Eric and Liv endured their full measure of agency consolidations and globalization, and in the early nineties they decided to return to where they had begun, with a small, sleepy agency in SoHo. They did local stuff, mostly, a fair amount of public service work, and for the most part, they had fun. Eric didn't do any writing anymore, which was just as well, because the zippy headline and smug humor that everyone liked these days—including Eric, when they were done well—were a young person's game. Instead, he schmoozed with clients on the "strategic and value leadership level"—whatever the hell that was—and he was content with his professional lot.

Eric made it to his office by nine, about typical for him but early by the standards of their business, and set about turning on lights, brewing coffee. The only person who was ever there at that hour, besides their preternaturally glum office manager, Sharon, was a young woman named Lilly DeLong. Eric had hired her away from a bigger firm as an account manager almost two years ago—offered her a good bit more than any of their current account managers—because she was smart and good, and also because she had grown up on a dairy farm in Wisconsin, making them perhaps the only two farm kids in all of New York advertising. He also hired her because she was sexy. Why deny it, to himself anyway? She was one of those short, hot packages, with long, curly, always just-out-of-bed hair, dark eyes, and her face, at rest, settled naturally into an infinitely sly half smile. Ever since Lilly arrived she had been providing small jolts of delight in his day and she knew it; she was not above flirting with him, but she flirted with everyone.

Lilly was in her office that morning, and as usual Eric could not resist poking his head in to say hello. He smelled the lavender soap she had bathed with this morning.

"Are we going to land FruitOut today?" he asked. FruitOut—not a great name, but their firm was proposing to ramp it up a little to FruitOut!—was a new brand of all-natural fruit drinks for the "energy/workout" beverage segment, an account they had all worked hard to get.

She held up crossed fingers. If they got it, it would be big for her.

She *was* a little small, especially compared to Gail's slender length, but she was a pistol; she occupied every inch to the fullest. The truth was, part of the reason Eric liked her so much was that she had never done a single thing in the shop that a worldly but chaste Jesuit wouldn't endorse, yet she still seemed vaguely untrustworthy; she was as sweet and dangerous as perfume. He didn't know much of anything about her love life: only that she didn't seem to be living with anyone. He couldn't imagine why not.

Eric lingered. "What's the milk quote today?" They had often spoken of farming during her first few months, but her family's operation was the real thing, not like his father's gentlemanly and politically useful pastime. She still followed milk prices like a trader.

"Under nine dollars a hundred," she said. "It sucks."

"What's your dad think?"

"Oh, you know farmers. He doesn't analyze; he just worries."

"It's a good thing advertising account managers don't worry." She smiled, but in fact, her right hand still held her place on some paperwork she was studying. Eric was being dismissed. "I'll let you get back to work," he said.

He moved down the corridor to his office. It was a warm place, his shop's digs, filled with color, framed ad campaigns, mostly the wonderful rejected proposals when the designers took the brakes off and did exactly what they wanted. Seated beside Liv's office, as if waiting for an appointment, was an inflatable love doll, primly dressed in a Laura Ashley print with a high ruffled collar, and with a cardboard voice balloon coming out of her mouth saying, "Hi. I'm Debbie. Want to party?" It was a joke most of the women took well enough. This was how an advertising agency was supposed to look, softly lit and full of extraneous, creative clutter.

Liv came in at ten. He was a big man with a classic Anglo-Saxon face that had put on too much weight at the chin. He wore, winter and summer, a blue blazer, jeans, and tassel loafers with no socks. "Any word from the carrot juice set?" he asked.

"They don't make carrot juice."

"Whatever it is, that stuff turns my urine the damnedest shade of yellow."

Eric had noticed the same thing; he'd mentioned it to Lilly, who seemed unaware. "Women don't observe such things in the same way," she said.

"We need this account," said Liv. He'd been making pronouncements like this for twenty years, make or break, like a football announcer describing upcoming plays. In advertising, with a small shop like theirs, the whole ball game could hinge on a single account, but the truth was that Liv liked the drama, or used to, before the living so close to the edge began to wear him out.

"If they choose on the basis of the work, we've got it made," Eric said.

"Yeah, but who does that?"

"We'll see."

"Our girls are better-looking than theirs," said Liv. He was talking about the account managers at WilliamsFriedman, their competitors in the final review round. "Don't think it doesn't help."

Liv was not ready to get to work; in fact, he'd never been much of a workhorse. "So how's the old man?" he asked.

"I think he's beginning to worry about the preservation of his soul."

"If I were your father, I would too." Liv was standing right next to Eric's desk and glanced down at the work he was doing. He always did this with a certain suspicious and hurt look, as if Eric had better, more interesting things to do, or as if he was cooking up a little side deal, a client he was cultivating for his own ends. This was not entirely unwarranted; just last week a firm they knew well had dissolved in a rash of desertions and coups, but Liv had to know that he and Eric were beyond that. "Stop it," Eric said.

He called Gail before lunch, to check in and take the temperature. Had she been scanning the apartment rentals this morning, or was all that over? He'd know in a second. He'd know as soon as she said hello; he'd know by whether she was distracted and answered on the fourth ring, or was impatient and answered on the first. It rang once. She was getting ready to go to work and was running behind, as usual. In the end, Eric pretended his real purpose was to tell her that if they got the FruitOut account he would probably go out for a celebratory dinner with the team, and if it was too late or too celebratory, he'd spend the night in the small apartment the firm kept for situations like this.

"What kind of celebration are you talking about?" she asked.

"Just taking the kids out."

Around four there was a sudden shout out in the cubicles. Someone gave a long blast on one of those earsplitting air horns, the kind of toy, like gumball machines and Nerf weapons, young copywriters like to keep at their desks. Eric's door burst open, and it was Aaron Allen, one of the copywriters. "The apple has landed," he said.

"We got FruitOut?"

"They just sent a fax." He held it up for Eric, a single sheet of paper with nothing written on it but a large exclamation point.

"That means yes? Are we sure?"

"Lilly's on the phone to them now," said Aaron, and Eric followed him out to the noisy gathering at her door. Eric did the businesslike thing, telling them all to shut up, but it was definitely yes Lilly was hearing on the phone, and she was thanking them with all the graciousness of a Presbyterian farm girl, as if no one would be wondering what she might have been doing beyond the haystacks in her teenage years. When she hung up there was another blast from the air horn, and then—because this is the sort of thing people did in advertising agencies, one of the reasons Eric loved them—the two copywriters on the team produced a present for Lilly, gift-wrapped in white and black Holstein-spotted paper.

She looked at it nervously before she opened it and discovered a cowbell, complete with collar. It was real; the bell was suitably stained and dented, and the leather was shiny with years of use. Lilly held it up and gave it a shake that produced the dull gong of beasts in the field. "Gee, guys," she said. "Thanks."

"You have to put it on," someone said.

"Fellas, where I grew up they put these on kids as a public humiliation, not as a reward." Still, she gamely undid the buckle and put it around her neck. When it was in place, she slumped her shoulders and looked up. "Satisfied?" she said. It was quite a sight, the heavy collar so loose around her small neck and the bell hanging down to her waist. It looked like an S/M apparatus.

A few minutes later she came clanking down the corridor to Eric's office. He was standing in front of his desk, and normally, in such a situation with a different woman, they would exchange a chaste little kiss, but not with her; her eyes were reckless with pride and pleasure: a big moment, not just a new account, but a win. Every ad agency in New York had taken a close look at this account. In fact, he had wondered several times why they were doing so well, such a small fish. He and Liv had already agreed that if they got the account they would have to hire up, possibly even rent the vacant floor above them in their building.

"I'm proud of you," he said.

"Thank you."

"Really, you don't have to wear that bell."

"It was cool of them to do it," she said. "Anyway, I wanted to thank you."

"It's your win."

"No, I mean it. Sometimes I think you don't know how much we all take your lead. Besides, we never would have gotten in the door without you."

That was true, but that's the way it worked, with balancing injustices: the kids do the work and get little credit; the farts get them the jobs and are treated as extraneous.

"You made it happen," she continued. "I know how difficult it was for you to work with someone like Rich Carlson."

Rich Carlson was the FruitOut partner none of them could stand. He was, Eric realized at the end of an endless luncheon with him, what Liv could be if Liv weren't ten times smarter: Liv was profane; Carlson was puerile. Guys like Carlson were the one part of the job that was almost intolerable. But Eric was a pro and he had done his bit, however distasteful, and the reward was Lilly, in his office flushed with triumph telling him he made it all possible. "Well, he's your problem now, honey."

The "honey" seemed right at the time—Eric was enough of a Southerner to claim it as idiom—but it surprised Lilly, and he watched her make a little mental calculation before she crossed over to him and gave him a hug. The bell kept their bodies apart, but she asserted the slightest—did he imagine this?—pelvic pressure. He could smell that soap again, or perhaps shampoo, now a full blast from the top of her head, and then she stood on tiptoes to give him a kiss on the lowest possible point on his cheek.

"Thanks," he said. One of those little bits of fruit from God's wonderful tree. It was her mood talking, her high after all those weeks of late-night high-energy labor. When Eric began at this trade those highs had lasted for days; he walked around town with steps lifted by sudden pulses of pride and satisfaction, a secret elation among the gray masses. What he had since learned, but did not tell her, was that most jobs were much more fun to win than to do. He did not tell her that these moments of triumph lasted no more than a few minutes for him now, and that these few minutes were really moments of relief, at best of thanksgiving, but not of celebration: he gave thanks that once again, he had been given something he hardly deserved. Instead of all this, he told her to gather everyone at six for a dinner at Fritz, and she went off excitedly, now perhaps relieved that this moment with him was over.

As the troops were gathering later for the party, he went next door to fetch Liv and found him sitting at his desk, staring out at the chessboard across the street: a woman working at a computer screen; a small conference in the window above her, three ladies pumping away at stationary bicycles in the health club on the top floor. It was not a cheery sight, these glimpses of other people's lives. "Ready to party?" Eric said.

Liv turned. He looked lousy. "Nah. You're there to grab the check. I think I'll pass."

"I thought this one was make or break."

"It was. We're made for another day."

"You sound worse than I do," Eric said. This really wasn't Liv's style, to miss a party. But Liv had so much more to trouble him than Eric did. His post-triumph crashes were deeper and more personal. He believed he had made a mess of much of his life. As collaborators and as partners they had made their share of business mistakes, and most of them had been Liv's fault: he had more creative flair than Eric did, but his judgment about people was flawed. Besides his own earned failings, one of his daughters was a manic-depressive living in a group home, and though no parent should feel the disease was his fault, Liv did, as Eric supposed he would, as any parent might.

"Hey, old friend. We'll miss you."

"Sure."

"I mean it."

"Sure," Liv said again, and waved him out.

They stood at the bar, ten of them, a boisterous group, but the waiters and barkeeps knew a good thing, and set up a table for them at the far end of the room. Fritz was their current camp spot in SoHo, a place in the bistro style, with plenty of dark wood and white tablecloths and, over the bar, an immense painting of a reclined nude in the Rubens school which they had all decided was Fritz, the owner. Eric felt happy to be there with these people, his troops. This was a celebration after all, and Eric could enjoy the moment now. What to do? Have a drink.

When they were shown to their table at a banquette in the back of the dining room, everyone waited for Eric to slide into the center spot. He felt justified in beckoning Lilly to sit at his right: it was her win, after all. He sprinkled the quick-witted and voluble copywriters around to carry the conversation. Amid the nice manageable buzz from his first martini, he thought of Gail, in the kitchen at home, alone, which seemed to be how she wanted to spend a lot of time in the future. He wished Liv were with them and figured the others did too; the two of them could do a pretty good routine, Eric the straight man, Liv the ironic counterweight, the one who delivered the punches. Few of these people suspected the darkness that was in Liv, was surely in him now as he headed uptown to his third bachelor pad, or sat alone in a bar somewhere. He'd be married again before too long, and Eric hoped this one would work out.

"So, Eric. Is this how winning is supposed to be?" This was from Marta Swenson, the other account manager besides Lilly, the other girl on the team who was prettier than the competition. She was blond, with big breasts that she displayed like Anita Ekberg swimming in the fountains of Rome. She was the one Liv had been referring to; Liv liked women he thought he could loll with. Lilly's high-energy, birdlike package, dark-eyed and sharp-chinned, wasn't his type.

"You tell me," Eric said to Marta.

"It's not quite on the level of winning a Clio," said Jesse, the copywriter with enough raw ambition to make Eric watch his back around him. Actually Eric had won two Clios, back before the award became something of a sham.

"Beats flogging home-equity loans," said Aaron.

"And the Neighborhood Health Plans," said Jesse.

"And the Bed Whorehouse, I mean *Warehouse*. 'Sleep with us.' " Everyone groaned. This account had been the pits; the tagline was the client's own idea, and they were very proud of it. In the end, the firm did what it could, which wasn't enough to save Whorehouse, which stiffed them for forty thousand dollars' worth of printing and ad space.

"Now then," Eric said. "No complaints. Let's remember the occasion here." He raised his glass. "To FruitOut!"

"And," added Aaron, "may our piss forever be the color of gold."

Lilly let out a good laugh at that one, and Eric realized she'd been silent during this back-and-forth, with not quite enough history in the shop to step in.

"I told you," he said to her. "Yellow."

"I'm sure it's healthy," said Marta. "It's like those cancer cures where you eat nothing but vegetable purée and then eliminate all those foul poisons. Right? I'm sure it's good for our kidneys."

"Let's stop talking about this," said Pat, the disagreeable designer, and Eric had to side with her, especially because their dinners, mostly steaks surely loaded with poisons, were now being served. His body had shifted toward Lilly, and he forced himself to face the other end of the table while she and one of their young designers talked.

Eric was left without a conversation, all these younger people around him chattering away, and suddenly he thought of Tom. Tom would have done fine in this group, such a funny, handsome man. God, how Eric loved him. Several of these people were not much older than he, and if they were accomplishing a good bit more in their careers already, Tom still had plenty of time. Eric hadn't gotten started in his career until he was twenty-six. He found himself wishing Tom still lived in the East. He wished, on a night like this, he could have called him up where he worked and brought him along.

He felt a nudge at his side. "Hey. Where'd you go to?" Lilly asked. The nudge was a little sloppy, but she wasn't slurring her words.

"Actually, I was thinking about my son."

"Thomas?"

"We called him Tommy when he was growing up, but now it's Tom. He's named for my wife's father."

"I bet you're a great dad."

In some ways this wasn't a topic he really wanted to be on, his paternity, but—maybe it was that face of hers—she seemed to be saying something more Darwinian: that he would be a good mate. She seemed to be referring more to the act of reproducing than to the issue.

"You've got to try, anyway," said Eric. "Having kids is what humans do, isn't it?"

"It's something I do my best to avoid these days."

He couldn't think of anything to add to that, and she was the one who broke the silence. "I just wanted to tell you something," she said. "You're a good man. I mean, you're a good person. I mean . . ." she faltered. Eric wasn't certain whether she had said the thing yet or not. "Shit," she said.

"That's okay. It's nice for you to say." He glanced around to see whether anyone was staring at them, but everyone else seemed noisily engaged in their own conversations.

"I mean you're good and kind, and you think the world should be a better place than it is, and sometimes you don't realize it just isn't."

This did perplex him: was she calling him naïve?

"I guess I'm a little drunk. Sorry."

"That's okay. So am I."

"I wanted to ask something."

He nodded noncommittally, but leaned in toward her. Her expression was young, and tentative, and a little fearful. This time, he knew what was coming. His heart began to beat loudly: he wasn't sure that this was what he wanted now. But he wasn't sure he didn't want it, either. That's what desire is, not a thing-in-itself but a state of being suspended between need and fear, the utter intoxication of uncertainty. That's why sex is wonderful, because it can't be done alone; because someone has to offer to do this thing.

"Would you like to come back with me?" she asked.

So that was the way it happened; that's the way it often happens. A little too much booze, an evening thick with celebration, a little too much freedom. The party was breaking up. It was past eleven but several of them—the copywriters and Marta, anyway—were making a plan to head out to a bar, and they asked Eric if he wanted to join them. He pleaded middle age and other responsibilities. Lilly stood up to go to the bathroom and staggered noticeably.

Pat, at his left, whispered, "Is she going to make it?"

"Sure," he said. "She's fine."

In the end it was Eric and Paul Ramirez remaining and waiting for Lilly to return. "She doesn't live too far from my stop," said Paul, a dutiful gentleman, with a Mexican brand of courtliness. "I'll make sure she gets home."

"There's no need for that. I'm staying at the flat tonight. Let's get a cab and I'll drop you both off."

"It's okay. We'll be fine on the subway."

"Paul," Eric said. "We'll take a cab."

He sent Paul off to find one and there Eric was, standing in the doorway of this restaurant, waiting for his date. God help him, but he felt great; here he was looking back in his life, back to when "he's fucking her and she's / Taking pills or wearing a diaphragm," as that old misanthrope Larkin says, back to "everyone young going down the long slide / To happiness, endlessly"; Eric knew, tonight, he was heading back into that dreamed-of paradise. He wanted to taste it, like this, youthful and heedless, again.

It was warm for March and the streets of SoHo were still full of activity, couples and small groups, blasts of music from open restaurant and bar doorways, galleries still open in blazes of light and splashes of color. He heard Lilly come up behind him and even though Paul might have been standing right on the other side of the door, he leaned down to kiss her, her thin lips, the dart of her tongue, firm and wet.

They looked at each other. "I'm glad we got that over with," she said.

They moved out into the street and while they were waiting, one of the waiters, a lanky kid with frizzy red hair and two earrings, came running out the door. For a moment Eric was afraid he'd forgotten in the excitement to pay the bill, but he heard a gong sound, and the waiter held up Lilly's cowbell.

A cab finally pulled up with Paul in the backseat, and they squeezed in beside him. They rode silently, and who knew now whether it was appropriate or indecent, but he gave the cabby Paul's address first, and when they dropped him off, he gave Eric a look so full of disapproval that he felt he had just been denied absolution by a priest. Paul slammed the door a bit too hard, and when the cab pulled away from the curb, Lilly said, "Oh dear."

"Yes," Eric said, "a problem," but they were soon making out, her dress hiked up to her waist. It had been maybe six years since he had last done this, and that last incident had been such a mechanical waste of time he had successfully sworn off temptations. He'd made love to five women in his life, not a lot by modern standards, but since Gail was the first woman he slept with before they were married, four of these had been affairs. But all that had seemed over for him. He was wrong, of course, and the pleasure he took in this fumbling—in the cab, in her building lobby, on the elevator, at her door—made him feel as if this was the first time all over again. And for a brief moment he found himself answering Gail's voice in his head. *I, mull? Whatever this is, it ain't mulling.*

Her apartment was the standard West Side one-bedroom, with a long corridor immediately inside the door running past the bathroom and coat closet and into the small living room, with its even smaller bed alcove separated from it only by a pair of French doors. She had decorated it with some care, a nice green velvet couch and two rust-colored chairs; a single Edward Hopper print on the wall, not many books, not much music. Eric liked the fact that it was all a little messy, magazines and mail in stacks here and there, a small basket of laundry waiting on the floor at the French doors. If she'd planned this, she wouldn't have left the laundry there.

They were on each other almost wordlessly, and he literally lost his breath when she unzipped the back of her somewhat prim dress—that's the way account executives have to look—and let it fall to the floor. He was like most men: he'd never gotten over his boyish fascination with girls' underwear, because he was, in the end, attracted most by the shape of women's bodies, by the form. He loved women's waists; that simple curve was the most erotic thing about the female for him, right up to the point of lovemaking.

When they were in the bedroom she reached into her bedside table and pulled out a condom and handed it to him.

He left her apartment about three, after dozing a bit, making love a second time, and then dozing a bit more. She did not stir much as he dressed—they engaged in no guilty prattle and made no declarations—but he couldn't help kissing her neck, and then her breast, and then her lips, before he headed out the door.

He waited a long time for an empty cab, and it was an old guy driving, an Irish cabby in a golf hat, too old to be out this late, or this early. Eric gave the address for the flat. Oh, he'd pay for this one, at the final accounting. Sooner than later, probably. Why do this? It was already not worth it.

There was hardly anyone on the streets, the city in its unreal early dawn, street lamps piercing the night and silencing all with their yellow glow. Would any of this hold up? Who knew, except that, in the end, Lilly would marry someone older, though not as old as he, and after not too many more years of success she'd find a way to pack up the husband—a journalist, a TV correspondent—and move them back to Milwaukee or Minneapolis. She'd take the Midwest by storm, and her kids would be small and coordinated and great hockey players, even the girls, and she'd get older and that curly black hair would turn a wiry gray. She might even send him Christmas cards with some kind of naughty code reflecting back to this night. Before Eric knew it there were tears running down his cheeks, tears without sobs; a release. Tears that seemed not for him or from him, but from another's heart, as if his eyes and tear ducts were simply being borrowed for a few minutes—tears for us all, for our hopes and sins.

THREE

"The word is 'mistake,' isn't it."

"No."

"Are you trying to deny it?"

Frank held up his flattened palm and wagged it side to side, a coy and perverse gesture. He'd been expecting this; perhaps he had assumed that sooner or later Eric would figure it out, this glyph that actually was not far from the intended word. His eyes were sparkling, poised above Eric's words. He was wearing a snappy red bow tie.

"You meant it last time. I think you let it out by . . . well, by mistake. You almost wept. You were telling me that you had made mistakes, and I guess you meant it as some kind of confession. Right? You're telling me that you have made mistakes in your life, but, Dad, that isn't exactly news to you and me."

Frank chose to ignore this last statement: he was too delighted to have been given the word at last. "Mistakes," he said, perfectly. Now he beamed; given the word, he could at last say it, days of frustration gone with just a few sounds, the right sounds. *Mottseck. Christ! How could I have thought that's the way you say it?*

"Over the last few weeks I've been trying to figure out what you meant, really. I was trying to figure out whether it had anything to do with Grammy. Remember? We were looking at those pictures when you said it—" He interrupted himself and fished into his briefcase for the copies he had ordered from the best photo lab in New York. He held up the two envelopes, the originals and the copies.

"Good boy. On the desk."

Eric was sitting in the old leather-and-wood banker's chair in front of the enormous rolltop, and he spun around to put the envelopes on the neat piles of paperwork. He stopped to glance over the letter at the top, a long unreadably convoluted form letter about some aspect of Frank's Medicare. "Is Alice going to take care of this?" he asked, holding it up.

His father nodded.

"But I was telling you I was thinking about mistakes. A lot, actually, and not just yours. Believe me, not just yours. But what were you saying? That's what I want to know. I got you onto something, and I remembered you said, 'Help.' At the time, I thought you were asking for help finding the word, but that wasn't it, was it. You wanted help with some mistake, right? Was there more to this Matt Billings thing? I haven't called him back, by the way."

Frank said, "Do it. A favor to him."

Adam poked his head in. "Miss Alice is coming over," he said. Adam loved calling her "Miss Alice"; he didn't mean it kindly.

Frank groaned, and hid his eyes in the crook of his elbow, his standard enactment for fear.

"What for?" Eric asked.

"Miss Alice didn't say."

Adam left, closing the door. It was warmer this week, almost warm enough in the house to begin spreading out into it, and when real spring finally took hold, out onto the front porch. The porch was where Frank ran the show in the summer; it was how Eric would always remember him from youth, because during the summer Frank was more often home and not—as Eric's mother used to say bitterly—"across the bay." It was easy for Eric these days to overlook how his father had been as a young man, the good and the bad, but he could always conjure that image of him on the porch in his seersucker trousers, white shirt, and bow tie. There were always people in the house in those summer months, always men in their ties and shirtsleeves, the odor of old-man sweat high enough to overpower the wafts of honeysuckle and cow manure flowing through the screens. Frank sat in the middle, the youngest man in the group, tipping back in his wicker chair against the shutters, smoking his Chesterfields, scheming. Eric liked watching, because it was a show he was seeing, his father behaving not entirely honorably. Maybe his district was just a bunch of mule-and-wagon dairy farms, but it was Eric's entire world and everyone knew who ran it. Sometimes Eric would peek out of his eavesdropping place behind the massive wicker settee, and his father would make sure to pull him in, make some joke or comment that went way over his head, and the men would all laugh. Good one, Frank, they said. Fine little feller. Now, about them Nigras . . . This was the Eastern Shore, after all, across the bay, a sliver of the Old South nestled right up to the Mason-Dixon Line.

Eric continued his monologue. "As I was saying, I've spent a lot of time thinking about mistakes, but it may be the first time I've ever heard you say something like that. That is news, if you don't mind me saying. Just acknowledging . . ." He stopped to gauge the reaction to these gentle recriminations: it could be rage; that was what it could be in the past, a sarcasm close to nuclear. But there was none of that now. Frank was breathing somewhat noisily, as if listening was costing him effort. Eric threw him a bone. "I've had to do some acknowledging of my own in the past few weeks," he said.

The morning after his night with Lilly they had both come in late, and the first face he saw was Paul Ramirez's. Paul fixed Eric with a look of such unbridled disdain that Eric had to go into his office and shut the door. He stayed in his office all morning. Outside he heard the continued high spirits of the winning FruitOut team, the young kids complaining of hangovers but still caught in the triumph. At eleven, in the conference room with the full team, there was Lilly with her files in her hand, and an absolute tidal wave of regret and horror washed over him. Their eyes met, and her demeanor was reassuringly professional, uncolored with recent intimacies, but Eric assumed that his face was all but purple.

After the meeting he asked her to come back with him to his office, and without weighing the symbols, he closed the door after her.

"Did you notice Paul?" he asked.

"Yeh. Not good."

"No." She waited for him to continue, but what to say? He fell back on his manners. "I guess I want to say thank you."

"I had fun too, but." She stopped.

"You're right. But." They looked at each other, and it did not really surprise him that she still seemed remarkably casual about the whole thing: she wasn't married. For a post-sixties kid, sleeping with someone was a smaller matter, a recreation for the moment, not a promise for the future. As far as that went, Eric himself was on the cusp: the impulse was there, but the reflection was still old school, church, priests, duty. She began to look a little annoyed as his silence continued.

"We were both a little drunk," he said finally.

"We don't need any big thing here, Eric."

"No. We don't."

"The thank-you was enough. I had fun, too. We're even. We just won't do it again."

When she was ready to leave, he took her small hand in his and gave it a slight squeeze, a last intimacy with this body, and then— now that all was safe again—the image of making love to her came pouring back to him, and once she was gone he was almost reassured by it, as if they'd simply go back to flirting, back to the time before, as if nothing had happened. And that, it seemed, was that, a proper parting, a modern accommodation, a mere episode. But in the days since then, this brief conversation had kept returning to his mind, as if there was something he had missed in it, and at length he had located the source of his unease. We're even. Even? At the time he took it as a sort of joke, something co-conspiratorial. But she hadn't really said it with any tone of irony.

Frank had been waiting all this time for Eric to continue, but a man who now spoke largely with his face was also a reader of faces, and if he couldn't see the entire memory of this office scene played out like a movie on Eric's forehead, he could get the gist. He fixed his eyebrows in a fatherly gesture of concern, an invitation to unburden.

"Oh, man," said Eric. "Regret is the human condition. It's not a religious concept, is it? Our religions are full of sin and error and forgiveness and redemption and atonement, but when all is done, when the priest has done his work and packed up his chalice to go home, you're left with regret to deal with on your own. 'Sorry, buddy, that's not part of the package.' " Eric had no stomach to continue into confession to his father. He concluded with what he hoped was a throwaway. "Regret is probably just a character defect anyway, don't you think."

Frank wouldn't let it go. "A reminder. Things left undone."

"Things left undone": perfectly spoken, that ancient liturgical formulation. Eric made a note to himself to ask Adam whether Frank had been speaking this well all week. Something was up. Frank's busy mind was focusing. And a small voice in Eric's own slightly tortured conscience began to be heard. "So," he said, "how do things left undone get done?"

"Dunow." Frank shrugged and raised his hand. "Lost. Lost." He fixed his eyes on Eric's to suggest that he was equally stymied. "Undone."

"Bullshit. Things never have to remain undone."

Frank returned his most noncommittal and, in this case, dismissive hand wave, a rare instance of patronizing.

"I'm not trying to diminish what you're feeling," Eric said.

Another wave of the hand, this one indicating it was time to move on to new subjects, but Eric wasn't ready to let it go just yet. If nothing else, he'd worked hard for that word.

"But what are you thinking about?"

Frank kept the hand down this time; he couldn't, it seemed, totally stonewall this one: it was too deep. "Your mother," he said.

Eric could not help audibly sucking in a mouthful of air. As far as he could remember, his father had never mentioned her, not in this way, as a person he'd give thought to. "Well, things left undone, and things done, too."

"Yes, yes." He was taking this without complaint. In fact, he added three more yesses.

Eric decided to let it go at that, and turned to the news: Tom went on a skiing trip and his roommate lost the car keys on the slopes. "Tom was very funny about it, a kid who has lost absolutely every conceivable category of things in his time."

"A good boy," said Frank, though he did not know him well.

"I have such faith in him. I wish he wasn't in Denver, but I must say, I look at your relationship with Alice and I wonder whether it really is advisable for a child to stay in the same town. I really wish you'd stop dumping on her, and I'm going to speak to Adam because this 'Miss Alice' stuff is really out of line. Jesus. Alice has done more grunt work for you than anyone over the years. Not just for you, but for Marjorie, too, and who the hell was Marjorie to her. Don't you think?"

"Mottsecks."

"Not that Alice would really notice. I know she's bossy, but that's the way girls are supposed to be, especially oldests."

They had run out of things to say at that moment, and they let a silence fall over them. Eric's eyes settled on the old framed family photograph on Frank's desk. It must have been taken in 1962. Poppy was in Audrey's arms; they were flanked by Alice and Eric—the latter cool and breezy and apparently ignorant of all the troubles buffeting the room—and behind lurked Frank, the smug patriarch, already planning to use this picture in the literature for his upcoming campaign for the U.S. Senate. It wouldn't have fooled the women voters. In this fading print Eric could still make out the despair on his mother's face: if this was the shot they chose for their Christmas card, what could the others have looked like? But if Frank felt an ounce of remorse for his accumulating list of crimes against this blameless family, it was going to take more than a local guy with a camera to pry it out of him.

They were startled out of this quiet by the sounds of Alice opening the front door, tramping in, shedding her outerwear, getting right to the task. "Hello, Adam," she called out cheerily. "It's me."

Adam responded with a muffled yell from the kitchen, and then they heard her footsteps approach. She stood for a moment on the threshold. "God," she said. "It smells like a locker room in here. Did you shower this morning, Eric?"

"Hi, honey. You smell rosy, as always."

Alice was a fine-looking woman, but even when she was a baby, her features looked older and more physically mature than her age; in her middle fifties, Alice looked ten years older. Sometimes it made Eric nervous, to think he might look as old as she, and maybe he did. Alice favored their mother's side, a bit dumpy in a pleasant sort of way, though their mother took a lot more care with her dress. Alice had always gravitated toward full skirts, jumpers in winter, functional garments for a functional person.

Eric admired the heedless way she dressed, as if she had no interest in competing with Poppy, the pretty one of the family.

"Hi, Daddy." She hugged him, and did not seem to notice that she got an unusually full hug in return.

"So how are things?" Eric asked, moving to the bed to give her the chair.

"Better since the rain stopped. I'm feeling much better." Alice was always recovering from some ailment. She spied the manila envelopes on the desk and immediately picked them up. "What's this?"

"Photographs. You've seen them all."

She opened a flap and peered in, as if she didn't believe him, but her mind was on other things, a mission of some sort.

"How's Alden?" Eric asked.

Alice made a disparaging scowl. "He's in Georgia, playing golf." This too was typical; maybe everything siblings do is typical. Alice and Alden appeared to have made a good enough marriage. Eric had always thought of his brother-in-law as an affable lug in the Southern style—fundamentally decent, would hurt no one if he thought about it, just needing a bit of enlightenment. For years Eric had been giving him books for Christmas—the Odyssey, *Beloved,* a history of the Ottoman Empire—even though he knew Alden hadn't read a book since he graduated from Vanderbilt. After years of this, Alden finally took Eric aside and said, mirthfully skeptical, "Tell me, Eric. You don't actually *read* this stuff you give me, do you?"

Alice turned to Frank and said loudly, "How are you?" Ever since his stroke, Alice had shouted at her father as if he were deaf, which he was not. It may have been one of the reasons that Frank cowered from her.

"Good. Good."

"You didn't get a chill during that bad weather on Friday?"

"No." He pointed to his trusty space heater of fifties vintage, the kind with dangerous-looking wires coiled around a glowing ceramic core.

Alice was full of news and gossip from town, and Eric was happy to let her take over; they often operated like a tag team in these conversations, and these local morsels were savories that Frank dearly loved. He had represented this district for thirty-five years until he was expelled from the Senate. A bimbo on his payroll, oldest story in politics, but a sensation in Maryland, a sour measure of the influence he had once wielded. For all the bitterness of the years after that, he remained interested in the district, a bitchy familial concern; there were people whose misadventures would give him pleasure. He remembered well the prehistory of every spicy tale Alice could serve up; he knew the parents of the local thug, who had been thugs themselves; he and only he recalled that a long-standing county feud between two prominent families had started over a duck blind.

In this arena Eric could hardly compete with Alice. Even if he'd still lived on the Shore, he wouldn't have noticed or remembered any of the bits Alice played out with such a fine sense of timing and bawdy detail. Most of these stories Alice picked up at "a time for fellowship and coffee" after services at her church, the church in town and not the little Episcopal chapel their father went to. Eric sat while Frank was being so roundly amused and he felt particularly pleased that he had spoken up for Alice. What worse and more relentless role in life than family caregiver?

Eric had taken a long vacation from the mess that was his family, about ten years in the seventies and eighties when he simply ignored the whole thing. That included his father's marriage to his second wife, Marjorie. He did not attend the wedding, and had really only talked to her at all during the last months of her losing battle against cancer. Tom was ten before he ever saw his grandfather's house in Maryland. Eric came back at the lowest point of all: the expulsion, the disgrace, but he did it entirely because Alice shamed him into it. So Alice had performed a miracle of sorts—she had preserved the loyalty of her father's issue, at least two of the three. It drove their mother to fury: "Well, I *know* you *children* are absolutely *devoted* to your *father*."

"And you left the Shore because you thought it was dull," concluded Alice to Eric.

"You're right. That's why I moved to Summit, New Jersey."

"I guess," said Alice. "Something like that."

Frank was tired out, and he was leaning back in his chair with his head against one of the wings. Soon he would be napping.

"Let's give Dad a break," Eric said.

As usual, Alice had brought a full basket of casseroles, a stew, some fried chicken. Only when she was really busy did she resort to the frozen entrees from the Safeway. Adam couldn't complain about this; he wasn't a cook and wasn't supposed to be.

When she came back from the kitchen, she suggested they take a walk. Eric loved this landscape in winter, the grays and browns stippled with sturdy evergreen of the box bush and magnolias and holly, the fields stretching away from the house covered with a lush, unlikely blanket of winter wheat. At this moment of seasonal turn, the frozen stubble was beginning to release its secrets, its perfumes and its beasts, a stirring from the core of life.

They set off toward the barns down the lane between the elephant gray of the beech trees and a line of small yellow sheds. "What's up?" he asked.

"Whatever it is, it's your fault."

"Isn't it written in the Constitution that before I'm punished I get to know what crime I committed?"

"Haven't you noticed?"

"Uh. No. Not really. What?"

"Those photographs. The family papers."

That was not what Eric had expected. "That's just family stuff," he protested. "He's been doing it for months. I'd think you'd approve."

She made a horselike sound that made it clear she did not.

Eric turned toward her. They were under a large black walnut tree, where she and he once had a treehouse: one or two of the weathered stepping boards were still clinging to the trunk. "I can't imagine anything more appropriate, anything more healthful for Dad than to be organizing all this stuff. I think you're being nuts."

"It's not the sort of thing he's ever done before."

"He's never been eighty-two before." They resumed walking, almost as slowly as if Frank were with them. "I think he's preparing the way, refreshing his mind, so he can gratefully and happily slide back into the past, live his last years as if he had speech, and legs. Maybe he wants to be sure he remembers everyone's names when he meets them in the afterlife."

"That's very poetical, but there's more to it than that."

Yes, Eric was certainly beginning to understand that there was a good deal more to it than that.

"Ever since you were here the last time, he's been distracted.

You stirred something up," she added, eyes narrowed with accusation. "He's being secretive and I don't like it."

"Has he said anything to you?"

"He never says anything to me. You know that." It hurt; it always had.

Eric stopped again to give her a comforting hug. "I'm sorry. Don't feel bad about it. It's just that he depends on you so much. We all know that if you weren't here, none of this would work. Okay? Honey?"

They resumed walking, past the old pigpen, down the gully where the waste from a hundred cows had once poured freely into the bay. "He did say something to me," said Eric finally.

"What?"

"A word. 'Mottsecks.' " He waited a moment to see if she could figure it out, but she had no patience for the game. "Mistakes."

"Whose?"

"That's just what Gail said. His own, I guess. He's talking about his mistakes. We were touching on it when you came in."

"I knew it." The self-pity was gone from her voice, replaced by a more steely calculation. She was getting strategic. She was playing out scenarios in her brain like a chess player three moves—so she always assumed about herself—ahead of her opponent.

They were standing in the barnyard now, old horse barns sealed tight, the abandoned milking parlor rotting away, the sheds full of junk, old boats, ancient farm apparatus; one bay contained a complete, uncataloged history of lawn mowers. This familiar place had once been a magical realm of hideaways, forts, haylofts to jump off, corn cribs to inhabit, pigeons to catch and keep, rats to shoot. Alice and Eric did all of that together; she could nail a rat in the head with a .22 from a hundred feet. As unlikely as it seemed now, she had been a tomboy, like most farm girls, if not like Poppy.

"The day after your last visit," said Alice, "he asked Adam to buy him a map, a road atlas, and he's spent the past few weeks studying it."

"Weird."

"You know one of the states he was poring over?"

"No. Tell me," Eric said, but he had already guessed the answer.

"Alabama."

"Aha."

"Oh, stop that 'aha' business," snapped Alice. "You know what's up, and you're not telling me."

"I don't. I didn't know anything about this map business."

"Hmmm," she said, her lips tight as wire.

It was Eric's turn to be impatient. "Cut it out, Alice. Did you say anything to Mom about this?"

"Are you kidding? Give me some credit here."

"It's probably nothing," Eric said finally. "It'll pass. He's reflecting on his mistakes, that much he has said." He looked up to deflect the accusatory widening of her eyes. "Really, I didn't think that much of it. He's admitting to himself that he regrets a lot of what went on. He should, but I think it's his own business. Maybe he wants to confess."

"Then let him talk to Brother Farley," said Alice, referring to the rather saturnine monk from Baltimore who conducted services in the chapel.

" 'Mottseck. Friggert. No. Yes. No. Shit.' Not sure that would get the job done."

"Just promise me," concluded Alice. They had completed the circuit and were approaching her car.

"Promise you what?"

"That you won't let him do anything stupid."

"Sure."

"Say you promise. Say if you break it you'll let me spit in your mouth."

"Okay. I promise. I won't let him do anything stupid and if I do, I'll let you spit my mouth."

Alice seemed to think she'd taken care of the problem for the day; a lucky thing she'd dropped in, taken Eric aside, gotten to the bottom of this. So much effort just to keep things on track. She put her hand on the door handle of her enormous Ford Expedition, an odd choice for her, but, typically, the basic model, bench front seat, no frills. She said she had to go. Choir practice for evensong; her pitch was uncertain but she sang con brio. "I wish you'd come sometime," she said. "You'd like the new rector. He's big on all that mystery and doubt you love."

"Maybe I will, sometime."

"I worry about you."

"Work. Life. Marriage." He shrugged. "But I know you're watching out for my eternal soul."

"Don't evade me. We all have to care for each other, don't we."

"We do. Thanks, honey." They hugged, a hard squeeze that felt good, and for the zillionth time in his life, Eric felt bad for all his mean thoughts about her, this big sister who was still watching out for him. He watched her head off, gunning her SUV through the rotting gateposts with only inches to spare on either side. She probably bought the car to haul altar flowers, meals-on-wheels, for outings from the local elderly day-care center. More Alices in the world, Eric thought; perhaps a more irritating place, but a better place.

Adam was in the kitchen making tea. Eric delivered a convoluted scolding for the way he treated Alice, to which Adam responded with only barely enough contrition.

"Alice told me about the road atlas," Eric said.

"I felt I had to tell her." *See?* he was saying, *I know my duty in this house. I know who signs my checks.*

"Can I see it?"

"To tell you the truth, I think he's hidden it. He saw me peeking at it and got right testy."

"What do you think?" Eric asked.

"I don't think he should plan any big trips. Doctor's orders, bad for the ticker. There's not that much holding it all together."

"But what if he wants to? What if he wants to make amends, or something like that?"

"I don't know about that, Eric. I'm a nurse, not a priest. I just know when people his age and condition start to go, they can deteriorate real fast."

"Well," said Eric, over the whistling of the teakettle, "let's go see if we can worm it out of him."

Eric went to the study door and cracked it open. He could see his father's face, mouth still open, but his eyelids were stirring. The gentle creak from the door, one of the voices in his beloved house, had whispered him awake, and he closed his mouth in a peaceful line. But his eyes popped open when Eric walked in, and there was a sudden flash of fear, and Eric knew what it was: this was the return of the wakened consciousness that knew how defenseless it was against any outside threat, any large quick form, dark as a bear, as if waking from the vigor of nightmare only to confront the helplessness of his reality.

"It's me."

"Eric," he said finally. Eric's name was one word he could never get right. The "r" sound in the middle was the problem: it demanded a certain agility, a quick half curl of the tongue after the breathy wide-open shape of the "E." The best he could do was "E-o-ick."

"You're tired. You were having too good a time with Alice."

His brow formed a question, a confusion: had he forgotten Alice had been there? It was times like this that made Eric nervous, when he had to speak to him as one would to an Alzheimer's patient: *You know, Alice? Your daughter?*

"Her gossip," Eric said hopefully. "The story about the Colleys?" This would have to do, and at least the confusion left his brow. He swiped at his face and then gave out a last cleansing breath. Yes, now he was back, straightening up stiffly in his chair, sweeping aside the glasses, TV remote control, books, and magazines on his table to make room for his tea.

"It's showtime," said Adam, his usual teatime entrance, but delivered with not much vigor. He put down the cups and then stood back.

"Coke?" said Frank.

"We're all out. Fire the help. I'll just have to miss this teatime."

"No. Sit." Frank pointed to the stool. He wasn't just being polite.

"Uh-oh. Am I going to get another whipping about Miss Alice?"

Eric glared at Adam, but he sat down. This was business. No one, Eric realized warily, was going to have to worm anything out of his father this time.

Frank took his normal first loud sip and then rolled the hospital table out of his way. He propped himself up by pushing against the chair back with his good hand, and then brought himself to his feet, his bad arm hanging down, the palm of the claw pointing backward. Watching this painful exercise, Eric had once concluded, was like seeing those old newsreels of inventors trying to launch flying machines, contraptions as unlikely and spindly as giraffes. But once Frank got up, he was relatively stable. Neither Adam nor Eric helped him as he shuffled over to his desk, swatting Eric out of the way so he could get at a drawer. "Good. Good," he muttered to himself, when the vinyl cover of the road atlas came into view. He took it out, closed the drawer, and made his way back to his chair.

He spread the atlas on his table and flipped through the first few pages until he got to Alabama. He smoothed out the stiff folds as well as he could, anchored the edges with the selection of brass weights that were part of his hospital table ensemble, and then looked up to beckon over Adam and Eric. When they were standing to either side, he traced the diagonal line of I-59 across the state to Birmingham. Adam let out a disapproving sigh. Frank ignored it and looked up at Eric.

"Birmingham," Eric said. "Capital of Alabama. The Magic City. Vulcan's Anvil."

Frank did not want to hear any jokes about this, and made his point by pounding his yellow fingernail on the spot.

"Do you want me to go to Birmingham?" Eric asked, though he knew that wasn't it. "There's some business you want me to conduct with my mother?"

"No. No. No."

"You want to go there yourself."

"Yes. You take me."

"To do what?"

"Mottsecks." He'd lost the word again, not that it mattered now.

"You want to go visit her? She's still a little peeved, you know. Thirty-five years hasn't been quite long enough for her." Eric did not know exactly why he was responding with these lame jokes; he could sense the irritation they were causing his father. But all through this long process of communication, Eric had been getting giddier by the minute. This plan, the image of them on the road, could only remind him of his earlier days, a cross-country trip from college for no reason but to do it, over and back all on one semester break. His father was more than a stand-in for his old roommate Steve Light; this was stranger, more unexpected. Eric

hadn't felt quite like this in years, suddenly punchy with life's pos-
sibilities. This glorious, perhaps mad gesture toward how things
ought to be. Why not do this? An old man, his father, stirring for
perhaps the last time, planning his escape from regret, a voyage of
redemption.

"Well?" said Frank.

Eric had recently made certain promises, and had just received a
small dose of paramedical opinion; he stifled his elation. "Couldn't
we write her? Wouldn't that be good enough?"

"No. It wouldn't."

"Mr. Frank—" started Adam, but he was shut off with a sharp
downward cut of the palm.

"When would you want to go?"

"Now," Frank said, in his command voice, the sound they had
always called Sergeant Bilko noises.

"I couldn't do it now," said Eric, his mind suddenly back in his
office: FruitOut. Lilly, Liv. "There's some big stuff brewing in the
shop."

"Next week."

"No. Maybe in a few weeks I could steal a couple of days.
When it gets warmer. Maybe. Do you know what you want to say
to her?"

"No. Yes."

"How are you going to do it?"

"You."

"I can't read your mind. This is uncharted territory for me. I
wouldn't have—shall we say—the context to go on. I won't be
able to translate for you."

"You will."

Adam broke in again. "How're you going to manage, Mr.
Frank?"

"You, too. You come, too."

Adam had not thought of this, and neither had Eric, but it
shouldn't have surprised either of them. "I don't think it's a good
idea," said Adam. "I told Eric that."

"You knew?" This pleased him totally.

"We guessed. But there's another problem," said Eric.

"Yes," answered Frank. "Many problems." He said "bop-
lems"; he was getting tired.

"Mom will never agree. She won't let you come. She won't even allow you to *ask* for forgiveness, if that's what this is about. I'm sorry, but I think you know that."

Frank did, had clearly recognized from the start that this was his major hurdle. His body, which had been rigid with determination, slumped a bit. "You," he said. "Help."

Eric could make the call, not that he had the slightest desire to do it. He could call, chat a bit, then clear his throat and tell his mother that actually, he had a specific reason on his mind, and that he wanted her to be—he was already choosing his words carefully—"open-minded" about what he had to say. Et cetera. He could make the uniquely privileged appeal of child to parent, *You must do this for me,* and she would protest and complain in her haughtiest and most matronly tone, but she would not and could not abrogate her compact with her children. And then she would spend a month stewing, and when the day came, if it ever came, that they arrived at her door, a block of marble would be waiting for them. She'd speak as if she were giving a news conference. Her phrases would be full of locutions like "most certainly" and "shall" and "absolutely insupportable." It would be awful, and pointless, and on the day Eric died, he would still be returning to this scene as the one enterprise in his life he truly regretted.

Or, they could simply not tell her they were coming.

Frank and Adam were both staring at him as he mulled, two fingers working the corners of his mouth.

"Well?" said Frank again.

"We'll get you there, Dad. The rest will be up to you."

FOUR

Love is patient, says Saint Paul, in the Epistles, one portion of the
Bible that Eric had continued to tiptoe back to, a little bedtime
reading now and again. The Epistles are where the sandal hits the
road. Eric liked the drama of it, Paul's calculations, feeding the
spiritual needs of his scattered domain, words of encouragement
to the most beleaguered outposts, threats to the most unreliable
distant fiefdoms. Most of the time, Saint Paul seems a little fran-
tic, extemporizing like crazy. Eric liked to picture him at his desk,
late at night. God help me, the Corinthians are missing the boat
again. So he writes that love is patient, love is kind, and sends this
message out with the next courier, sends those isolated souls back
to their huts to confront their own faults, where they discover
that the wisdom and truth of this observation only grows in rela-
tion to the wisdom and truth of the opposite statement, that love
is impatient and unkind, something Saint Paul knew all along.

Late the next week, they held the first firm review on FruitOut
in the conference room, though it was clear by then that Eric
was being nudged out of the loop. The copywriters were proposing the tag "Get the fruit out!" and he had told Aaron earlier that
it sounded as if they were telling people not to use the product.
Aaron allowed that Eric could have his own opinion, but that

so far, the team liked it. Lilly was wearing what he had always thought his favorite outfit, a somewhat old-fashioned wool flannel dress with a wonderful hourglass silhouette. She could make business wear from Talbot's look like lingerie, but so what: the female form is everywhere these days, in underpants on the sides of buses, a flash of buttock in an ad for hip replacement surgery. Eric didn't have time for sex, didn't really have time for further regret.

After the conference he could not avoid a short meeting in his office with Lilly on other accounts, and he told her he would be taking some time off in the next few weeks. "I suppose that's for the best," he said.

"Yeh," she answered, but since their single conversation on the morning after, she had been all business with him; on personal matters, she affected a careless indifference.

"I'm just telling you this because I want Liv to take the lead for the FruitOut presentation."

She seemed mildly surprised that he said this. "Liv already is," she pointed out.

"That's what I'm saying," he said, working a little not to be snappish, which was a not unfamiliar tone in the office. But in fact he was equally, if mildly surprised to hear her state this. He turned the conversation to the other concerns of management. "Don't neglect the other stuff, Beckman, and give Arnie Traber a call, will you? Don't let the big new account make you lose sight of the others, which are the real bread and butter."

"Sure," she said. "Is that all?"

The tone was not all that different in his conversation with Liv later in the day. He repeated his uneasiness about the tag, and asked what other candidates they were preparing, and Liv brushed him off. "We'll be ready," Liv said about the presentation, which was now only three weeks away.

"I'm going to be taking a few days off. Next week, I think. Just a few days. My father. He—"

"He calls. You come," interrupted Liv, supremely uninterested in the details.

"If you say so."

"I wish to hell you'd get a beeper. Or a goddamn cell phone like any other adult. Get into the nineties."

"I'm going to be in Alabama."

"Alabama. Christ, I'll have to reach you by pigeon."

"I'll check in."

He left work feeling extraneous, which he could appreciate in the place of those weeks and months when it seemed that the solvency of the whole operation and the lives of twenty-five people rested entirely on his shoulders. Gail was out for the evening. She left a note that she and Rebecca Walsh and Amy Aronson were taking in dinner and a movie, and that she would be home by eleven.

He put on a pot of water for spaghetti, which he would eat with an extra chunk of guilty butter that Gail would not have allowed. He went upstairs to change. The house seemed extraordinarily empty. When he entered the bedroom he called out the dog's name, and all he got was a single desultory thump of the tail from under the bed. This was not good, this emptiness. He went back downstairs, turned on some Mozart at high volume, poured himself a drink, and tried to interest himself in the mail. He overcooked his spaghetti, in part because he'd come to think that the cooking instructions on all pasta had now become an affectation: eight minutes, two minutes for fresh ravioli that would come out stiff as a potato chip. Even the extra butter didn't help. From then on he was just killing time until he could call Tom, and when he did, about nine, he was a little too joyful when Tom answered on the second ring.

Eric hadn't spoken to his son in a few weeks; usually he had a purpose, but Tom realized soon enough that this was just making contact.

"So how's things?" Eric asked.

"Good. I have now seen the depths of hell."

"What's there?"

"A gray steel desk in an office that looks like a front for an FBI sting, and a temp job as a dispatcher for a courier service. I got yelled at in four Eastern European languages."

"Sounds hellish enough."

"Well, that's my life." He said this in his accusatory way.

"Come on, Bear. All you have to do is set a goal and you'll have a good job in a month. You've got plenty of time. When I was your age I wasn't even trying. It's just that we had the war and the threat of the draft to let us pretend that we were making choices."

Tom let out a grunt; he'd heard all of that before. "How's Mom?" he asked. There was always a tentative note in his voice when he asked Eric that question; he probably used the same tone when asking Gail about him. What was meaningful was that he always asked, always had to take the temperature.

"She's fine. She's having dinner with the girls."

"Really?"

"Yes, really."

"I understand you're taking Granddad to Alabama." Tom gave this a mean twist. He didn't know his grandfather well and didn't like him; Tom was one of the very few children Eric had ever known who weren't immediately attracted to Frank's gruff bluffing, his playfulness around children. A holdover, or maybe the source, of his years as a magnetic campaigner. It's all bullshit, Tom had said, at age twelve. You can tell he doesn't mean it.

"It will be quite a show. You should take some time off and come with us. I'll send you a plane ticket."

"Not me. Too many rednecks." He didn't like the South, either; he didn't like the way waitresses called him "baby."

"Whether you like it or not, a quarter of your people are from Alabama."

"Dig it. Hey, I've got to go."

"Got a date or something?" Eric said hopefully, trying hard not to sound hopeful.

"Just got to go."

"Okay. I love you."

"Yeh, Dad. I know you do. Thanks."

Eric hung up. He was sitting in the hall, or at least what they had always called the hall. It was a vestibule broad enough to swing the front door open without having to back up the stair. For some reason the previous owners had put a telephone there, on a tiny bedstand with an uncomfortable straight-backed wooden chair. The sellers had thrown this uniquely suited ensemble into the deal, and though Gail and Eric had planned to move the phone to a more comfortable place, they never had. The arrangement seemed to fit in this house, a "center-hall colonial" as the Realtors say, with a garage and a family room above it. "You'll love the family room," gushed the Realtor, but they didn't use it much. There was a Ping-Pong table in the center that no one had used for years. Though the proportions of the whole house were small, it was still too big for the three of them, but it, and the backyard, were what they had concluded they needed in a snap, midsummer decision—better schools and a neighborhood with lots of kids for Tom to play with, though he hadn't really expressed the need. For a couple of years, Gail and Eric had been talking about selling, and soon they probably would, but the house had been good to them, as good as they let it be, and it contained the spirit of their only child.

Eric considered wandering aimlessly into his study—the mood is bad when the best choice seems to be something you know is aimless—but on impulse he made the call he had promised his father to make, to Mike Billings, to see what he had on his mind. Mike, the faithful servant who had gone down with the boss, the dog curled at his feet on the funeral barge. It was late to call, even by Eric's standards, but though he had come to feel sympathy for this man, this project of his was nothing Eric wanted anything to do with.

Eric had checked out of Frank's orbit in his twenties, had wanted nothing to do with this arrogant, deceitful, sarcastic monster, and he didn't even know how bad it had gotten toward the end, because if he had, he never would have come back. But in the many months of the final tale—it had taken over a year from the time that someone had alerted the attorney general that there was a no-show typist on Senator Alwin's staff for the public execution to be completed—Frank had already been an outcast, and so it made sense to Eric, at Alice's urging, to take pity on him, do the right thing, do the *patient* thing, and pay him a call.

How well Eric remembered that day, coldest day on the Shore for many years. Frank was still fit, in his sixties, and he'd finally gained enough weight to look as if he couldn't be knocked down by a gust of wind. His second wife, Marjorie, had just survived her first bout with cancer, and in a year would die quickly from its blistering return. Frank had been expelled from the Senate in January, and a month later the boxes of senatorial mementos and papers were still piled high, untouched, in the hall where the movers had dumped them. It had been long enough since Eric had seen him that he was unsure about what to call him. They shook hands on the landing wordlessly, and then Eric followed him past the boxes into the kitchen. It was mid-afternoon, and Frank poured himself some Scotch without offering any to Eric. The whole time Eric was thinking: *You selfish son of a bitch, you brought this on yourself.*

"So," Eric said, after watching Frank's Adam's apple work a good hot wash down the throat. That was all he could think to say, and as the seconds ticked away from that lonely hanging conjunction, it struck him he had said everything he could say: the past acknowledged, a future of some sort implied.

Frank still had his glass raised, and he gazed at Eric over the rim. He waited for Eric to say more, and when nothing came, he said, "Precisely. Not exactly a gubernatorial proclamation, is it."

"No. It's not." Eric didn't like the waspish tone, but wasn't sure what he might have preferred: blubbering would have been ghastly; a heartfelt confession would not have been believed. Eric looked around to see if they were alone.

"How's Marjorie holding up?"

"She's behaving splendidly," he said, dropping the tone for a moment. "I have no right to expect it from her."

"This will give you some time, won't it?" Her doctors at Hopkins had made it clear that the cancer she had was a nasty one. "I hope a long time."

"We do, too."

It seemed to Eric that now was the time for some of the lines he had prepared on the way down, as unfamiliar as it felt for him to be offering any comment or opinion on the way his father lived his life. Eric was in his thirties, a little young to be delivering a sermon, but still, he thought he ought to make the effort as a form of—well, the word was more original then—closure. "Dad," he said, "I hope you can just let it all go now. No revenge, no cloakroom stuff. Just come home and be retired." He got no response, so he came to his conclusion. "You could reassess and get ahold of yourself."

Frank had been listening with his drink raised—later Eric recalled the whole conversation through the image of Frank holding this heavy crystal highball glass, brown liquid lapping its color onto the clear ice cubes, the glass held chest high, close enough to his nose for him to sniff the smoky flavors of the Scotch for comfort. Eric was seated at the small kitchen table, in front of the lazy

Susan packed with prescription bottles for both of them, some jams and jellies, and a glass honeypot topped with a small silver bee.

Eric looked directly into Frank's eyes as he delivered the last statement; he'd been avoiding his father's gaze since he arrived. As he said "get ahold" Frank's eyes widened into shock: who was his son to say such things to him? Eric thought he might go into one of his rages, and was ready to meet him face on, fists ready. Instead, Frank let out his breath and took another quick sip of his drink. The anger passed, and perhaps he was now planning to brush Eric off with a perfunctory *Thank you, I appreciate your concern*. Either anger or this response would have been okay, but what he got was worse.

"I intend to fish and hunt a good deal," he said. "You can quote me on that," he added, as if Eric were a reporter for the local newspaper.

"You hate hunting and fishing," Eric said, trying to play along.

"Ah, but perhaps I was wrong." He beckoned toward the Scotch bottle. "Forgive my lack of manners. Can I pour you a cocktail? Are you allowed to drink while on duty?"

"Dad."

"My wife, as perhaps you know, is dying of cancer. We shall—"

"Will you stop this?"

"—devote a great deal of time to the grandchildren, and if I am asked to comment on the great issues of the day, I shall respond, 'No. It is the next generation's turn. Let them decide on the proper path.' "

Suddenly Eric was spinning into a rage of his own. Even as he had imagined every possible scenario for this visit, he had never suspected he would completely uncork, but he did. Yet he would not surrender completely enough to scream; instead, he spoke calmly, as if the answers to his questions were of no particular concern or use to him. "Is this what you're going to do? Drink? Feel sorry for yourself? You pull this shit all your life, and now you think you can buy it off with prep school sarcasm and Ballantine's? This is . . . the plan?"

"Mea culpa."

"Oh, fuck you."

"What?"

"You heard me. Fuck your mea culpa. It's your fault, every bit of it. You lost everything that was handed to you." Eric got up; he'd never taken off his parka; never even, as he realized later, taken his hand off the keys in his pocket. He was shouting now, and didn't care that he had lost this small battle with his own emotions. "You know what? I despise you. I hope you fall down sometime drunk and break your fucking neck." He strode back through the house and out the door. He reached his car still in fury, and drove off, spattering icy pea-sized stones all through Marjorie's meticulously kept plantings and perennial beds. He reached the state road before he could quiet his breathing enough to remember exactly what he had just said, and when he remembered the word "despise"—it was right, he wouldn't take it back, but still, it was incomplete—he slowed down, and in another five miles did a U-turn across the median and headed back.

What was the impulse? He didn't know. Maybe it was because he felt it was inexcusable to spread that gravel through poor Marjorie's things. Maybe it was simply the hurt of it, this final brutal chapter, and the child's never-ending hope that parents can make such hurt go away, even—maybe even especially—when they have caused the hurt in the first place. Or maybe some passing breeze had whispered to him the less solipsistic truth, that what he had just witnessed was pain. Pure pain seeping out of that man. A howl of pain from the better man inside, the man who had been, despite his faults, a loving father to Eric.

When he drove back into the lane, Frank was sitting on the top step of the stoop in his shirtsleeves. He'd been there the whole time, long enough for his nose to be tipped with a white dot of frostbite.

They stood again, face-to-face, in the cold. "How did you know I was going to come back?" Eric asked.

"I didn't. I was saying good-bye to you."

"Oh, cut the crap," he answered, not in anger, but because that is what you say to a man you despise and love with all your heart, your father.

Mike Billings's wife answered, and said "Hello" with an aggrieved accent on the "o." Eric had always thought that, against type, Southern women of a certain age bore a heavy resemblance to Frenchwomen of the same type: the bitchy concierge. There was a pause while she processed his name, and then there was a sudden and infinitely suspect transformation. Oh yes, she said. Mike's right here.

"Young Eric," he said, full of his own intimacy, patronizing Eric from the first breath.

The sound of his voice, not heard in many years, made Eric shiver. "Dad asked me to give you a call. What can I do for you?"

"Well, slow down, boy," he said. "I hope this ain't a telephone solicitation." He sounded each syllable of this last word and then laughed at his own joke. "Tell me. How's your dad? How *yew*? I *h'ain't* seen *yew* since you were about *fov* years old."

So there Eric was, trapped with this blowhard and regretting powerfully that he had made this call. They ran through everyone: Frank, Alice, Poppy—"damn cutest thing you ever saw in your life," he said, which was his code for saying it was a shame that she had turned into a dyke—finishing with Eric himself.

Finally they got down to business.

"I was wondering if you could help me fill in some blanks."

"I don't think I can, but shoot."

"Well, now. Frank was discharged from the Navy in 1945, right?"

Eric said that as far as he knew, this was true, but only because the war was over in 1945. It might have been later, because he had joined up late, been protected by his father's pals on the draft board, under the dubious proposition that Frank was a farmer. The campaign tale held it that Frank, horrified by what had happened to so many sons of the country, had left a safe deferment and joined up. The whole thing seemed like a calculation: the old patriarch knew that Frank needed a war record to inaugurate his political career, but held off until the U-boats had been largely eliminated, the *Bismarck* had been sunk, the Japanese fleet had been all but wiped out at Midway.

"And him and Audrey were married by then?"

"Yes, when he was in training. In 1943."

"Here's a small thing I'm curious about. He was released in 1945 and first ran for office in 1950. What was he up to? I've never known."

"Hanging out, mostly," said Eric, purposefully using that slangy and unrevealing term.

"Uh-huh," said Billings, not convinced, as well he shouldn't have been. What Frank did in those years was resist his father's plans. He returned to run the farm, to farm and write, of all things, to write fiction, to speak the truth. His father let this go on for a couple of years, because a little background in agriculture wouldn't hurt a bit in this rural district. He consented to read a manuscript of some sort—Eric never knew what sort—and pronounced it trash. About farming he said, The niggers have it under control. Frank considered going to law school then, and his father said, Fine, fine, but get the seat first and see if you need all that lawyering mumbo jumbo. In the midst of all this, his perfect young wife was enduring at least two miscarriages. Why Frank didn't, in all those years, tell his father to fuck off was a mystery clothed in earlier times, but he didn't, and the soul of a fundamentally decent and shy man was taken by the devil. By 1950, the year Eric was born, Frank had given up; he ran for the seat that was virtually reserved for him.

"Seems like a sort of blank spot in there," said Billings.

"I can't help you on that one. I wasn't even born yet. Mike, it's getting pretty late. I shouldn't have even called you at this hour."

"No problem at-tall." He then ran through a quick thumbnail of Frank's legislative career, putting out names of committees he'd served on, bills he'd entered; he mentioned a few details about the narrow loss for the U.S. House of Representatives in 1968—he'd lost primarily because he was, by then, in the process of being divorced by Audrey—and made reference to the aborted ramp-up to a U.S. Senate run in 1974. Billings pretended he was airing these understandings just to be sure he wasn't "dotting the t and crossing the i," but he knew perfectly well that he knew a great deal more about this than Eric did or ever would.

Eric listened, but offered no corrections to the record. "I guess I can't help you much," said Eric.

"Just one more thing." He made a loud, probably staged scuffling of notes right next to the receiver to make Eric think he had to track down what he wanted to ask. "Now, about Myra Podesta."

It was a name Eric hadn't heard anyone speak in a long time, not a popular topic in their family. "Mike. My understanding is that this is not what you are going to write about."

"It isn't, it's just—"

Eric interrupted. "No dice. Come on, what's the point? You might even piss me off here."

"Now hold it just a minute"—he was still trying to jolly and patronize Eric into speaking of this matter—"she worked for your dad for six years before she left and there are—"

"There's nothing I'm going to say."

"She wasn't the first little bimbo we had to take care of. You know that. But he wouldn't let her go. Why?"

"Ask Dad, not me. Better yet, ask her."

"She's dead. She's been dead for ten years."

"What's the point of all this now?" said Eric. "You got hurt enough by it yourself. You deserve to let it go as much as anybody, don't you?"

Mike deflected the tone of sympathy—it was genuine; Eric had long felt bad for him, someone he and his sisters were so nasty to and about all those years—and made as if he were continuing his research, but then he let everything out. "Why did your father behave like that?" he asked. "You know, that's just what I can't figure. Why did he fuck everything up like that? What exactly was it that she had on him? Myra Podesta, you know, was no beauty."

"Maybe he was in love with her. Maybe all she had on him was that. Maybe it was worth it to my father, to throw everything away for her."

"I guess," said Mike. He'd given up.

"I'm sorry the way it worked out for you, Mike. It wasn't fair, I know it. But please, whatever you write, don't go there. It's as bad for your heart as it is for his."

But Mike would never let it go, and as they were saying good-bye, he let out one final bit of the story that had clearly consumed him for years. "Who blew the whistle? That's the thing we never figured out. Who blew the whistle on the payroll?"

"Why would you ask me?"

"Because it came from someone close. I used to think it could have been you."

"Whoever did it," answered Eric, "probably saved his life. That's all that matters to me now."

And that was the spirit, the morning of the departure to Alabama. A typical late-April day, a foggy drizzle, a wet and mild Tuesday after a last day in the office preparing for this four-day absence. The FruitOut presentation was far from finished, as far as Eric could discern, but that was as always, when the team finally focused and began to ask themselves the questions they should have spent the last two weeks answering. Maybe mess was good, in his trade; maybe the charette, as the architects say, is the only way to do it.

Once Eric had persuaded Alice that there was nothing they could do to derail this trip, they argued for two weeks over what car they would take. More accurately, Alice had stated categorically that they would be far safer and far more comfortable in her immense SUV, and what's more, it was the car Frank wanted to take. Eric had responded—for no real reason but to argue against her preemptive tone—that it was too high for Frank to get into comfortably, that it used too much gas carrying at least two hundred cubic feet of completely wasted space, and that, being a Ford, it would crap out somewhere in Tennessee. This made her angry and then Eric realized, much too late in the game, that the car wasn't the issue and neither was standard sibling chafing, but that Alice had not been invited along. Alice was insufferable to travel with: her schedules, her lists, her miffed silences when things didn't go exactly as she planned. But she should have been invited, and would have come if she had been, because this was her life they were confronting too, going back to the dark truths of both their childhoods. Above all—all, all of it warranted—she was furious that Adam was going in her place.

"He needs Adam," Eric argued in a subsequent call. "What happens if Dad falls? What happens if something goes haywire?"

"That's why I was against this from the start. Anyway, if something happens, you and I could manage fine."

"He'd never let you help him bathe, or get him dressed."

"That's not the point," she said bitterly.

She was right, but he was trying to make her feel better. "It's really a small thing, this trip. Isn't it really? I just think it's something he wants to get done."

"You're such a liar, Eric. This is your show and you're not going to share it."

He had an easier time with Poppy. When he told her of the plan, there was a long pause on the other end of the line, until she said, "Bring something to read."

"Why?" he asked.

"Because in the rest of the world people ask you what you're reading. In Alabama, they ask you what you're reading . . . for." Poppy could say this: she'd lived in Alabama after she and their mother moved there, had gone to college in Tuscaloosa.

He told Poppy he missed her, missed her often and wished there were two of her, one to live in her live-oak-shaded neighborhood with Ricki and do her librarian's work at Rice, and another to be with them. She said that was sweet, but that she'd just as soon stay whole, in Houston. They all admired her, someone who, it seemed, had endured turmoil in her childhood and had emerged with the clearest sense of what she needed: a great deal of distance and space, touched only by an occasional brotherly kiss on the cheek.

When Eric and Gail drove down the lane, the Expedition loomed into view. They could go all the way to Tierra del Fuego in that rig, and who knew? Maybe once on the road Frank would decide to keep going, to the Everglades, to the Grand Canyon, places he'd never seen and always wanted to visit. His old-fashioned suitcase—his big one—was waiting under the shelter of the entrance way, and beside it was a small red nylon athletic bag that Eric knew would be Adam's. To the side there was another mound of luggage: a duffel bag, two large gaily wrapped presents, two pillows and a blanket, a picnic basket complete with a red-and-white-checked ground cloth, folded neatly on top. For a moment he suspected that Alice had won a place after all, but no, these were the things she was sending along in her stead: extra coats and raingear for all three of them, spares for the spares that Adam would be bringing anyway for Frank, sandwiches for today in the basket, tea in a thermos for Frank, coffee in another thermos for Eric, Cokes for Adam, birthday presents for God knew which cousins or aunts in Birmingham.

Eric was standing on the porch, surveying the heartbreaking thoughtfulness of these items, when his brother-in-law, Alden, a fleshy sight all done up in pastel golfing clothes, came out to find him. "There's the tour guide," he said. "We were wondering whether you went AWOL."

"No. I've signed on for the full tour, wherever it goes."

"Frank's hot to trot."

"Really?"

"Seems pretty spunky about the whole thing to me." He followed Eric's gaze out at the car. Alden regarded it with evident pride. "Fucking monster, ain't it."

"It's nice of you to lend it to us. I'm sure we'll be more comfortable."

"You bet. Besides, you're so high up you can sometimes see a fine shot of leg in passing cars."

"Alden," said Eric, "you make being a teenager sound fun all over again."

"Hey," he said, maybe a little hurt, but undaunted. A good old boy, reliable as a priest. A kind husband, a patient father.

"Who's here for the bon voyage?" asked Eric.

"Just us. Alice is planning to house-sit."

Eric glanced again at the luggage. "You know, I'm sorry I didn't make sure she was invited."

This was as close to intimate as they ever got, but Alden was pleased to hear it, even if the ardent tone made him nervous.

"She's over it," he said. "Come on in."

They were all in the kitchen, with Alice at the stove making crepes. Adam's fanny pack was dense with supplies, and he had three or four fresh steno pads in his hands; overkill, thought Eric, for a four-day trip. Frank was in an old blue tweed suit, a little heavy for the weather, almost Victorian with its fat lapels, but he'd made it sporty with a red gingham shirt and a bow tie, as if he were going shooting. He had his best silver-tipped cane at the ready, and would not have tolerated this extended farewell if Gail hadn't been beside him. The mood in the kitchen was bright and festive.

When Eric walked in Gail had just asked one of those questions the others might have been avoiding, which was how long since Frank had been in Birmingham.

He traced the answer on the table with a fingernail: thirty-six years. Thirty-six years since he had made his one final gesture to save his marriage, to bring Audrey and Poppy back. He had been met on the porch of her family's home by her father, who would not let him see them, not let him enter. "You, sir," the old Alabama gentleman had said, "are a cad and a rotter." But coming back from impossibly long odds was the theme of this trip.

"It's a dump," said Frank.

"Don't tell Audrey that, or you'll get the whole visit off on the wrong foot."

Frank bellowed with pleasure about this and happily thumped on Gail's forearm. He had always enjoyed jokes at his own expense, especially small ones that brushed lightly on places that hurt. Alice and Eric traded looks: what a mood he was in. It was a Saturday-morning kind of mood, a feeling that Eric could recall from some years ago, heading out the door for errands with Dad, or later, with Tom—Eric the son and Eric the father.

Alice handed Eric a plate of crepes, and he thanked her and said, "Yum," standing aside while his father lavished his attentions on Gail.

"Come with us," Frank said to Gail; he thought he was being playful, but actually, if she had accepted, he would have been delighted. Everyone in the room knew this was true. Eric wasn't sure whether he gasped audibly, but Alice did. Maybe it was more of a gulp, and was followed by the clatter of a spatula hitting a griddle, and then by Alice's footsteps leaving the room. Gail looked horrified. Alden looked as if he had missed the whole thing, but the recognition was slowly and visibly working onto Frank's face.

"Christ, Dad," said Eric. "Use your head."

Frank pulled himself to his feet and shuffled after her, leaving behind him a silence sustained only by a thumping of hearts. The remaining group, an improbable foursome, avoided each other's eyes until Adam said, "Takes two kicks from a mule to knock sense into that head."

"That was my fault," said Gail.

"No," said Alden. "It was his. Forget about it. Alice will." What he said was almost true—she would soon act as if she had—but worse than almost anything else.

"I guess he's going to get some practice begging for forgiveness," said Eric, going over to the sink to flush Frank's uneaten crepes down the disposal.

They waited somewhat wordlessly for ten or fifteen minutes, and when Alice came back, it seemed as if the old man had done well enough, because Alice was willing to say to the group, "He doesn't mean it. I know that."

Frank might have prepared a small parting elocution—it was the sort of thing he had done in the distant past: a few often-repeated lines of his favorite poets, Kipling, Tennyson perhaps, phrases he dropped into speeches with a slightly impish nod to the few in the audience who might be expected to recognize them. Today it would be Whitman: "Allons! the road is before us!" Eric could hear it now; Frank would only have to get out a few words before Alice and Eric knew what poem he was reciting. But the mood for such things was now past. They all went out to the porch, where Alice told them Frank was waiting, and Alden had already pulled the car around directly opposite the stoop, with the passenger door open. They found Frank gripping the wrought-iron rail of the steps and looking uncertainly at the car, as if he had doubts whether he could make it up to the seat. He refused help and clambered in, relatively smoothly, and closed the door. He looked tiny, a child's face peering through a school bus window. Adam followed into the back, pausing to take his choice of six places to sit and exclaiming, "Whoa, this place is plush!"

Eric said good-bye to Gail, a lingering hug, and he whispered into her ear that he loved her. She whispered back that it would be fine, life, life would be fine someday again. Then Eric looked around for Alice, and saw that she was not there.

He found her in the kitchen, scraping the rest of the crepes off the platter. She had a brush of powdered sugar on her cheek.

She refused to look over at him, so he came up behind and put both his arms over her shoulders. "Honey," he said. "I love you."

"You do not," she said.

"I do. That's why I threw the cake at you." At her eleventh birthday he had thrown her birthday cake at her, for reasons nobody could remember. She'd beaten him up for that, the last time they fought physically.

She couldn't help a small laugh at that, and she dropped one cheek onto his arm. "It's never going to be different. I just have to get used to it."

"Maybe. But maybe he still can change. Maybe we all can change, but not without your help. You're our rock."

"Don't patronize me. Just go. You've got a long drive."

Adam had taken up his place in the third row, more than ten feet behind the front seat. He was far enough away to suggest that he wanted to give them privacy, though the household situation never permitted much privacy anyway. Maybe he was trying to signal something to Alice, that even if she wasn't coming, he wasn't going to muscle into the space she left. Eric got in, spent a few minutes poking the dials and switches to make sure he knew exactly how to operate this thing, and then they drove off, down the lane, past the gates, and onto the road.

Frank was sitting stiffly, good arm stretched across the bench seat as if to give him balance should he be lurched around, or the door beside him pop open. Eric understood that pose; riding as a passenger still terrified him, even all these years after his stroke. No one, not his son, not his nurse, could truly understand how vulnerable he felt, how helpless he might be in an accident, when an able-bodied person could squirm out a window or jump before the gasoline tank caught fire. There were lots of terrors away from the farm. If he got lost, he wouldn't be able to say his own name. Over the years Alice had registered him with numerous Med-Alerts and elderly hotlines, but the one gesture of that kind that he seemed to truly appreciate was a laminated card she'd made for his wallet including several telephone numbers and the words "Hello. Sorry to bother you. My name is Senator Frank Alwin, and I am unable to speak."

Eric reached over and tapped his shoulder. "Everything all right?"

He looked back a little hopelessly, the festivity of earlier completely gone. "Alice," he said.

"Yeh. Not very swift, I have to say."

"Not swift. A shit."

They left it at that for a few miles, while his eyes darted around at this familiar landscape: the old ice plant, the Southern States grain elevators, then the beginnings of what would in a few miles become a garish and unregulated strip of outlet centers and malls, the Chesapeake Bay Bridge's gift to Kent Island, once so sleepy.

"Are you scared?" Eric asked as they finally began to mount the bridge. "About Mom."

"No. I waited a long time." He looked at Eric and asked. "Long enough?"

"I don't know. Long enough for whom?"

"Yes."

"But it's right, Dad. It's right to do this. It may be a disaster, but I think you're doing what we are all called to do."

"Thank you. A good son."

"You're a good father. Sometimes."

"Father. Gak. Husband. Gak."

They were now on the western shore, across the bay, the place where Frank had committed so many of his sins; in a second they'd catch a glimpse of the Naval Academy, and perhaps the spire of St. James Church, if not the statehouse dome itself.

"When was the last time you were here? Annapolis."

"When Marjorie died."

Eric had forgotten that they had not made it to Baltimore that night, with her hemorrhaging in the back of the ambulance. Eric had come down the next day, still tentative about this thaw. He came down because Frank had asked him to, asked for his help, for the first time in Eric's life. So he did, took care of the funeral home, was standing with the small crowd at her graveside when they lowered her down. Frank had cried.

"You were a good husband to Marjorie. Weren't you? Really?"

"Bad."

He didn't bother to try to answer that, and they settled into the drive. Eric already felt comfortable in this car, and understood why Alice liked it, with its bulk and power, perfect for someone who thought the only way to get through life was to dominate. It wasn't her fault. Alice: the eldest child of divorce, unsure who she was, baffled by the way the world—and her own father—treated her. She made herself into such a mark. Perhaps that was why Eric had thrown that cake at her, such a transparently troubled thing to do, even if they both now regarded it as a high point of their childhoods.

They reached the beltway around Washington and turned left to skirt around to the south. In an hour they hooked up with Interstate 81, which took them down the Shenandoah Valley west of the Blue Ridge, toward the mountains of eastern Tennessee. "Virginia," said Frank admiringly. He'd always felt the Marylander's twinge of envy toward the Old Dominion, for being a place of history, the father of Washington, Jefferson, Madison, and Monroe; for Robert E. Lee and Stonewall Jackson; for its firm place in America as the source of an honorable if myopic democratic tradition; for its loyalty to its principles even when they were wrong. Maryland was home to second-rank revolutionaries, aides-de-camp at best, a border state always calculating the odds, making its deals sometimes to the north, with Pennsylvania, sometimes to the south, with Virginia, a rather bland and boggy piece of territory whose main claim to fame was not its land or its people, but a body of water thrust into its midst. Rather like Rhode Island, a small, inconsequential state split in two by a bay.

Eric had been raised in the deep awareness of Maryland's status as a border state, and his mother had pulled some of his sympathies into the Deep South. But when the time came for him to choose where to live, after prep school and college in New England, after marrying a Bostonian who would happily have moved anywhere above the Fortieth Parallel and would consider nowhere below it, there really hadn't been much to debate. He stayed up there, got used to it: a decision maybe, but not really a choice.

But this was the landscape he truly loved to visit, the plunging hills of red earth and scrubby oaks, the rounded mountains off in the purple haze; it was a landscape that suggested one could live in magnificence and become a better and more loving person for it, not a harder and more independent one. The shapes of the mountains: maybe that was the real reason for the differences between Northerners and Southerners. A simple pleasure to be in this landscape. Well, he'd like Gail to come down here with him, for a weekend in Lexington. They'd rent a canoe for a day's paddle down the river, then maybe head over to Charlottesville for dinner and a walk through UVA. He'd like it if Gail could understand the South, and not be afraid of it, and not condemn it for its mistakes.

He was driving happily now, free on the road. Somewhere down there, in Tennessee, they'd find a motel for the night. The next day they would be up on the highway cutting across the northwestern corner of Georgia, and by mid-afternoon, at the latest, they'd pull in to Birmingham. This journey was a trip rich in history, dotted with the mysterious names of a country almost ruined by war—Manassas, the Wilderness, Lookout Mountain— and of those names still infamous from the twentieth century— Scottsboro, Selma, Birmingham itself.

"The South," said Eric, a shorthand for all these thoughts. They had finished a rest stop, had eaten Alice's picnic, and all felt pretty good.

"Norfolk," Frank said. It was a hard word to say, but there was no doubting it; speech was coming well to him these days.

"That's right. That's where you met, you and Mom."

"In love, so in love."

"We all are, when we marry, aren't we?"

"Supposed to be."

"But you were, when you married her. Or was it really just the war, with you shipping out? Was it"—he hesitated before saying the word—"a mistake?"

"No. Mistakes later. Mine."

"But she can't have been a perfect wife. She can't have been completely blameless. Marriage doesn't work that way."

Frank thought a long time about this, almost long enough for Eric, as he drove past Roanoke, to think he was dropping the subject, but he had not.

"Never said good-bye."

He never did, that was sure, as Eric had learned long ago from Poppy. As far as Eric could tell, nothing had been planned. It was early May and Poppy was in second grade, and any parent as dutiful as Audrey would have waited out the school year to move. But Frank was in Annapolis, or somewhere, two days overdue and not so much as a phone call, or not much of one. It was Saturday morning, and perhaps Audrey had decided to give him one last chance to show up for the weekend with his family. At twelve sharp she said, "That's it." As Poppy remembered it, the words came out in the calmest possible tone, a simple statement and a simple concept upon which to end a marriage. When one debates for years about doing something, the decision comes not in passion, but in the dry voice of reason. No need to buttress oneself with anger and indignation when the answer is so clear, when the evidence has been there for so long and the counterarguments finally wrung dry. The moment she heard Audrey say it, Poppy knew exactly what she meant, and she went outside and climbed into the car and an hour later they were on the road. They took the route Eric was following now, perhaps stopped at the very gas station they had just left, because there couldn't have been many gas stations on the road back then. Later that day, to hear him tell it back then, only a few minutes late, Frank entered an empty house. He was shocked, he had said, and when he wandered into Poppy's emptied room and found a single white ankle sock on the floor, he cried. That's what he had said, back then, and Eric was too young to argue with him.

"I let her go," he said.

"Was that a mistake? You couldn't think of preventing her."

"I wanted to change. I didn't know how."

"Who does," said Eric, spinning now back into his own agenda, listing the mistakes he had made with Gail. His affairs, certainly. Moving to Summit—yes, definitely, in retrospect, bad for her, making her into a suburban wife. Making her feel unloved, maybe. A foul and useless kind of list, an unpleasant sort of register, and surely not the sort of list that she was asking for at their disastrous—but maybe not so unproductive—dinner a few weeks ago. So he switched his direction, and for many minutes he pondered what she had asked at that dreadful meal, to tell her what she could do to bring him pleasure. What could she do for him that she wasn't already doing? She wasn't any more perfect than his own mother, and Tom, for one, would be happy to cite chapter and verse about Gail, but what would make life better? Not just salvage what they had, but make it new, shiny as a coin. The faults, the thoughtlessnesses, were still his: didn't think about her when he went to a bookstore, didn't buy her a scarf he saw that he knew would be perfect. Why? Why not? But—this was sudden, a spark of electricity in his musty brain—these were, after all, things he *could* do for her.

They spent the night in Knoxville, the home of Eric's earliest literary love, the writer he had tried to emulate with such lack of success that winter years ago, James Agee. Frank had insisted they avoid the many motel chains, and Eric had begun to see his point. As they had wound through the mountains, each exit had been marked with four or five grotesque lollipop signs, a froth of litter just above the treetops screaming out the marketing messages of corporate America; the repetitions of colors and logos of brand awareness were beginning to seem almost scary, how these companies were screwing right into the hamlets and hollows, corporate planners hunting from the air like eagles. What was Eric doing in a career in advertising, anyway?

They ended up at a modest place called the Motel Buford. It was just the thing Frank had wanted; a sign advertising air-conditioning and free TV, a single-floor building, L-shaped, bare as a barracks, cars with Tennessee tags pulled right to the picture windows to allow people to enter unseen, couples heaving and pumping just a few feet from public view, risking all for a few moments of pleasure.

It had been a long time since Eric had spent the night in a place like this, but he had been in one, in New Rochelle, with Fran Bradford, a woman he hardly knew except for the kind of coincidences that seem so meaningful when one meets on an airplane: her brother was a year behind Gail and Eric at Middlebury. A week or two after they met they were having a drink in Manhattan, and they ended up at that motel, at seven in the evening, shedding their clothes. It was Eric's first infidelity, and they came together like an implosion. They had no reason to spend time together other than as sex partners, and they had made the most of it, so much that he could actually imagine leaving Gail and Tom for more of it. Fran Bradford. The safest thing he'd ever done in his life, really, and when he called an end to it after a few hair-raising weeks—or maybe she did—they had a drink and screwed one last time. The things sex will make you do; there is no limit.

FIVE

How to atone? How to cleanse the soul?

Eric stood on his mother's stoop, a brick platform slightly too small for the accoutrements she had placed there: sandstone planter, boot scraper, and bench, furnishings reminiscent of entrances to more commodious Southern homes. His mother and Jackson had built this house, a colonial if it was anything, when they were married; there were no ghosts in the residential developments of the new South, in this expensive neighborhood called Mountain Brook, just a glancing look backward, a few architectural details and design features: winding staircase; chintz upholstery and velvet drapes. And this stoop.

There was a fine rain, a gloomy mist; the air was chilly. Eric was all but hyperventilating as he stood for a final moment of panic before pressing the doorbell. He could imagine his mother's slight alarm when she heard the chime: *Who could that be?* she would wonder, noting that the laundry wasn't due back until Thursday. Audrey had always been flustered by unexpected or unplanned events, though she had spent her life insisting that she loved things spontaneous, madcap, and gay. "Just surprise me," she would say, when discussing her birthdays or other celebrations, though what she was really saying was "Don't disappoint me." Well, Eric had a surprise for her today. Jackson's Cadillac was gone, an astounding mercy: maybe he was off trying to play golf in the rain or getting the oil changed, or whatever retired Southern bankers do.

Behind him, at the curbside, the Ford was parked, with Adam and Frank waiting in their seats. That had been one of Eric's conditions for this day's plans, that he would greet his mother alone, speak to her in private for as long as it might take to gain entrance. They had discussed this over breakfast at the Tutwiler, a meal Frank had consumed with relish, a bracing start for a big day. Frank had slept well, it seemed, which was good because it meant he might have an easier time finding his words. He'd waited long enough, and made effort enough, to say them, whatever they were.

Eric reached up and pressed the button, and then stepped back to the edge of the stoop. Soon he heard her footsteps and saw the quick brush of her face through the muslin on the sidelights, a quizzical peering, then the beginning of amazement. *God help me,* thought Eric, as she unbolted the door.

"Eric. What's wrong?" she said, quite apparently reflecting on their last few communications to determine if she'd missed something, a plan, impending bad news.

"Hi, Mom. Nothing. Nothing's wrong." He leaned forward to pull open the screen door.

She wasn't in her nightgown, that was one good thing. She was in a light blue dress, small string of gold around her neck; she looked as if she were just heading out for a lunch, but she always looked that way, dressed like this, red-tinted hair in a tidy arrangement. Still pretty, her sharp jaw unsoftened, even if she had become rounder, as, Eric thought, we all will. Still pretty, and still tough: that this woman became anyone's victim was a testimony to Frank's dark powers.

She still looked alarmed, but trusted his assurances. "What a surprise," she said, offering her cheek, smiling. "Eric."

"Yes. I'm sorry to bust in on you like this."

She had now adjusted to the fact that her son was at her door, and that whatever the reason, it was not life-threatening. "It's lovely. Come in. Have you had breakfast?"

"Look," he said, meaning, perhaps, that he really wanted her to look over his shoulder and figure it out for herself, though he was still standing squarely in front of her to block the view. "This is one of those moments in life . . ."

She had now picked up his obscure tone, and her eyes scanned him anew, as if checking to see whether she had missed some injury, whether his clothes could give her a hint of what was to come.

"I have Dad with me."

"Dad? Your father?"

He nodded, and then stood aside. He turned his head to invite her, at last, to see what was about to present itself at her door. They had already begun to descend from the Ford; Adam was outside the car, his arm at the ready, as Frank pivoted in the seat and slid himself quickly to the sidewalk, the powerful fingers of his good hand clutching the doorframe for support. He was trying to look spry, but still, he wavered when he landed, and he had to lean back for a breath. He stood for a second, long enough to appear to be reconsidering, but then reached back into the car for his cane.

"Eric. God in heaven. What is going on? What does he want?"

"He needs to see you. It's a long story. Just a few minutes."

She was watching Frank arrange his dead arm, straighten his rain shell. Crystal droplets of moisture were forming on the delicate wisps of her hair. Her face registered shock and her eyes were narrowed, and Eric could imagine the lens of memory and anger that she was looking through as this invalid demon of her former life began to make his way up the walk. He was shuffling. It had been years since Eric had been so aware of his father's painful gait, the one reasonably confident step, then the pause to pull around the leg on his bad side, the knee permanently crooked, the foot pointing out at an angle and landing uncertainly on the instep. What a long thirty feet this was. This was a person after all, not a stroke victim, not even a father, but a person with all his vanities and his regrets intact, and all of his ghosts plaguing his mind. For all of his aged infirmities, he was approaching her like a child. There was no way for Eric to fill these seconds with anything but the slow progress of the event, the exquisite delay of time and space. For his mother, Eric was no longer there. About halfway up the walk, Frank stopped, took a breath, met her eyes for the first time, and tried to smile. He tried to make it winning and sly, but there was no way to mask his many truths, that he was old and feeble now, and not a young Navy lieutenant; that he was terrified; that only she could set him free from his mistakes and regrets, but that there was no reason on earth why she should.

Eric heard her gasp slightly—her first sound for a full minute—and she put out her hand to steady herself on his arm. "Oh my God. Look what has happened to him," she said, mostly to herself.

Suddenly, Eric wanted this to work; he wanted to know that something like this could work, a test case of atonement. For the first time in decades it seemed to matter to him, what his parents thought of each other; it mattered that they had once been husband and wife and Eric wanted them to acknowledge it, right here; these things suddenly seemed necessary to acknowledge and accept, along with all the other ordinary human failings; this was important to the family and its future, and his future. These two people were his *parents*. If they couldn't forgive each other in some measure, who in his world could?

Frank had made it to the bottom of the steps. He was breathing hard, and his mouth was slightly open as he took time to look up at her, gazing at her without apology; and in fact no apology was necessary, because she was looking at him, both of them auditing the years that stood between them, and bound them. Eric could only wonder what he would feel if this were himself and Gail. He wondered what part of the woman he had once known so well he would look for first, her eyes, her hands, her body. Would he be thinking of the time she threw a book at him?

His father was trying to speak. "Owder," he said.

The sound settled into the mist. Audrey didn't respond and suddenly Frank looked over for Eric, looked over for help; he realized the word hadn't come out; he'd practiced and practiced and practiced, and at breakfast must have been sure he could do it, and on his way up the walk he was sure, and now, it didn't come out.

"Owder."

"Eric, what's he saying?" Audrey asked.

Frank's eyes begged for help, yet Eric could not speak. But then, a small—perhaps just tiny—miracle, a high cry deafened by its own explosion at the lips, unlike any sound Eric had ever heard before from his father, maybe from any human throat, but clear, clear as a voice speaking from the burning bush.

"Audrey!"

Audrey seemed to sway in the air, but then responded the only way she could. "Frank," she said.

He had the sounds now firmly fixed, and said her name again in the tone he had wished for in the first place: respectful, correct, but with a slight ironic dip, the reference to the years since they had last met. He then brought his hands flat together in front of him—cane hanging at the edge of this ritual gesture—and bowed slightly, his version of a Japanese show of respect, of homage, of submission.

"Mom," said Eric, "are you going to let us in? We're all getting soaked."

"Yes, yes. Of course. Good heavens. Can he climb the steps?"

From behind, Adam said, "You can do it just fine, can't you, Mr. Frank."

"This is Adam Miller," said Eric, and he started to say that Adam was a nurse who took care of Dad, but that seemed disloyal to Frank, and an unnecessary admission. "Adam's come along to help with logistics."

Audrey backed into her house while Frank pulled himself up along the railing, and the three of them followed in a line.

"We've just come for a short visit," Eric said, taking the lead in shedding his coat. His father was trying to do the same.

"Why don't you show your father to the living room and then come out and help me get some tea."

"Good. Good. Thank you."

Audrey scrutinized Frank as he forced these few trusty words out, an almost professionally neutral eye, like a rehab specialist or a social worker, and then shook her head. An unpromising case, she seemed to have concluded. But when she spoke, her voice was warmer, if still wary. "This is crazy," she said, before heading to the kitchen. "This is one thing I never in a million years would have expected."

Eric led them into the living room, with its pink floral patterns and sea-green wood trim.

"Whoa, totally Hilton Head here."

"Oh, Adam, knock it off."

"Hey, I'm just here helping with logistics."

"What was I supposed to say? That you're here to help him bathe and cut his food?"

"Stop. No."

"Okay. Sorry," said Adam. "She seems like a nice lady."

"Audrey."

For the first time, Eric allowed himself a slight pause. They had made it inside, at least. "You got it out, Dad," he said. "That was good."

"Lucky thing. Close run thing."

This was a hopeful sign: two phrases together, said pretty clearly. Even his mother would have understood them, and she would remember—perhaps with dismay at the echoes of her life with him—that he liked to call complicated procedures close run, as Wellington had described the Battle of Waterloo.

"Is it going okay? Is this what you expected?"

"No."

"You mean yes?"

"No. Easier."

"I wouldn't spike the ball, Dad."

"No. Good. Good."

Eric took a few more moments to buttress his strength, relaxing here with the comrades—Adam had won a reprieve by calling Audrey a nice lady, because it was a genuine compliment for him, for most people in the South—but then Eric departed for his next confrontation, in the kitchen. As he was entering she was saying good-bye on the phone, but not, as Eric might have thought, to Jackson.

"I've just spoken to Alice," she said, after hanging up. "She was in on it too. All of you?"

"No. Alice was just being honorable. She knew about it, but I was the only one *in* on it. Don't think that Alice was for it."

"Then what is it for?"

"He wants to make amends. I think. I think it's that simple. Because a few weeks ago he seemed to be saying that he regrets what he did. Honestly, you don't have to do or say anything. Just listen for a few minutes." She was reaching for the teapot. "You really don't have to serve us anything."

She regarded her hand on the teapot. "No. I guess I don't." But she went ahead anyway, turned on the gas, went to the cupboard; Eric realized this was not only about hospitality, but about diversion, about time. She prepared a tray, and then sat down opposite Eric at the breakfast table, in front of the remains of Jackson's breakfast—yogurt, All-Bran, decaf. Just as at his father's kitchen table, there was a lazy Susan laden with jams, a sugar bowl, and prescription bottles. The same things on all lazy Susans all over the country, and who under seventy used one of these old-fashioned conveniences anyway? His parents had that in common, and pills for the heart, for the blood, for the digestive tract, bodies no longer pumping out all the chemicals and substances they needed to stay alive.

"Why would he care, Eric? Why?" She was no longer angry, maybe not even angry at Frank.

"I think he's afraid of his own regret. I know it sounds unlikely. None of us really believed it at first. He kept talking about mistakes."

Surprisingly, she did not respond to this the way he expected: with anger, with the bitter assertion that Frank had never apologized for anything in his entire life. Instead, she seemed to consider it as a possibility, asking herself, perhaps, how she might respond. Still, when this reflection was done, she said, "No one has asked him to apologize to me. I certainly have not."

"Of course you haven't. But you must have been curious to see him again? To touch that part of your life, the father of your children."

She was inching the lazy Susan around with her fingertips, stopped opposite a particularly large prescription bottle. "You're always trying to make things right, aren't you?"

"I guess."

"I still have dreams about him, now and again, about still being young and married to him. More and more, actually. But that doesn't mean I would go back to Maryland and descend on him like this. And to bring along this young man. Couldn't he wait in the car?"

"No. We need him, and he's in this family until Dad dies. A half hour. Then we'll be gone. Before Jackson even gets home for lunch. How bad can it be?"

She took a moment to process this. The teapot was whistling, and she stood up to pour. When it was done, with a ginger ale for Adam, she turned to him. "Well then, dear," she said. "What do you have in mind?"

"Just let him say whatever he can say. It's not easy to understand him."

"Yes," she said.

"I'll try to translate if necessary." He was ready to get this over with, but apologized once more. "I hoped," he added, "that in some way this might be good for you, too."

"To get closure?" she said, full of sarcasm.

"No, Mom. Not that. Maybe just some insight."

She stood up. "Okay. I'm ready to be illuminated."

When they returned Frank was sitting comfortably, his bad leg propped on a footstool. Adam was prowling as usual; he'd come across Jackson's collection of big band music, vinyl relics, and was reading the names to Frank: the Dorseys, Ellington. "Who's this," he said to Frank, not aware that Eric and Audrey had returned. " 'Bob Crosby and His Bobcats'?"

Audrey put the tray down on the butler's table in front of the couch. Courtesy, perhaps, impelled her to answer him. "They were very popular during the war." She handed Adam a ginger ale, which was the closest she had to Coke; she always believed that it was uncouth and unhealthy to drink sodas before mid-afternoon at the earliest.

"Hip hop," said Frank. "At the O Club."

She glanced up in surprise to hear him speak intelligibly. "That's right. I'd forgotten."

She handed them both tea. Eric waited for Frank to sample it and say that it was perfect, but he did not. She took her own cup and sat in a chair at Eric's end of the couch.

"I'll wait outside," said Adam. "In case you need any . . ." He paused, ready to add the word "logistics," but did not, left the room to camp somewhere, though Audrey had not told him where. On the way out he gave her one of his merry smiles; he could go far on that smile alone.

"A nice young man," said Audrey. She meant that, when it came to it, if not a second earlier, he knew his place. "Eric and I have been talking," she said, to the room.

"Yes. Good. Eric."

She paused when he did his closest version of Eric's name and figured out what he meant, that he was proud of their son, who was a good person and someone to be depended upon. She seemed to be seeing the light, that there was a responsive person in this damaged body, that he could be understood—at least on a mono-syllabic level—if one tried. Besides, Eric couldn't imagine that she had not had friends and acquaintances who'd suffered the same cruel fate.

"Alice. Poppy."

His enumeration of their children reminded her that they— Alice, anyway—had plotted against her. A scowl appeared briefly, but she could not deny that she and Frank shared love for them. "Yes. They've turned out very well, haven't they?" She almost let it go at that, but she was finding her way now, beginning to decide how to act, or to react. They sipped their tea while she came to this final decision to relent slightly—her thoughts were frighten-ingly visible; this whole event, so transparent in its pains and its yearnings, seemed spookily evident even if implausible, as if it were all in retrospect. "Poppy is very well. But it's hard," she as-serted somewhat absently.

"Yes."

Her eyes narrowed, as if he would have little way to know this, considering how rarely he saw her, and as if he had little right, or nowhere near as much right as she had, to make any comment at all. Poppy was private for her. Eric didn't know why she men-tioned her at all.

"Life?"

She was trying to understand now, but didn't get this. Eric in-terceded. "He's asking if there is something particular on your mind about Poppy, or is it just the way she's living, with Ricki and everything?"

She seemed a little mystified and dubious about how Eric had divined this from a single word, but it was the right question, after all.

She gave her answer to Eric. "I love Ricki," she said: none of them could even mention Poppy's name without defending her life. "Poppy's just so separated. She keeps so much to herself, don't you think?"

"Yes," answered Eric, "but you have to talk to Dad. He was the one who asked."

She was stung by this correction of her manners. "Oh, this is all so impossible." She took this moment as a chance to indicate the door through which Adam had departed.

"Don't worry about Adam. Pretend he isn't here."

"Yes. I suppose we must." She turned now fully toward Frank. For the first time she was confronting him straight on, without the deflections of the arrival, without the busywork of tea, without hiding behind continued protestations and chilly locutions. She said nothing for a minute or two, and that was fine with Frank: he was used to these pauses in conversation with others, especially with Eric, when the silences could last for many minutes. At last, she asked the one, perhaps the only, question that made sense. "How are you, Frank?"

"Old."

Eric had expected him to tip his hand from side to side and say, "Good, good." What he heard was the suggestion from Frank that this would never happen again and that he, and perhaps she if she were willing, should make the most of it.

Audrey was not impressed, but there were a few things on her mind, the few stray, sympathetic stirrings she'd felt for him over the years, a few "Christian impulses," as she would say, though she was not much of a churchgoer. "I was sorry to hear of your stroke. You don't look so bad."

"From the good side."

"You always were so photogenic." She paused, and—perhaps unwillingly—a succession of early photographs, from youth, their courtship, the young family, seemed to shuffle across her eyes. She blinked, as if to stop them. "I was sorry to hear about your . . ." She was avoiding the word "expulsion." "About the way the Senate ended up. Though—" Here she cut herself off sharply.

"Though?" he asked. "Though?" This was the sort of thing he'd come to hear her say. He wanted it, this *though*, the dividing line between the good and the bad, a bill of particulars concerning his mistakes, the things he regretted.

"Oh. I always thought that your life, this career, was what led you astray. There's so much falsehood in politics, it seems."

She was realizing that in these conversations one needed to push forward and get the whole thought out, less a dialogue than a series of statements. "It's public service, and important to do and all that, but too public. No wonder those Clintons are such a mess."

"My fault."

"I wasn't saying that it was not." Chillier now, redolent of past sins.

"Gone. Over." He nursed each word out, and Eric watched him intently; Audrey's emotional twists and turns were there for all to see, but Frank's remained hidden. He took a sip of tea in order to avoid Eric's stare, not trusting his own eyes to keep his secrets in this private moment. A clock ticked somewhere; Eric's mother's and father's houses alike in this additional anachronistic detail.

"Happy?"

"To see you?" she asked. "I should—"

Eric cut her off. "No. He's asking if you're happy with your life."

"Oh. Yes, I am. Jackson and I are very lucky."

"Good. Good. You deserve it. Always did."

She did not thank him for this; she did deserve it, with or without his blessing. Eric fiddled with his teacup, the Spode china that he remembered from his early years, the good china brought out for a party, the bustle, the smells from the kitchen and his mother's perfume, the cigarette smoke and the loud laughter of adults with sweet bourbon on their breath.

"Orfick," said Frank, into this calm silence.

"What did he say?"

"Norfolk. Virginia."

"Oh good heavens. Do we have to start all over, back in Norfolk?"

"Dad?"

"Love."

"Yes, we fell in love." She would not deny that.

"Maslo."

Eric repeated the sound to himself: starts with "M"; ends with "o," maybe. "Try again."

"Masliso."

"Gee," Eric started to say, a hedge on an impasse, but his mother was ahead of him now. "The Monticello Hotel," she said. "It's where we met. In 1943."

This moment in the distant past hung in the air for a while, and it seemed the whole visit would die there. "What were you doing there?" asked Eric.

"It's a long and not very interesting story."

"Tell it?" said Frank.

She might have resisted: she did not have to do Frank's bidding. But she didn't hesitate too long, either; she was a Southerner, after all, and could not resist a family story no matter the circumstances, especially if, as in this case, she had someone to tell it to. And the truth was, Eric knew almost nothing of his parents' courtship and early marriage; he'd been too young to ask or care when they were still married, and after they divorced the subject was forbidden by his mother and apparently of no possible interest to his father. "Well, I was there," she said, facing Eric, "with my cousin Rachel—you don't know her; she moved to California centuries ago—my cousin whose fiancé was going to sea that week."

"Nick."

"That's right. Nicholas." She stopped, lost in the memory now. "How mad we all were for him. He was so . . . excuse the expression, dear . . . he was so dreamy, and Rachel loved him so much. Rachel and I used to take turns describing him to each other, hour after hour, us innocent Alabama girls, sitting on the porch on Waverly Street. I was madly jealous of her, but that was okay, because there seemed to be enough love to go around. You saw those couples back then, two girls and a boy, and you knew that two of them were sweethearts but the other girl was part of it. Back then, it was enough for me that I could dream of moving in with them after they were married, the maiden lady in the back bedroom. That's real love. Young people now just go to bed, don't they?"

"I don't think that means that people don't fall in love."

"Maybe not. But it means they don't have time to anticipate it." She seemed pleased with herself for this retort, and picked up the story again without prompting. "Rachel was eighteen when they announced their engagement, and her father"—she turned to Eric—"your great-uncle Frederick, do you remember him? He wouldn't permit the marriage until she was twenty, and she was nineteen and eight months when he got his orders. It seemed cruel, but in the end it was better for her."

"Sad. Nicholas."

"Yes."

"Because she couldn't marry him?" asked Eric.

"What happened was sad. He was killed in the landing in Sicily. His ship was bombed or something, I forget what it was. Rachel knew it was going to happen. That's why we were in Norfolk to see him off. She wanted . . . oh dear." She stopped.

"Please. Tell Eric."

"If you must know," she said to Eric, but she didn't mean it, didn't mean that she was saying any of these long-forgotten words reluctantly, "Rachel wanted to make love to him. I'll never forget the night she told me. I was so shocked I cried. It scared me, as much because she wanted to give herself to him as because of her certainty that he would die. She had it planned, that I would come as her chaperone. Imagine! I was nineteen, just her age. Our parents all got together and debated whether we should be allowed to go. Rachel and I sat in the kitchen with Myrtice and waited, and I was secretly hoping they would say no. But they didn't, and I've always wondered if our mothers knew what Rachel wanted—not that they could share this with each other, even with their husbands. So there we were in Norfolk."

And there the three of them were, suspended in this moment in 1943, when almost anything could happen, when nineteen-year-old girls could be sent off to a Navy town to lose their virginity, with their mothers' assent, a cousin sent along not to stop her, but to give her cover.

"And?" said Eric.

"Well. That's when I met your father. Frank. Wasn't it?"

"In the lobby. May . . ." He drew the numbers in the air: May 19, 1943. "Blue dress. Pearls. Beautiful."

"You should understand the time," she said to Eric, as if he might be shocked, as if the rigid expression on his face meant that he was. "Men shipping out—I haven't used those words in years: 'shipping out'! They were a death sentence to the women, their boyfriends, husbands, shipping out. Being left behind can't have been comparable to going to war, but we thought it was."

Eric could catch hold of that terror, not from anything he knew or had experienced, but he could make it up out of the gifts and losses and turns of his life. Of course, Frank had shipped out, too, later, but if what Eric suspected was true, it wasn't much more dangerous than a passage on the *Queen Elizabeth*.

"So I was sitting in the lobby. The Monticello was one of those grand hotels, just like . . ." She stopped and said to Frank, "You're staying at the Tutwiler, of course."

"Yes. Old days."

"I would have guessed. Is that what this visit is about? All these old memories?"

"No."

She was perplexed by this, and Eric wondered how to explain his father's uses of "yes" and "no," the strange syntax of his reasoning, because he knew this "no" meant that these memories were definitely part of what it was all about, but not all of it. Still, she seemed to believe that all she had to do was finish this story and then Frank would leave.

"Rachel and I were sharing a room—do I have to spell everything out for you?—and I was sitting in this uncomfortable little side chair right in the pathway to the bar, and there were men in uniforms going in and out, some with women, most not. I think I had a book with me, but I couldn't concentrate, and then I looked up and this gawky, skinny lieutenant was staring at me. His ears looked big." She glanced over at Frank as if to check whether it was still so, though Eric had never noticed it if it was. "Just in case you were going to ask," Audrey picked up quickly, "I never knew if Rachel and Nicholas actually made love, and Rachel never told me because I never asked. There wasn't any"—she paused for the right word—"evidence, and that's all I'm going to say about it."

"Did he talk to you? Did he pick you up?" asked Eric. He glanced at Frank to make sure that this was where he wanted the conversation to go, and he returned a rather ambivalent nod: *Sure*, he seemed to be saying, *let's hear it out.*

"Well, yes. He asked me whether I was waiting for my date. I told him I was waiting for my mother to get dressed."

"Nasty and unfriendly," said Frank.

"When he came back out of the bar I was still sitting there. He asked if it always took my mother an hour and a half to dress. He was . . ." This was coming less willingly now that it had turned to them, but her own pleasure at imagining these hours so deeply overcame her resistance. "He was very charming, not pushy. He looked a little lonely. That's why I talked to him. I felt sorry for him. I suspect that's the way a lot of love affairs start, the girl feeling sorry for the boy. It's hard being a man. I could never understand all those feminists, wanting to be men."

"They didn't want to be men. Really, Mom, even for you that's grotesque."

"I can have my own opinions," she stated.

"Sure. But about Dad . . ."

"We had a drink at the bar. The rest we all know too well."

"A Manhattan," said Frank.

Once again, the intimacy of remembered details drew her back. "Was it? It was certainly the first time in my life I had ever sat at a bar with a man and ordered a drink like that. I'm sure I didn't have a clue what a Manhattan was, I must have heard of it in a movie. All I remember is that I was tipsy when I said I had to meet my mother, and he walked me to the elevator and asked if he could pay a call for breakfast. I said yes. Back then, you had dates at any time of the day or night."

"It's a great story," said Eric.

"I suppose, but it didn't turn out very well." She had snapped back into the present, on the other side of the gulf that separated her, and him, from these cherished memories. "It's silly to speak of. I don't know why he"—unloading the ammunition here, *he,* this nonverbal invalid—"wants to go into any of it."

"I was a fool. I lost you."

"You didn't lose me. You rejected every fiber of my being, Frank. So I left you." The sweet rhythm of memory was gone in a second.

He said something she couldn't understand. She looked at Eric. Surprised at the turn, he translated. "I think what he was saying was that he behaved hatefully." Frank nodded vigorously. The word had been "outrageous"; the sound had been "oragus": Eric was sharp this morning, almost spooky.

Her hand went nervously to her mouth, to her hair, and she turned her gaze out the window. The rain was heavy now under a very black sky.

"Do you agree? Did you hate him? Do you?"

"He can't expect me to answer that question. I don't even know why *you* are asking it."

"Seems like a reasonable thing for him to want to know."

"What difference would it make?" she stated sharply. "No. I don't hate him. It's all so long ago, or was, until this morning." She turned her attention back to Frank, angry now. "No. I don't hate you, Frank. I hated you during those years, when you treated me so horribly. So cruelly. Why? What did I ever do besides try to be a good wife to you? God, all those miserable, wasted years."

Frank stiffened; a surge of hurt. Words battled at the bottleneck of his damaged mouth; Eric could almost hear the tumult of their jostling, syllables being snatched from each other and reinserted backward, words elbowing each other like soldiers insisting on their right to pass unimpeded, brandishing their arms. The sounds came out in a faint gargle like the whistling of phlegm. Audrey was staring at him, almost taunting him as he struggled in this way. But then it was over, another defeat. He waggled his hand, meaning only that he had much to say and no way to say it, which was not news. Eric said nothing. His stomach felt thick. This is what they had all expected; it was what both he and his father deserved. Eric felt adrift in this middle ground.

"Worse," said Frank at last. "Mottsecks."

"What?"

"Mistakes. He means that he made mistakes."

"He certainly did."

"He's told me that he regrets the way he treated you and by making this trip, he means that he can't finish his life without this, this moment. He's not asking to be forgiven. He's trying to atone. I guess he just wants you to acknowledge that he is here, that he made the effort."

"Yes," Frank said.

"And I believe"—here Eric could only take a big breath and step out onto infirm ground—"being here in front of you, with all your memories, is a way of confessing. Because he can't do it himself. The confession just has to be wordless. It's that simple."

She took this longish speech without comment or change of expression, and made no motion or response. Her mouth remained fixed in an irritated but not angry downturn. Eric had said almost everything that seemed worth saying. Perhaps it was time to go, whether she wanted it or not, but he could feel a change in the room, which was that Audrey was no longer trying to throw them out, but had now begun to exert a different pressure, a captive force. Frank wanted this meeting, and now, by God, he was going to get it.

"He's just trying to tie up the loose ends." Eric had never been able to endure silences and often said the first thing that came to mind, especially in a silence like this one, as dense and brittle as a block of marble.

"You would not like it, dear, if you were one of the loose ends."

"No," said Eric, "I'm sorry. An awful thing to say."

"The question, of course, is which loose end he might be referring to." She was angry now, she wasn't performing for Eric or anyone else, but a person angered by the past. "I was twenty years old when we married. I trusted him with my soul."

"I know," said Eric, not answering for his father now. This was no longer a conversation that included Frank.

"I was beautiful," she said, a strange turn, though not, from her, an unfamiliar vanity. "I was a beautiful young woman and there was nothing I wouldn't have done to please him. I was young and wanted a full life; I wanted pleasure and was eager to give it. I wasn't some innocent, frigid belle, you know." She directed this small aside at Eric, which made him squirm a bit. "No one should have tolerated what I did. His unfaithfulness. He taunted me with it. I tried to understand. I thought it was all my fault, so I tried to behave the way he wanted. But the fact was, he didn't want me. So explain that to me." She looked again at Eric, as if he really might be able to explain the mystery and perversities of desire, but he could not, could only think of Gail, as beautiful a woman as he had ever known, and of his own infidelities. "It has taken me years to understand that I was not at fault, that I truly offered him everything a man could want. In the end, what happened had nothing to do with me, did it, Frank?"

"No. Audrey." He fought again with his mouth; the intolerable moment. "Scared" was all that came out.

"You? Scared?"

"Yes. Too much."

"That's absurd," she said.

"Then why," said Eric after a suitable pause, "didn't you leave him earlier? I know divorce would not have been something you wanted, but gee."

It seemed that her answer would be brisk, but whatever her first impulse, the inrush of air stayed inside for a time, and then came out as simply air, a long-drawn-out exhalation that now seemed to be an effort to remove entirely the impulse from her mind. "I didn't know where to turn. I didn't want to come back here to Birmingham in disgrace."

"There it is."

"No, it isn't. Because he admitted to me that his behavior was evil and kept insisting he would change."

"But he didn't?"

"Eric, why are you putting me through this? What is the point?"

Yes, it was now Eric who was leading her, forcing her back into those years, not sure for whose benefit, but believing that it could be for hers as much as anybody's. "I don't know what the point is," he said. He looked over at his father, and there was no sign from his eyes: fright maybe, but no sign. "I guess because you've never told me any of this. Because you should tell me this, so I understand my own life better."

"It is the little things that are hard," she said, and there was wisdom in that, perhaps enough to put an end to this, a reference to a thousand small hurts, too numerous to name. But she was not done. "One time—I forget whether this was the first time, or the tenth—he had come home and promised that it was done. He begged to be taken back, and I didn't have much choice—did I, dear?—but to believe him. A week or two later I decided to go to Annapolis to shop, which was something I never did because I was afraid of what I might see. I put on my best hat and gloves and went over, and I was walking along Church Circle—that was the closest I could get to the statehouse. I was being brave; I thought I was reclaiming these places, and it was a beautiful day. It must have been in the early spring." She stopped here for a moment, perhaps thinking of that suit, which Eric could recall quite well. "And there he was, sitting on a bench with a girl. Their ankles were entwined. They didn't see me. She was smoking a cigarette. I cannot describe what it felt like, that instant that bored into my heart like a dentist's drill."

From the side, from Frank, Eric heard a sharp groan almost as if a fist had just struck him in the chest. It was the sound of his mother's instant, decades later.

"And you knew she wasn't something legitimate?"

She waved that argument off. "I was pregnant with Poppy, a big old pregnant hag, and she was this cute little thing, some eager little intern from College Park." She turned to Frank. "Did you have interns back then, Frank?" she asked with a sneer. "Had you men invented interns yet?"

"Dunow."

She turned back to face Eric. "I didn't want that pregnancy. I hadn't consented to sleep with him when it happened. After I got pregnant he never bothered me again." She stopped while the implication of her last statement settled over the room. There was thunder outside now. For the first time in several minutes, Eric glanced over at his father, and it was there in his eyes, a horror at these facts, a horror and an admission. His lifeless arm twitched, as if long-dead neural paths were stirring on the narration of these stories.

"I wanted to die. On the way back over the bay I realized that I could die in childbirth, that the baby would be stillborn, and that would take care of everything. I wanted that. I would have prayed for it, but what was to become of you and Alice?"

Eric didn't know; it had never before occurred to him to wonder what his father would have been like, if Audrey's death or the circumstances of divorce had left him and Alice in Maryland, to be raised by Frank. His mother had stayed married to Frank long enough to get Alice and Eric through their childhoods, and from the day she had left with Poppy, Eric had ceased really to have a home at all, other than a prep school or college dorm, and a choice of two places to spend his vacations, but by then he was old enough to survive it.

No one spoke for a few moments. Frank was folded deep into the cushions; this couch was too soft for him; it made his body seem even more unconnected than it was; he knew it made him seem pathetic, but he could hardly complain. Still, he tried to straighten up. "I'm sorry," he said. "Only sorry. Just so sorry. All of it."

It was all anyone could imagine to say, at this point. Eric looked over at his mother. She had a firm grip on herself, on this room, which she regarded with a stiff, unwavering gaze. Eric waited for her response, and was surprised by what came out.

"If you have apologies on your mind, Frank, you should make them to Poppy. You know that, don't you?"

"Yes. Yes."

"What happened between us is long gone. There's no longer any pain for me in this. If there is for you, then I'm glad. I'm glad regret has finally come to you. I don't mind that you came here." She glanced at Eric as she said this. "Eric did what he thought was best. But he doesn't understand, does he?"

"No."

"He doesn't know that this trip to see me isn't the trip you should take."

Eric could not help himself. "Why? Why Poppy?"

Neither of his parents answered.

Eric tried again. "Is that right, Dad? We should be in Houston?"

Frank tried to deflect the question with a dart of the head, one of his long library of helpless, equivocating shrugs, but Eric saw it anyway, the terror in his eyes, and after the terror had cleared somewhat, Frank began to cry. Not a few tears, but a deep sobbing, a choking of breath behind the heaves. He clasped his hand over his eyes, and when Audrey finally offered him a handkerchief, he took it with gratitude and began to mop up. Eric appealed to his mother—*What should I say? How can I help?*—but she shook her head. *Say nothing. Just wait.*

Frank handed the moist handkerchief back to Audrey, a clear thank-you in his eyes. He coughed a few times to clear out the last of it, and then looked at Eric. He shrugged again, but there was relief now in his face; a suggestion of a smile, as if acknowledging that he had been silly.

So what now? Audrey wasn't going to say any more. Eric tried to see where she was now, but she was staring out the window, her eyes dry, one wrinkled but still-elegant hand raised to her chin, the other hand clasping a handkerchief moist with Frank's tears. Eric turned then to Frank, and all he could see was the top of his head, gray with the stubble of his once-thick brown hair, his glasses down on his nose, but it was as if he, too, had checked out of this, his gesture made. But no one moved, and no one seemed to feel the need. The conversation was now silent.

"I'm sorry to put you through this," Eric said finally, to his mother.

But this did not move them, either. Still staring out the window, she flicked her raised hand to dismiss this final unnecessary, or irrelevant, apology from him. What was happening here? Why wasn't his mother brusquely shooing them out, *I'm sure you have a great deal to do;* or his father grappling himself to his feet saying *Go. Go?* Eric considered making some noise about something, but at last it dawned on him that whatever this stasis meant, it had nothing whatsoever to do with him, that if this strangely peaceful impasse contained messages, none of them were his business. This part of the conversation was theirs. So he did stand up, and said he was sure they might want to be alone—and since neither of his parents said anything, he left the room.

He walked across the hall to Jackson's study and found Adam there, sitting at Jackson's desk leafing through a banking trade magazine. This room was perfectly decorated for the man of the house: dark woods, brown walls, two small windows. The architects and builders of these upscale tract houses seemed to believe that they had a perfect sense of the needs and tastes of the two genders, and an unquestioned grasp of their roles in any marriage: the man working late into the evening, paying bills, doing taxes, perhaps completing the day's business with a briefcase full of files spread out on the maroon carpet. Eric's house in Summit had a similar room, smaller and less lavishly outfitted, and he had indeed worked late at night in it over the years, bills, taxes, business, while Gail put Tom to bed and kept their mutual friendships alive on the telephone at her bedside table.

"So," said Adam.

Eric shook his head and slumped down in the love seat.

"Rough?"

"Please, Adam. Just let it be."

Adam accepted this request with a nod: *You are a bit of an asshole,* he seemed to be saying, still angry about the remark about logistics, *but I know you don't mean to be.* "Okay," he said. It was no longer raining, but the cloud cover was still thick and it was so dark in the room that Eric could barely see his hands.

"Pretty rough," said Eric, at last. "But kind of miraculous. I may have just heard the sound forgiveness makes, and I'll tell you, it's all but silence. A bit of a miracle," he repeated.

Adam seemed pleased to hear this. He cared about Frank; for the first time, Eric saw how much Adam had hoped that this would not be awful, that it would give this man some peace. Yes, much more than logistics and a paycheck was driving him.

"I'm sorry for that 'logistics' bit," said Eric. "You know. I was a little nervous."

"That's okay."

"It's not as if I ever was confident that this wouldn't be a complete disaster."

"No. But it wasn't, was it?"

Eric nodded as he reviewed a little of this recent event: the stories. Poppy. Yes, what the hell was that, about Poppy?

"This was good," continued Adam in kindness. "It's meant a lot of wear and tear, but if this went well, it will give him strength. We'll see."

Eric snapped into the moment; there could be only one next step. "We're not going home yet, are we?" said Eric.

"Well. Not sure."

"We're going to Houston. Right?"

"This is not good. This is pushing himself too far. I don't approve."

"But we're going to Houston," Eric repeated, "because that's where the work is." But as soon as he had used the word "work," his own labors and responsibilities rushed in on him. What was happening in his office; who was leaving enraged, bombshell messages on his voice mail at this very moment, *Where the hell are you, you bastard, we're putting the whole damn account up for review. . . .* Out there, people were mad at him: *That asshole Alwin off in Alabama*—Liv's voice now. Time to wrap this up and get the hell home.

Jesus, he thought; it was Thursday. There was no way he could get them down to Houston, get anything meaningful with Poppy done. But that's what had to happen; he'd figure it out, he'd do it for Poppy. His office, his career, would have to wait. Any occasion with Poppy was a gift. Back into that big Ford. Frank's mission: a rolling thunder review of his life.

When the door to the living room opened, both Eric and Adam leaped to their feet, like husbands in a maternity waiting room. Audrey looked serious, maybe a little grim, as if there were good news and bad news, but when she spoke, she was relaxed and content. "Your father's ready to go."

"Did it go okay? Could you understand him?"

"He knew exactly what he wanted to say. It wasn't that difficult, really. It's fine."

Behind her, Frank was working into the hall. He was tired, and when he was, his balance wasn't very good. Adam moved forward to give him a hand, and Eric stood face-to-face with his mother. "Are you okay?"

"He has nothing to be afraid of from me, Eric."

He told her he thought she'd been incredibly fair about this, courageous—both he and Adam thought that, he said. He told her he'd been dreading this and now that it was done he hoped something good would come of it for her as well as Frank.

"Yes, dear. How's Gail?"

"She's fine. She sends her love."

"And Tom?"

"Oh," he said, "you know. You worry about the kids, don't you. For the rest of your life."

Adam had gotten Frank into his raincoat and was holding him very firmly by the arm: Eric had never seen him do that before; he'd never seen his father need it and accept it so fully. His skin looked gray, but he flashed Eric an all's-well smile, a couple of quick raises of his eyebrows, and he said, "Picture."

"Dad, I don't think so."

"Picture," he said.

"What does he mean?"

"He wants me to take your picture."

Audrey's hand went immediately to her face, running her fingers across her cheek. She was still very pretty; Poppy's beauty had come from her, her sharp and graceful chin, her clear skin. But the idea of being photographed was not a hit.

"Picture," he said one last time, too tired to bellow it, as he would have at home.

By now Audrey had dropped her hand from her face, and had

run both of them over her hips, smoothing the nonexistent folds in her immaculate blue dress. "Oh fine," she said. "It's positively mad, but you know me, Eric. I like surprises."

Eric still disbelieved, but he went to the car to get his camera anyway, and in the meantime they had clambered back onto the stoop, where Eric had stood in trepidation a century ago, and if there had not been so much ornamental clutter on that platform they would almost certainly not have posed so close together, but there they were just the same, side by side, a couple under the threatening skies of the storm, and Frank was already smiling, and it wasn't the smug or drunken expression of the young groom or philandering husband in earlier photographs, but a look of gratitude. Audrey was still composing herself in a slightly distracted way as Eric took the camera out of the case, opened the f-stop in this gloomy, sodden light and sighted in on the scene, but she was not bitter now, and she was not miserable: she had won at last. She had gotten justice from the only person who could give it to her. When Eric snapped the shot, a smile formed on her lovely face, and it shone, her features glowing, everything right there on the surface, a full display for the camera. Maybe there was a hint of triumph on his mother's face, but it was not victory on his father's: it was joy. Eric took a few more pictures, and then, feeling that he would never take a more valuable photograph in his life, he moved a few feet for more of a close-up, and kept the shutter clicking until he used up the entire roll.

"That's one," said Audrey, "that will confuse your grandchildren, won't it?" She was pleased. "If they care at all, of course."

They did not speak on the trip back to the Tutwiler Hotel, and as soon as they arrived, Adam had Frank in the elevator, and they were gone.

Eric checked his messages and when he reached him, Liv acted as if he didn't know why Eric was calling, which was strange: normally, he would be heaping on the guilt trips by now. He ate dinner alone in the hotel, reading a book; he always liked eating alone in restaurants, as long as he had a martini and something to read, but he was getting tired of solitude after the stunning human interaction of the morning, and when he called Gail he was relieved, almost surprised she was home, but he was eager to talk.

"Tell all," she said, and he did.

"We knew it all, didn't we really?" said Gail.

"Yeh. We did. No real surprises. But God, how could he behave that way? It wasn't a single event, something out of character. That was him. That was this man, my father."

"Well. Now you know."

"Yes, but I do think he got somewhere. There's another thing. This thing about Poppy. We're going to Houston. Tomorrow, I guess."

Gail whistled. "Cool," she said.

"I don't know. We'll see what happens. But I'm getting worried about work, the presentation. I *have* to be there for it; clients like to see the whole team. Monday morning, nine A.M. Liv's acting weirder and weirder on the phone."

"I don't see the problem. Drive them to Houston, get them settled, and then fly back for the meeting. Come back on Sunday and we can have the evening together."

He had not imagined such a simple plan; that had always been one of Eric's failings, in business especially, and in his marriage, especially; he could get stymied by small conflicts. Gail had said he behaved this way because he could not bring himself to admit to his own needs, that he was terrified of people finding fault.

"That's fantastic," he said. He stood up in his hotel room and paced happily at the end of the phone cord. He wouldn't have to miss a thing. "I don't know why I didn't think of it."

"Sure. But what about Alice?"

"What about her?"

"Eric, come on. You would consider having this family reunion and not include her? Even Alice would never forgive that."

She was right. And there it was, the full plan. Eric flies up, Alice flies down about the same time, and Eric comes back down to Houston after the meeting. They spend a couple of days with Poppy and then head on back, a mini vacation if there ever was one. His mother's triumph was his triumph; his father's release was his release. There were mysteries in the air again, a hint of magic, a working of grace, and of love. Eric hung up, amid several "I love you"s, sincerely stated, and got ready for bed. He flicked on the television, and hesitated for a second at the adult offerings and then turned it off, a peaceful dark descending upon him. Outside, Birmingham, a place that had been kind to him this time, honked and sirened its way into its own night.

SIX

Eric had been ten when his mother became pregnant with Poppy, and he was old enough to regard his mother's fate with true alarm. He did not know how miserable her life had become, which was one of the many signs of her strength and courage in those days, but he did realize that this addition to the family was not part of the plan, and that his father, so often absent, did not want it to happen. All that hot summer Audrey's body swelled; even an Alabama girl suffers with pregnancy in the heat, and she took cool baths often. One time Eric surprised her getting out of the tub, and what he saw struck him with horror, his mother's distended flesh, the violence of this slow force, a fierce concentration of irresistible forces played out on his mother's helpless body. He retreated from the room, sought out Alice, and cried. Alice was just thirteen and had become aggressive about the holy mysteries of the female body. "What are you crying for?" she asked. "I think she's beautiful."

And she was beautiful, not Audrey—what boy would notice that about his mother, pregnant or not?—but the sister, Penelope. She was the kind of baby people stared at. Eric found himself lingering around her crib, her playpen, astonished by the articulation of those tiny hands, the porcelain perfection of her mouth as it closed so firmly around the bottle, the wide eyes scanning the room with such interest. Even at the time, Eric realized that this fascination was odd for a brother, who was supposed to complain about her screams, about the grossness of her diaper, about the loss of his mother's attentions. But he could not resist the order and calm, the innocence that radiated from her person. He noticed that whenever Poppy was in the room, a family was there, all smiles and cheeriness, an *us,* where otherwise—despite his tight alliance with Alice—their family seemed a collection of *them*s. His mother laughed freely in her presence, because Poppy was a funny baby, impish and almost sly as she mastered those first skills, rolling over, sitting up, walking, and speaking. She seemed to understand her received task, and played it to the hilt. From those ghastly beginnings in his mother's belly had come a gift.

But children are selective about what they focus upon, even though they see everything, every minute fold in the fabric around them, and what he finally began to piece together as an adult was the fact that from all this familial cheer his father was totally absent. Not just absent during his long weeks in Annapolis—Eric had grown up with those—but here in the center of his family. In the heat of that summer, 1962, Poppy's playpen was set up at one end of what had been Frank's domain, the water-side porch, to be cooled by the breezes, to hear the birds during the morning and the locusts during the day, to see the fireflies in the evening. Frank sat at the other end, smoking his Chesterfields. At the time, Eric noticed that he and Alice and their mother closed around Poppy; even today, he had no real memory, could conjure up not a single likely incident, of his father so much as touching his youngest child.

A few months after Poppy was born, Eric went along with his father on one of his political events, one of those constituent gatherings that are the centerpiece of a local politician's career. It was a church picnic in the 4-H Club park in the next town, an assemblage of livestock sheds and exhibition halls under the deep shade of tall loblolly pines; once a year the park was filled with farm animals, and the children who had raised them, and the parents who had raised the children. For the rest of the year, the place was free for the asking to local organizations. On that day, the games and barbecue were well under way when they arrived, and as usual, the men in suspenders and white shirts and straw hats all gathered around Frank, lots of laughs, a jostling for position, and a few who had lost out came over to Eric, and one punched him on the arm and said, "Son, you're so skinny you're going to slip down a straw and drown in your tonic."

Eric pretended he thought this was funny. He had heard and seen all this before, knew that nothing an adult ever said to him was truly directed to him. He followed the crowd over to the picnic bench that had been cleared for the Senator, and the crowd gathered around in a ring. This fuss would not occur for just any state legislator, but Frank Alwin was on his way to D.C.; everyone believed that, including Frank. He made a show of wiping the seat, saying he didn't want to sit on "no" chicken bones or sweet potato pie, just the right amount of comfort and hilarity to legitimize the serious matters on his mind: traffic on Route 50, the Berlin crisis, the colored. Who knew what the hell it was that day? But that was to come after an interval accorded precisely by some collective clock, and they started with the heat, veered toward Eric himself, a prop in this theater, and then moved on to the new arrival in the Senator's family.

"Pretty little thing," said one of the men. "I seen her at the Acme with Miss Audrey the other day."

"A lovely child," said Mrs. McMaster, the librarian.

"Dainty as a china doll," echoed Mary Watkins, a woman of well over three hundred pounds.

Eric watched as his father beamed, deflecting what were obviously compliments meant only for him. "She gets her beauty from her mother," he said. "Imagine a baby that looks like me."

Everyone laughed at this tired joke. From the crowd a coarser male voice said, "You the stallion in the family, Mr. Frank."

"That's right," said one of the favored ones in the front row. "We figured that you were a little old for this, but you can't keep a good man down." More laughter, as the woman to this man's side, his wife no doubt, gave him a slap that knocked his hat to the ground.

"Can't take him nowhere," she said.

Frank waited patiently for this to play out, and as it did he let his expression firm up a bit; a sign of wisdom on the way.

"Thanks for the compliment, Bobby," he said. "But I'll tell you this. At night when she's in her crib—"

A woman's voice interrupted with a slight taunt, "*After* she's washed and diapered," but this woman clearly had a less meticulous sense of timing, and she got only a few polite chuckles, even though Eric now thought what she said was perhaps the only real truth of this exercise.

"Well, at night after everyone else has turned in I just go in there and watch her sleep. I don't need to tell you that each breath is a miracle. And then once in a while she lets out a little sigh, like this"—and he mimicked the sound, but this was not supposed to be a joke, it was a masterful detail of manipulation, and no one laughed—"and I know the love in my heart is the love of the Holy Ghost." He paused here, for emphasis. "And I know that this is what matters. Nothing else. It's why we're here today, for the children in a place for children, ain't it?" A murmur of agreement. "It's why I do what I do. It's why these things we talk about amount to more than a hill of beans." This was the cue for absolute silence, except for the buzz of insects and the crackling of chicken skin over the coals. And then, "Speaking of beans, Mr. Thompson, what price you figure you're going to get this year?"

Eric heard this with profound confusion: Dad goes into Poppy's room at night? When the talk turned firmly to business, he wandered off through the fairgrounds, through the empty, fragrant pens, past the well-trodden ground where a few months ago he'd ridden the Ferris wheel and the loop-de-loop, and as he approached the far end, he heard and saw another gathering, Negroes this time, the same chicken on the fire, a slightly louder and milkier sound to the voices. His father went to those picnics too, now and again, though Eric had never accompanied him to one. He stopped, a small white face looking in, a turn of heads directed out, children in their Sunday clothes, and he wondered about what his father had just said, that he went into Poppy's room at night. It didn't quite add up, not that Eric could have organized and reflected on the evidence at that age. Eric couldn't quite imagine it, but all sorts of things happen at night after the kids are asleep, and he decided that it was true. His father had said so. It didn't really make much sense, but maybe that was just what fathers did. Even forty years later, when much that he had learned argued otherwise, even after he had raised his own child in what seemed to be such a different manner, he still was not sure that it wasn't true. He could imagine it now as he had not been able to do as a child, imagine it as a crossing of a barrier that had been put up by history and confusion and fear, and knew now that what Frank was experiencing, watching Poppy breathe, was not the light of the Holy Spirit but the dark side of despair, a knowledge that through his own acts and will he had already destroyed his place in the only thing that amounts to more than a hill of beans, your own family.

So what can you make of your father, this figure connected to you physically only by a few thrusts of that part of him you can hardly bear to envision? Does he really love you? Why bother with him? Leave him alone, the old fool, and let him live out his life in peace. Visit him on Thanksgiving. Send him a birthday card. He doesn't owe you anything for his single nighttime visitation, not now anyway, not after he'd fed you and clothed you, and if you're lucky, done his best to raise you. What do you owe him?

But still, what can you *make* of this man? And what can you make of yourself, trying to do your best in a job that's hard to grasp?

Eric was asking himself that question, and remembering this incident forty years past, as he guided the Ford out of Birmingham and turned now for the deeper South, toward the Gulf and Louisiana's spongy delta lands, on to the hard-rock soil of East Texas and then Houston. They'd spent a layover day in the Tutwiler while Frank rested, and in the afternoon, before joining his mother and Jackson for dinner, he went to his father and told him that he was on board for Houston, that he'd take him there since it was clear that was his plan anyway, that the hurt Eric had seen in Frank the day before must be tearing him apart.

"I don't know what you'll get from Poppy," he had said. "I'll tell you the truth: I'm even less sure of what you'll get from Poppy than from Mom. And I won't be able to translate for you. With Mom, well, it was sort of my business too. I have no place in a conversation between you and Poppy. But we're going."

Once Alice understood that she was a key member for this part of the trip, they debated what they would say to Poppy. They didn't remark on it to each other, but though arriving unannounced at Audrey's had seemed—and in fact, had been—the only way to do it, this would never fly with Poppy. They tried to remember the last time she had seen Frank, and agreed it was two summers ago, when she made one of her lightning visits to Maryland. She did that, now and again, sometimes with Ricki but most times not, came in late, accepted without complaint Frank's lavishments of attention, returned her typical distracted affections, endured with more warmth Eric's own love for her, and was gone in the morning before anyone was awake. This was Poppy, it was what they knew of her even if Alice and Eric truly didn't understand why she made these trips: what impelled her? What force drew her there? Not as a stopover on the way north for business or something, but as a trip she'd booked only for this and precisely to this plan. On the telephone it was different; safe in Houston, she called Eric and Alice often, long calls asking mostly for their news; it was on these calls that Eric had told her about his life, his affairs, his struggles with Gail. Eric's true intimacy with the person he had loved longer and more purely and faithfully than anyone else on the planet, was, he realized, entirely long distance.

So there was no question that they would call her first and tell her what was happening, but who should call? Alice? Eric? Both, on a conference call? No. In the end, Poppy herself had made it easy: she called Alice for news about the Birmingham visit. As Alice relayed the conversation to Eric, Poppy had accepted the plan without real complaint. *Sure. Why not? Eric and Dad think they're going to fix everything, right?*

On the drive they were taking the old route through the hillsides covered with kudzu and the flaky buildings of the little towns. Adam would participate in none of it. "What's on for tonight, boys?" he said through the window at four young men, fat and longhaired, glaring at this vehicle from the Outside. "A little gay-bashing? Cross-burning, maybe?"

Eric did not argue with him. That was the way it was. Alabama, a place most other Americans speak of as a foreign country, like Nigeria or Singapore, where you can run afoul of local custom or law and end up dead or in prison. A state represented by senators and congressmen who were wrong on every issue that remotely related to truth and justice in the world. Martin Luther King, Jr., began his career in Alabama, but when he described his dreams, he could go so far as to predict freedom in Mississippi, but he was silent on Alabama. Too many dead for that, and more to come. Eric was in Birmingham during the summer of 1963. Audrey often went down for a long visit—the reverse, she pointed out, of the typical vacation migrations—to stay with her parents in their age-less outpost of Confederate calm on Highland Avenue, and that year she had decamped with all three children for their entire vacation. Eric and Alice hated it there, hated being away from the farm and their farm children's games. A revolution was going on, said Grandpop, on the phone before they arrived; when the wind was right, he said, you could smell the tear gas rising up from downtown. Why this gentleman would tell this to a child, scaring him out of his wits, giving him nightmares about the "lovely long visit," as his mother put it, Eric could not figure. But when they came in that June, there was nothing going on. All placid: leafy tree-lined streets up the hills, people going about their business, pale little boys and girls swimming in the pools, favorite restaurants as always: black waiters, white diners. If things were tense and simmering, he wouldn't have known of it in the family's white cocoon. All remained quiet until the Sunday—September 15—they were packing to return to Maryland, and a whispering began to move through the adults, and Myrtice, who was there to prepare their roadside picnic, left so fast that eight slices of bread with mayonnaise on them remained on the counter, and even Grandpop looked ashen with fear and grief, and Eric heard the news that someone had blown to bits the Sixteenth Street Baptist Church, and four little girls with it.

But today Eric was on a different course through that sleepy terrain, down the Alabama River, into Mobile and then on to Pascagoula, Mississippi. They wound through the hamlets and villages, some prosperous enough to support a modest line of local stores, others looking as if mules and wagons would still be parked at the loading docks in back. They drove through the verdant and little-marred landscape, a creamy roll of small rises and dips. People—white and black—stopped to stare at the big car as if it were the luxury liner of a country music star; it wasn't so hard to understand: the tourists normally never left the interstate. When they got gas, two boys asked to sit in the car. Eric said they could, but when they saw the old man, they backed off.

Frank rode mostly silently. He peered at the sights with mute interest, this gradual unfolding of antebellum scenes. They were in the swing now, each stop a close-order drill, bathroom, gas, something to eat. Adam was always pushing Frank to eat, whatever reasonably healthy snacks he could find in these roadside palaces of convenience if not sustenance, and Frank usually resisted before acceding to a few crackers, a handful of trail mix.

The sun was starting to redden as they rejoined the interstate across the mouth of Lake Pontchartrain. Eric had never been to New Orleans—though it was a favorite destination of Birmingham's cosmopolites—and, without asking, he took an exit ramp into downtown.

"No," said his father. He had no interest in the ugly neon sights of this or any city.

"Just a drive-through, Dad. You know, places to go, things to see?"

"Ack," Frank answered, his all-purpose expression of displeasure and disgust. As soon as they were off the ramp they were in the thick of a steamy Louisiana rush hour.

"Stupid," said Frank.

They were waiting through a third light change to get through an intersection, and all they got to look at was a Wendy's, a Taco Bell, and a liquor store with grates over all the windows and a handwritten sign advertising po'boys.

"Okay. A bad idea. I admit it."

Adam had moved up to the middle seat and was studying the not very helpful detail of Central New Orleans in the road atlas. "What's a 'vex car'?" he asked.

"What?"

Adam spelled it out: "V-I-E-U-X C-A-R-R-E."

"French," said Eric, nosing ahead in the line of traffic. " 'Old Square,' or something like that. Must be the French Quarter."

"Ack," said Frank again, loudly.

"We'll give it one try," said Eric, and Adam navigated until they were driving down the narrow streets, with their wrought-iron balconies and tile roofs. They were so much like the photographs

Eric had seen that they were almost completely without appeal. He recalled a movie he saw far too young and hadn't seen—or even heard spoken of—in over forty years, Elvis's *King Creole;* in the opening scene, Elvis was awakened in one of those second-story rooms off the balcony by a street vendor yelling "Crawfish," the opening word of the movie's first musical number. Eric tried to hum a few bars. A great movie; he must find out if he could get it on video. In *Easy Rider,* Peter Fonda and Dennis Hopper had come through New Orleans on their motorcycles, and had taken acid in a spooky aboveground graveyard. Eric had taken acid once, at Gail's prodding, and didn't have a whole lot of fun; it felt like sweating through a high fever.

Frank had had enough. "Go. Now."

"Okay. You win."

They stayed at a Holiday Inn—there was no "locally owned" alternative—in a town well west of the city, maybe twenty miles short of the Texas border, a barren swash of neon and oil equipment. They got an early start for the longer leg into Houston. It was Sunday now, and Eric had to catch his plane at Hobby at two-fifteen; the old seep of anxiety was reclaiming him and he kept on the highway, following its harsh arc through the increasingly arid landscape. Adam kept them distracted with a story of the trip he took with his two aunts—Aunt April and Aunt May—to Dallas to see Southfork, a landmark he was too young to appreciate. Adam's mother—the youngest of the three—was named June. On the road, each day at three they had to find a television set so the girls could watch their favorite soap. "*General Hospital,*" said Adam, "or *Love of Life*. Whatever it was. They watched them all." Adam described them, nearly panicked as the hour approached, busting into the sleaziest bar he himself had ever entered and then cowering in shame while April demanded that the TV be tuned to ABC. When they left, the bartender gave all three ladies a kiss. "Those three," said Adam. "They've always gotten exactly what they wanted."

Frank had sat entertained for the whole long story. A love of stories, almost anybody's, had always been one of his peculiar graces; unusual for a man otherwise so self-absorbed, so strategic in conversation, to have such patience for another person lost in the intimate anecdotes of a beloved memory. It was as if from the first buttery tones of narrative some of the demons in him were put to sleep, and others, the shards of memory of his first career ambition, were brought back to where they belonged. Eric had known this about his father from the moment he could talk. When Frank was away, Eric would save up the tales of playgrounds, or books, things he heard secondhand, and later of more meaningful college days, and then spend an entire weekend playing them out, and unlike the distracted "Uh-huh"s and "That's nice, dear"s he got from his mother, he'd receive rapt attention and "Then what?"s and roars of laughter, and if a story was interrupted by a phone call, or a visit from cronies, his father would return to it later, prompting Eric on where it left off. Eric treasured this as a child, and when he became a parent and learned how tedious, despite endless love, these stories from a child could be, he was further mystified by it. Now he had lived in the North awhile, where wisdom gets exchanged more in the form of disconnected ironies. The failing, then, was Eric's: he had lost the wisdom of stories. Perhaps his father would now listen to him as raptly as he once had, as he had focused on Adam, as indeed he focused on Alice's bits of gossip.

Listening to Adam tired Frank out, and he snoozed for a while, now and again making energetic little yips like a dog dreaming of tasty things; and when he awoke, he reached over and grasped Eric's shoulder.

"Well?" he said.

Eric knew this single word was a reference to Audrey. He drove a few more miles before answering. "Do you think I was surprised to hear what she said about what you did? I wasn't, you know. They were all just details of a story I've known all my life."

"I know. But she said them."

"And I heard her. That was the important thing, right? I sat there and listened, as if you were the one talking."

"Yes."

"So are you satisfied?"

"Yes. Blessed."

"She said something that released you?"

"Maybe. Maybe yes. Don't know yet."

"But Jesus," said Eric, now in a rush. "What did you think you were *gaining* by behaving like that back then? You've never done anything in your life without calculating the pluses and minuses, so what was the calculus for this? Mom can't have been perfect, and I don't judge you except by what you are now, a good man, a kind man. But in the prime of your life, you gave it over to such mean-spiritedness. What was it *for*?"

Frank was quiet for a while, now and again cocking his head, raising his hand as if he would begin to respond, but then dropping back into his private conversation. The answer, when it came at last, was the only one that made sense. "Can't tell you. Wish I could."

"I wish you could too," said Eric, first as a continuation of the note of recrimination, but he soon realized that what he said was not a judgment, but a question, a plea. "Jesus," he said. "I wish you could, because I wish I knew why I've done half the things I have done. I wish I knew why I think half of what I think. Why it all gets so fucked up, so often."

"Dunow. Dunow."

"I think you do. That's your stroke talking. God, I wish you could tell me what you've learned. I wish I could go into your brain and mine it. You could help me."

Frank reached over and patted his shoulder, the usual way he expressed sympathy, his standard nonverbal reference to the cruel fate of his condition. What would he say, if he could? Eric thought about this, this mystery. Frank would quote a few lines of Saint Augustine, perhaps, someone who had asked himself such questions. Or Frank would speak for himself: *We don't know why we do cruel things to the people we're trying to love, only that, at the moment, some false logic has persuaded us that we should.* And then Eric would say, *I don't want to know about humanity; I want to know about myself.* Frank would cogitate on this a bit, defend the statement but admit it wasn't the whole answer, and then tell Eric that he had done his worst when tired, when afraid, and that if in the past he'd been able to say out loud, for Audrey, or for Eric, or for the world to hear, "I'm tired," or "I'm afraid," things would have gone a lot smoother. And then Frank would add the kicker: *Solitude of the mind is what destroys us. A human alone is the most ignorant and dangerous creature in creation.* Eric would try to understand exactly what this meant, and then it would come to him, the two parts of this wisdom connected in a single sentence, and he would say *I'm afraid of being alone.* Oh. So that's it. He'd say it to Gail. He'd say it to Tom. He'd write it to his wise friend Sheldon, who would respond with a single-word e-mail: "Bingo." Oh, how Eric wished he could have this conversation with his father, and then he realized he just had, and it was time to return the gift.

"Don't worry about Poppy," he said.

"My one unforgivable sin."

"The way you treated her? Leaving when she was so young? Withdrawing from her life?"

"It was all lost by then. I couldn't bear it. Had to get it over with."

"Yes. Afraid. And tomorrow, you'll start anew. You have nothing to fear from her."

"I was a monster."

"Not to Poppy. You were just Daddy. You're Daddy now. A bad one, maybe, but you're on the way to make it right. What you get from her is not the point. This is giving, not taking. She knows you're coming. She didn't refuse us. She and Ricki are planning a dinner."

"Thank you," Frank said. And then he made the connection that was always part of Eric's thinking and mulling on the topic of Poppy. "Tom?" he said.

"Yeh. You're right. He and Poppy are kind of similar people, anyway."

"Not a similar story. Only what we think is similar. Why are you worried about him?"

"I want things to be easier between us. I want him to be happy. I love him." What Tom was doing was the right thing for a person in his twenties to do, to "separate." There would indeed be time in life, later, to come back, if Tom wanted to. And really, he was still giving them a lot more than Eric had given his father at that age. Tom could make them both laugh, magnificent equipment for an only child keeping his parents at arm's length. But, God help him, Eric could see it the other way, too. An unloved shared apartment in a neighborhood that even Tom described as "chancy." His two friends always out, to judge from the fact that

Tom always seemed to answer the phone in the evenings, always seemed alone. No "someone" ever mentioned, just dates now and again.

"What says he isn't happy?"

"Nothing, I guess, really. It's just speculation."

"Then stop it."

Eric nodded. Perhaps easier to say than to do, but maybe not as hard to do as he thought. "It does plague one, caring so much and having so little control. Maybe the thought of a child's loneliness is even harder to bear than one's own," said Eric finally.

"If he's lonely." "Olney," Frank said, which Eric recognized would be his private code for this condition for the rest of his life.

"I suppose it's too easy for us to imagine anyone else is olney."

"Don't impose olneyness"—he seemed to use this malapropism deliberately, a sign of mastery so rare for him—"on anybody else. You don't know."

"No, you don't." Eric went back to his driving feeling better. He studied the road signs coming up, yelled over his shoulder for Adam to get out the atlas. Eric passed some time reviewing the plans, making sure they worked. They drop him at the airport, Alice arrives twenty minutes later. They find their way to the War-wick: easy. From the Warwick, they're a short walk to the Rice campus, and to Poppy and Ricki's live-oak-shaded bungalow in Montrose. But when they had made the right turn for Houston, he turned to his father one last time. "Dad?" he said.

"What?"

"Your speech. I've never heard you speak so clearly. Not since your stroke."

"Yes. I know."

They made it to the airport by one; Eric had hardly noticed that most of the time they were doing eighty. They pulled to the curbside at the departure area, and Eric unloaded quickly, said his good-byes, and sent them off into the haze. He was immediately dripping with sweat; he'd always thought that the Chesapeake Bay area was the muggiest place on earth, next to Calcutta, but that was before he visited Houston for the first time. The most air-conditioned city in the world, the Houstonians seemed to take pride in pointing out, an odd claim; no one called Nome or Moscow the most heated city.

He was back now in his world, if not, perhaps, his favorite part of it: the spacious airport halls, with their dense tiled floors and array of banners all proclaiming the joy of nonstops to places Eric could never imagine needing to go: Spokane, Washington; Green Bay, Wisconsin. He was back at work, on the airplane, spreading out his papers on his seat-back table. He'd seen nothing of the work on FruitOut. He'd asked Sharon to fax him some of it, but none had reached him. He'd go into this meeting blind, a test for his ability to adapt; even though he was no longer on the account, he would be at the presentation carefully stage-managing the clients' anticipation as Liv began to flip through the concepts and campaigns and storyboards sketched out on two-by-three pieces of foam-core. He'd always done that well, lowering the expectations by stressing that all of this was exploratory, a work in progress, allowing Liv to move somewhat quickly through the first idea or two, the ones that they all liked, the ones that really showed the creative side of the thing, but which no one thought there was a chance the client would buy. He'd call a small break after these, risking unease as the participants went to the bathroom or milled about the boardroom credenza for Coke and coffee, and then they'd spring the good stuff. Sometimes he felt like a fool, especially when the good stuff wasn't all that great, but that's how he made his living. That's how he kept body and soul together through the long nights, in hopes of a day or two of joy, like the ones that had just passed.

SEVEN

What is forgiveness? Is it choosing to ignore and overlook? Water under the dam? Is it a test, or an embrace?

Gail was waiting for him at the gate, and it felt as if he had been away for weeks. She was wearing a short red-flowered skirt, and she looked as tanned, healthy, and radiant as a girl appearing for cocktails on the deck after a day at the beach. Eric's clothes were rancid from his initial sweat bath in Houston, and his hair felt crusted by bad airplane air and grimy seat backs. She seemed not to notice, or not to mind, as she hugged him, so he hugged back hard: her body felt wonderful; she smelled like lilies.

They had parted four days ago with a kiss and a hug that implied their fights and disagreements were about the trivial stuff, that their hearts were pure; it had been in a spirit of denial, at that time. But that was four days ago, a long time ago. Now they seemed to him nothing more or less than a married couple with no more hurt than many, and with more intimacy, at times, than many with no hurt in their past. They would get home and after getting settled they would make love; she had said on the phone yesterday that she was missing him, and that was what they meant when they used that word to each other. Still, through all this, through the wait at the baggage carousel, she seemed tense.

"Is anything wrong?" he asked, finally.

"No. I'm glad to see you."

Things felt a little better when they got into the car, with her driving. She loved to drive, used to redline his delicate old Triumph TR3 in college, and she drove the same way now that she had a Taurus station wagon; she often scared him and Tom out of their wits.

"Liv called today," she said.

"Uh-huh," he answered. "It's about time someone in the shop remembered me."

"He wanted to come out and see you this afternoon."

That wasn't like him, but FruitOut was a big account, potentially the biggest one they'd ever had, and maybe Liv wanted to bring the boards along and map out the meeting.

"I told him no," she said.

"No? You're kidding."

"Whatever it was, I thought it could wait."

"I hope you said it nicely?" He could see Liv's eyes rolling now, hurt and angry. He'd always felt wary of Gail, easily wounded by her, as if she thought he was a shill. Whenever he mentioned her, he called her "your wife."

"I told him you were getting home late and you'd be tired and we needed to spend some time together. I'm glad we have this time."

"So am I," he said.

When they got home she left him to look through the mail while she got a couple more plants into the ground. He took his shower, long enough to exhaust the hot water, and toweled his body off carefully. He was proud of his body, lucky that it had stayed reasonably firm, though it was spotted here and there with new blemishes, which the doctor had pronounced unworrisome, part of growing older. "Just wait until you're eighty," the much younger man had said, as if it weren't going to happen to him. Eric took his penis into the harsh grip of terry cloth. Outside, through the small bathroom window, he could see Gail, keeping her plants and trowel at arm's length, away from her clean clothes, and when she bent over, the red skirt rose so high in back that there couldn't be any more of it left. His penis stirred, but he suddenly doubted there would be lovemaking in the golden late-afternoon sun. Suddenly he was afraid. He wouldn't call to her, an impish little invitation: "I'm wai-i-ting." He didn't have the courage. She'd know that it was what he wanted, and she would come to him because she promised, but she wouldn't want to. Sex seemed to be fueled by nothing but his own familiar male tug, a jolt of need from the gut. But. But he loved her, wanted to be in her glow, wanted to feel as if he were part of its source.

So, what? He dropped the towel and stared down the front of his nakedness. This body, these hands, this penis. What had Lilly really thought of these parts of him, his penis soft, limp as a kitten, or hard and impossible to ignore. Oh, that got a burst of blood flowing into the erectile tissue, Lilly naked on her bed, her breasts and small black patch of pubic hair. For a moment, Eric thought he'd keep this going and then masturbate, park it all in a washcloth and then rinse it down the drain. Then he'd be done for the night, and he wouldn't have to ask Gail, could forget about sex for the evening and concentrate on what worked better: her affection, her patience, the thirty-year history with his family and the guidance she gave him because of it, her love for their son. He knew he couldn't live without those things from her.

She called to him to get a drink and come join her in the backyard. He pulled on a pair of shorts and a T-shirt, stopped to make himself a gin and tonic, and came out the back door. She was standing, beholding her arrangement of mums, begonias, and marigolds, her hands caked with soil.

"I'll just go in and wash up," she said.

"Don't change." She glanced down at her linen shirt and skirt. "Why are you dressed up so nicely, anyway?" he asked.

"I had a vestry meeting. It lasted forever."

"You wore that skirt to a vestry meeting?"

She glanced down again, this time trying to step aside to see better what he meant. "Do you think it's too short?"

"No. I like it. You can get away with it."

She went off, still inspecting the fall of her hem. She came back with a glass of wine and sat beside him in the other green Adirondack chair. They rarely sat in these chairs, which held their places on the lawn through summer and winter, patient as old souls. Tom's old wooden swing set was still there, beside the garden, as if waiting for grandchildren, though neither of them could imagine wanting such a thing anytime in the near future. The peepers were out, and the breeze was blowing the highway sounds toward the other direction.

"Aren't you glad I told Liv not to come?"

"I'm glad he's not here."

"You know me. I was sweet."

"You were not. You were abrupt and chilly, and Liv's going to be making hurt little asides about it for months."

She was unrepentant and uninterested. There was a pause, a full one, which Eric finally noticed with unease.

"It seems like a long time that you've been on the road," she said.

"Yes. It does to me, too. Long in time and space."

"I've done a lot of thinking, while you've been gone."

"Oh?" In the failing light, her new flowers were losing their color.

"Well, it's time for me to tell you something."

In a marriage, that means only one thing. Everything stops in this moment; the blood in the body becomes still; the stomach locks down. Eric took a breath, and took in what she had begun to say. Yes, she had been having an affair. "Sleeping with someone," is how she put it. "Not many times, but a few times over the last year." Most recently—well, she said as much to herself as to him—"the other night when I said I was out with the girls."

He took a sip of his drink, and then drained it. *Who is it?* Eric wanted to ask, but did not. He imagined the scene, that beautiful body under a man, any man. The image tugged at him, like an invitation. *Was she telling him because it was over?* he wanted to ask, but did not. He didn't have the right. He recalled Lilly DeLong, under him, and then scenes from a soft-core movie he had watched the second night in his hotel room in Birmingham. Sex is what people do.

She was waiting, looking at him. Was it serious? He needed to ask, but the answer to that would be clear in due course. Who else knew about it, what friends in Summit? Who pursued whom, and was it a courtship, or an explosion? She took a sip from her wine and stared off into the pines. He could hear her swallow. Where did it happen, his place, a motel, or here, in their shared bed, when he was away on business, or entertaining clients deep into the night. Was it to get back at him for, for— Christ, he couldn't even remember the name of that last episode, the last one she knew about, the one he had admitted to in a very different scene, blubbering out his guilt and shame, begging for her to forgive him, to take him back, because it was over, over, over. When was the last time she and Eric had made love, how infrequent had it really become? Was this affair—is it—fun? An almost generous impulse on his side: Was it good for her? Did she have pleasure, more pleasure with this man than with him?

He looked over at her, a perplexity on her face now. "Do you want to ask me anything about it?" she asked.

He let his own silence, and the wind through these suburban trees, answer that last question. But where to go from here? He thought he might say that he knew she had made mistakes. "No. I guess not," he said finally.

"Well," she said, disbelieving, unprepared for this turn, thinking perhaps that all that was left was to go have the nice salad she had prepared for their dinner. But that would be ridiculous, and it would be the end of their marriage. "Then what do you think?" she asked.

"I'm not sure. I suppose you have the right to do anything you want."

"Eric, I've got to figure out what to do, and I need your help."

"I understand. Of course."

"Will you help me?"

"Later, I guess. Sure. You deserve support from me, if I can give it."

"Nothing's decided. I'm not holding back any decisions I've made or even want to make. No one's talking about leaving anyone. I promise you."

"Isn't that sort of what you were saying that night in the restaurant?"

"Maybe. But not really. Not leaving you for him or for anyone else. I was just trying to find out how to tell you this."

"Do you feel better now?"

"Yes. I guess. What do you feel?"

"I'm afraid of being alone."

She was now standing in front of him. He could just sit here if he wanted; he couldn't be faulted if he sat in silence in this chair deep into the night. Self-pity was always attractive, even when it required you to ignore your own manifest sins. But he would lose her for sure. He gave a small prayer to perhaps nothing more than his own unconscious will for guidance, and then, when the answer came, as perverse as it was, he followed it.

"Gail?" She turned quickly at the sound of this first response. "Let's make love."

Her hand went to her face, as if sampling the flesh he seemed to desire. "Really? Now? After what I told you?"

"We're still married. Yes. Really. I'd like to."

"Then let's. Why not?"

When he arrived at the office the next day, a little later than he planned, the team was gone. Liv, Lilly, Aaron the copywriter, and Steve Rabinowitz, their hottest new art director. That was it: in one taxi, with a trunk full of their precious boards, was the real talent in the shop, the future of the business. The place seemed lifeless without them. Even Marta, the tireless junior account executive, was acting withdrawn and sullen.

"When did they leave?" Eric fumed. "Christ. I haven't seen a goddamn thing."

"About half an hour ago. The presentation's at nine-thirty."

He'd thought it was at ten; that was the plan. He looked at his watch. Perfect. If he had luck getting a cab he could arrive at the meeting with about five minutes to spare, and he and Liv could take the boards into the bathroom, set them up on the urinals and Eric could figure out just what he was supposed to be saying for the next two hours.

"Why didn't someone tell me?" he shouted, enraged. He caught Sharon, the office manager, lurking in the background. "Goddamn it, Sharon, why wasn't I informed? This is the sort of fuckup you're supposed to prevent." That wasn't entirely true, but she was there.

"Liv said he was going to see you over the weekend," she answered, hardly concealing disdain.

He held up a finger and pointed at her; if she had been close enough, he would have poked her chest. "I'll tell you one thing. If we lose this account, you're out of here. Understand?"

Paul Ramirez had come in now; they were all in early, all of them gathered to send off the A-Team on their biggest mission.

Sharon appealed to Paul, and he told Eric he'd better get going. "Do you want me to flag you a cab?" he asked.

The meeting was at TT Associates, FruitOut's venture capitalists. Their office, mahogany and artwork screaming out their success with other people's ideas, was in midtown, on the top floor of a new high-rise. Eric made it at nine-thirty sharp, composing himself at the glass doors lest he snarl at the TT receptionist. "I'm just catching up to the FruitOut presentation," he said, trying for a casual tone. She showed him into the boardroom, and there was the team, making small talk with Rich Carlson, the FruitOut executive whom Eric had courted for months.

"Eric," said Liv, standing up. "I tried to tell you about the schedule change, but your wife—"

Eric waved this aside. He had to be a pro now, smooth and on top of the unexpected. All was in order, he was saying. He looked around at his colleagues. Liv, as always, was dressed in his jeans, blue shirt with white collar, no tie, a cashmere blazer. Eric didn't have to see under the table to know he was wearing tassel loafers with no socks; that was the way they had always done it, Eric the straight man in his suit with just a hint of Armani, and Liv, heedlessly cool and creative. Until about three years ago, Liv still insisted on smoking cigarettes during meetings, which he stopped when he realized they were losing clients because of it.

Lilly had her head down in her notes now, preparing a last few items. She was wearing a blue linen dress with a crewneck collar, short sleeves, and gold buttons; it was a little to the Villager end of the spectrum, but that was probably the right choice, and the two young artists, Aaron and Steve, were looking properly uncomfortable in their ill-fitting suits. There was a reassuringly thick packet of storyboards propped on the easel at the end, and a slide projector at the ready, pointing at a mahogany panel that would, no doubt, disappear at the push of a button. No tacking old bedsheets on the wall for this outfit.

"Have some coffee," said Rich Carlson, pointing to the credenza, with its obligatory basket of fruit, plate of croissants, pump pots, and cans of soft drinks. "I didn't pay for it."

Liv followed Eric over to the breakfast items and tried not to look as if he were whispering. "Hey. Sorry."

"You're damn right," said Eric, through his teeth.

"Look. We agreed I'd make the presentation. It made sense."

He was right about that, but there seemed to be more to it, something off.

"With you in Alabama," Liv felt compelled to add.

"Sure. Fine," said Eric, cutting it off because the others were entering the room.

How many times had Eric done this? The team all ready, appropriate piles of papers and writing instruments laid out in front of them on the gleaming table; Steve with his big pad and markers, as if he could fill in the work with the last flash of genius, on the spot. In the middle of the table was a line of eight bottles containing liquids in a range of fruity colors, with the labels pasted over, like statues awaiting the big moment. The team stood when the bosses approached, smiled confidently, and shook hands firmly in turn with the other two FruitOut principals, Mike Ivey and Gerry Russo, and with Trevor MacRae, whom Eric had never met, the young Scot from TT who was making all this possible. "Made it back from Alabama?" said MacRae, pleasantly, as if Eric had just returned from the Australian outback.

After the introductions, MacRae went over to the end chair in front of the easel and stood with his hands resting on the leather back. Eric took a seat beside Gerry Russo, the silent and seemingly least influential partner, with the real focus of the meeting lined up—Carlson, Liv, the kids—on the other side.

"The big moment," said MacRae. "I'm sure we're going to have some fun."

Eric hated it when clients said that; normally, he could picture each board, each slide, each piece of film when they had it, and would feel sure they were lousy. Let's see what the wild and crazy guys have come up with, people sometimes said. Let's see how you're going to make us a million bucks. But MacRae wasn't going to take that any further. He got right to business. "As you all know, we decided last week on a schedule to go national with the product."

Eric nodded, but he hadn't known that. Hadn't heard a peep of it. Liv gave him a nod, but it was an odd look, not a "We'll talk later" but a "Things have changed." Eric wanted to grill him on the spot. He could hear his first words when they finally busted out into the safety of the building lobby, after remaining mute all the way down the elevator, as if it were bugged. *What the fuck, Liv?*

Eric wasn't listening to the rest of what MacRae was saying, mostly because he'd heard it all before: tight schedules, spot markets, intricate rollout: didn't matter if it was computer software or baked products. If it was true, and sometimes it wasn't, it meant the big break was really happening, but Eric wasn't in any place to celebrate.

"I know," continued MacRae, "that Liv and Rich have been working closely this week, and that Rich has reviewed what we're about to see."

Eric didn't know that either, and didn't like it. They always tried to give someone from the client a sneak preview, just to make sure they had not made a real howler mistake, but rarely someone so senior, and never a loose cannon like Rich Carlson.

MacRae finished his remarks, turned the meeting over, and sat in the next seat down the line from Eric. His presence restored a little of the balance of the seating arrangement, but Eric suddenly felt trapped on the wrong side of the table, pinned between the clients; he'd have to sit on his butt for the rest of the presentation.

Liv and Carlson stood up, each offering the other an "After you." Eric should have been part of that pantomime, not Carlson. Those two were acting as if turning over the first board was like opening King Tut's tomb, the first sunlight to fall on these fabulous treasures in three thousand years. They looked like a circus act, with Carlson in his plaid third-rate marketeer's suit, and Liv was descending to his level; Eric knew the value of rapport with a client, even a sleazeball, but this was disgusting. Something was very wrong here. Eric glanced over at Lilly, but she and the two men were staring forward at the act. Liv wanted to come out here, Gail had said; in twenty years he had been to their house in Summit exactly twice.

Carlson finally turned to his little spiel, reviewing the marketing plan, listing the many aspects of the product and its "lifestyle-intensive appeal," its ace in the hole as "natural," just what this new generation was after. *Yeh yeh yeh,* thought Eric. *Natural as the spring rain. This guy Carlson, he's so natural he pisses pineapple juice.*

And then there was Liv. The old creative presentation shtick.

Flip over the boards, stand back as if he, like everyone else, was appraising them with the skeptical and thoughtful eye of people with money on the table, the occasional invitation to Lilly, or the creative guys, to interject a detail, or to pump in some enthusiasm. Liv was using all those terms like "market appeal" and "perception management" and "ego activation," all this fake marketing psychobabble that they both mouthed at times like this without a clue whether it actually meant anything.

Eric said nothing, even when Mike Ivey—the one person in the room whom he actually trusted at this particular moment—made an effort to look down their side of the table and solicit his opinion about a rather off-color third-string concept. "It's aggressive," said Eric, but he was in the midst of crisis here: his horror at what his old partner was saying, his sudden absolute disdain for the way he made his living, his hatred for Rich Carlson. He believed in advertising as a good and useful profession; he'd taken care over the years to avoid what was unethical, or merely distasteful. It would take years for him to recover from this, from this epiphany of loathing. He tried to think about Gail, about their wonderful sex last night, his hopes that she would drop the affair, anything to drown out this terrible stuff, his father and sisters waiting for him in Houston, but it was as if all these people he loved were down at the end of a very long tunnel, echoing specks in a small circle of light. For the first time in his life, Eric believed he knew what it felt like to go mad.

During the break he talked with Gerry Russo about golf courses; Eric had never swung a club in his life, but from hearing Alice's husband, Alden, talk all these years, he could share stories about the third hole at Pebble Beach like a pro. He felt Lilly trying to amble over from the snacks for a word, but he didn't want to talk to her. There was something going on in this room, and it wasn't just the thundering pressure of his skull about to blow up. He was seeing looks and glances, people talking about him; if this kept up they'd have to walk him out in a straitjacket.

They reconvened. Liv flipped over their número uno, the firm's champion: "Get the FruitOut!" In one version, the exclamation point was an apple and a banana, which Liv allowed was just them "funning around." "Those creative types," he said, waving his hand toward the kids at the end. They'd done their work on this one, headline emblazoned over young exercisers so perfect and brimming with health and so inhuman that it seemed you could order both them and their treadmills straight from the Home Shopping Network. Liv was doing this well, building the campaign for them, all of it springing forth from those three words and one immutable punctuation mark. As he spoke, Steve unveiled the bottle labels one by one, a sideshow orchestrated as a tantalizing extra. When the presentation was done, Liv sat down.

Mike Ivey was the first to speak, a demur. "But doesn't the headline suggest that they shouldn't eat fruit, or something like that?"

Lilly was ready for that, as well she should have been. It was, she said, "the contrariness" that gave it legs. "As a headline," she said, "it gives us the chance to play with a very rich palette of responses. On the one hand, it's a joke. On the other, it's the simplest ad copy that's ever been written: 'Buy our product.' I like this one the best," she concluded.

"Yeh," said Carlson. "Besides, this is just preliminary. They'll iron it out as soon as we get them set up in their new shop."

And there it was. Eric felt this bombshell as little more than an aftershock. Four pairs of eyes from across the table met his, all involuntarily.

"Yes," said MacRae, British sensibilities sharp enough to realize he had to give the nail the final whack, "we think when the team really gets to focus solely on FruitOut in their new shop, we may well see some new thinking. But I agree with Lilly. I think this works."

Again, Mike Ivey leaned forward to speak to Eric. "You knew about this, didn't you?" It wasn't really a question; he was seeking reassurance that he hadn't just seen a public execution. None of the eyes from across the table were on him now: he was a dead man.

"Yes," said Eric. "Of course." Gratitude from Liv; a shot of triumph for Carlson.

"We didn't want to leave too much of a hole in your agency," continued Ivey.

"Not a problem. We're deep enough to take it," Eric said. He took a second to reflect: Sharon, Marta, Pat? Not a lot of fun maybe, but good enough to lead the rank beginners; they knew how to work. Randy Steele, the best traffic manager in New York, a miracle they still had him. Paul Ramirez? Even if Paul still hated him, he trusted Paul, everyone did. Paul was the key. Maybe he always had been now that, in this unique circumstance, with everyone in the room looking at him, he thought about it. "This happens in our industry," he resumed finally. "Clients get a look at talent like this"—he pointed to them, not resisting a mildly ironic tone on the word "talent"—"and they all try to hire them away. Sometimes it's for the best."

Eric still had a reserve of passion left to feel a final jolt of hatred for MacRae, who snapped his folder shut and stood up. That was it; a fine meeting, a good morning's work. Time to head back to the phone in search of new capital-starved, neglected geniuses dreaming up the next Microsoft. The small talk was brief, the boys gathered up the boards into their portfolio cases, no hanging around in the reception area while people went to the bathroom, a frigid ride down the elevator, and at last, the release onto the street. They all stopped just outside the revolving door.

Eric looked at them all and Liv suggested the other three go on ahead. The two men started to walk away briskly, tugging along their portfolio cases, but Lilly lagged behind until she turned, perhaps in apology, perhaps in defiance, and then rejoined her team.

Good-bye, thought Eric.

"Thank you, Liv. Thank you for that, old buddy."

"You want to go have a drink?"

"No."

"I tried to tell you. But your wife just blew me off. I'll tell you, I'll be glad if that's the last time I have to take that shit from her. I was pissed enough to think you deserved what was coming."

"She didn't blow you off. It's just the voice in your own head speaking. It's what you hear the world saying. It's why you did this."

"I did it because I had to—"

Eric interrupted. "I could have squashed that deal for you, you know. I don't know who the power is, Ivey or Russo, but it ain't your friend Rich Carlson. I could have put the brakes on your whole deal."

"I know. That was big. I owe you."

"So why did you do it?"

"Carlson said he couldn't connect with you. He said there was no chemistry."

"His chemistry is all foul smells. Shows a rare bit of perception on his part."

"This didn't just start last week, Tonto. He has been complaining about you from the beginning. He says you're cold and arrogant. He said if he had to work with you he'd take the account to WilliamsFriedman."

"So you were the one that got the account?"

"You're right. Me and your girlfriend Lilly, and the kids. We all busted our butts to get this, and you were off in your family haze. When was the last time you really gave everything to the shop? Fuckin' A." Two passing women in business suits heard this, and both looked up.

"Happens all the time, ladies," Eric said to them. "Someone cutting off a partner's legs." They diverted their eyes and kept going.

"You lack the common touch," said Liv. "All that Southern gentility. Carlson's got a job to do."

"Yes. You and he showed the common touch up there with those last boards: 'Ready to show them where the sun don't shine, Rich?' "

"Jesus. Did I say that?" Liv reached for a cigarette.

"It's a cliché, but I never would have dreamed."

"This is big, Eric. And not without a hell of a lot of risk. It just seemed like the time was right for me to make a go, you know what I mean? This sounds like melodrama, but you don't have alimony to pay. You don't have to keep your daughter in a halfway house. There's plenty left in the shop for you and it's more dependable stuff. Give you plenty of time to head off to Alabama."

"Texas."

"It's Texas now?"

What does a man say to his business partner, one of his best friends, after that friend has shot him in the back? They stood face-to-face, holding their briefcases while the early lunch crowd, secretaries in their running shoes, young execs in their shirtsleeves, swarmed around them.

"So what now?" asked Eric.

"We need to stay in the office until we get set up. Maybe just a couple of weeks."

"Sure, but with one condition. You have to take Sharon with you."

"You hired her. Just fire her, for Christ's sake."

"Maybe."

"When are you heading back to Texas?"

"Today. This afternoon. I came in just for this. After—"

"After what?"

"Well, I've got to go rally the troops, right? They all know what's up, I assume."

Liv nodded.

"Which means I've got about twenty people who now depend on me alone. They deserve to hear something from me, or have I missed something? And by the way. You try to take Randy Steele with you and I'll sue your ass."

Liv nodded again, this time through a cloud of cigarette smoke. "We'll stay out of the way for a few hours," he said. Yes, the three coconspirators had stopped at the other end of the plaza, wondering whether they might see a fistfight. Later Eric might wish he had taken a swing at Liv, but violence wasn't on his mind now. Maybe he didn't care enough; maybe he didn't have the energy to "go national," to move back into the big time of advertising. He didn't want to do it. Liv knew that perhaps, may have sensed that. Liv was now appealing to him with the hooded eyes of a whipped dog. Eric put down his briefcase and gave him a hug. "Asshole," he said into Liv's ear.

He took a cab back to the office. The receptionist—a very young Barnard girl whose name Eric had momentarily forgotten—took one look at him and then darted down the corridor behind her desk: a lookout, or a messenger to the rest. No one was working. He went straight to Paul's office and closed the door. "You've heard, of course."

Paul turned slowly in his desk chair; his broad Latin face was blank. On his desk were some sketches for the latest public service campaign for water conservation. At a glance, Eric could tell they were okay, but not very interesting. Never the best designer, but at firm conferences, who invariably had the most solid suggestions?

Who reeled the kids in just enough to make the work fly? Whose office seemed forever to have some slightly downcast colleague in it asking for advice? And who, after all, exerted moral force around here? This all came to Eric in a flash. And to top it all off, Paul was far too sharp to answer a loaded question like the one Eric had just asked.

"Heard what?"

"Liv and the others and FruitOut. They're going. The question is"—and here, Eric dug deep back to those days listening to his father on the telephone, and asked the question that seemed to be the close for every one of those conversations, as inevitable as the good-bye that would follow it—"are you with me?"

"In what way?"

"I mean, will you help me put this back together? I need you. I can't do it without you. You're the key."

"What's the offer, Eric?"

Again, the right response. "I haven't had time to think about that. You tell me what you need. Junior partner. Something. We'll figure out what that means when I get back from Texas." In answer to another blank look, Eric admitted that yes, in the middle of all this, he had to head out this afternoon for more family business. "And Paul, there's something else we have to clear the air about a little, sometime."

Paul made no reference, at least not a direct reference, to this last acknowledgment of things done. "Well," he said, "family is important." And at last he smiled. He was cagey, but not inhuman.

Before Eric assembled his dispirited gang he found a crisp letter of resignation on his desk, from Sharon, enumerating certain incidents of coarse language and abusive behavior to women, an opening salvo for some sort of suit, no doubt. Eric didn't care; he was so relieved to discover that she had already cleaned out her desk that he decided it was worth the hassle; he'd already decided that the next thing, after cementing Paul's loyalty, he had to do in rebuilding the firm was get rid of her. By God, this coalition building, this cloakroom stuff, could be fun after all.

Paul had gathered the firm in the conference room, and when Eric walked in he saw those faces, worried, skeptical, angry at these people, Eric included, who were fucking with their lives.

Some of the older ones had been in such places before, whole firms evaporating in an hour. Pat was knitting, something she did compulsively when nervous. Liv called her Madame LaFarge. "Not knitting a shroud for the firm, are you, Pat?" Eric said. A few laughs; the copywriters knew their Dickens; something to work with.

He went over to the place that had been left for him, and made a show of inspecting the seat. "No whoopee cushions, I see," he said.

"That's for later," said Jesse, the ambitious one. He knew what all this meant for him: with Aaron out of the way, he was top dog on the copy side. There were more laughs. None of this was that funny, but it helped.

Eric sat down. He looked around the room once more, and said, because he felt it in his heart, "This fellowship we have, even in times that might seem a little bleak, is why we do this. Human beings aren't meant to be alone." He continued with this, and without having planned any of it, he told them about his first year in this business, taking the job as a temporary matter while applying to graduate school, and then, when the choice was upon him, when it was time to leave that old firm, he couldn't do it. He had fallen in love with this collaborative enterprise, with the irreverence, with the fellowship. "We see the inside of a lot of industries, a lot of firms. We see how all sorts of offices run, and there isn't one of us who doesn't walk out of some suite in midtown, get into the elevator and cross that lobby with all that marble and faux luxury, get out on the street, and say to himself or herself, 'Jesus, I'm glad I work where I work.' Right?"

"Amen, brother."

"So, I'll tell you, nothing has changed in any of that. We like each other. We respect each other."

"Well, Eric," said Randy, to Eric's great relief, "as we've all been saying, Get the Fruits out."

"Okay. They're gone, and we wish them well. And now we've got work to do. As the philosopher Wittgenstein said"—this would have never flown in a 4-H park, maybe not here, but the tone was right, the rhythm of the reference was right—"old philosophers run out of problems. Things get stale when you lose the comfort of problems to solve. Well, we're young. At least, you are,

and our new firm is, and we've got the comfort of a few chal-
lenges." He went on to enumerate every job, every client in the office at this moment, singling out people for questions: Where are
we at with them? Have they paid us yet? It took a while, and in the
end, it was a reassuring list: nothing national, but decent clients, a
good backlog of work, a going business.

"So that's where we're at, and in my experience, we're in good
shape. I can sleep well, which I wouldn't be doing if I were one of
the Fruits. Two more things. First, I have to go out of town again.
A week, probably. I have the comfort of family problems, good
problems, problems I hope all of you will have when you're my
age, and your parents and siblings are getting on, and your marriages have faced the normal stresses and strains, and it seems time
to get a few things straight before it's too late."

A few faces fell at this; no one would have thought it ideal, certainly not Eric. But problems were problems.

"And the other thing is this. I have asked Paul to become junior
partner, president, office manager, executive something—well,
we're not sure what he is for the moment, but he has accepted.
From now on, he's the boss. And to celebrate this"—he had to
shout over the sustained round of applause—"I want every person
in the shop to take a two-hour lunch. Paul will pick it up on his
corporate card. If the phone rings, they'll just have to press one for
more options."

He made it to La Guardia by two, passed his time for the most
part pacing up and down the concourse, staring occasionally out
the window at the people and airplanes moving back and forth in
the watery clouds of heat. It was good at this point, he figured, to
be virtually brain dead, rather than reflect on the events of the past
twenty-four hours, but images still popped into his head, images
from the bright side, lovemaking, office fellowship, a business that
seemed healthy, a popular choice for a promotion. Each of these
had corresponding shadows—he knew they were there, all right,
but they weren't the ones offering themselves to him.

When he landed in Houston he took a cab straight to the Warwick, found his room waiting for him, cool and clean. The message light was blinking and he sat on the bed as he dialed his
"personal voice mail." Three calls, none from Gail: Poppy, rather
cheery, telling him they were all there and to come over for supper

as soon as he could. *It's like a family wedding,* thought Eric; *a rehearsal dinner.* A call from Alice asking him, if he could, to get into Dad's room and bring a sweater, because Poppy kept her house like a deep freeze. And a call from Lilly. "It's Lilly. I'll call back."

He was not going to join the family scene; he was too tired and had too much baggage to drag around tonight. Alice would have improvised by now. His father would survive Poppy's AC. He called Gail, and she answered, and he told her what had happened, and they began to think it was funny, in places, and at the end of the call he told her he loved her and wanted to keep trying to win her back.

He ordered a club sandwich and two Heinekens from room service, and was watching TV when the phone rang.

"It's Lilly." She stumbled through an explanation of sorts: torn emotions, rival responsibilities, how—well, to tell the truth, how angry she was at him after that night. That comment about being drunk. "Well. It made me feel cheap."

Eric was past apologizing for any of that; in fact, all this apologizing was starting to get him down when, really, what he wanted to do now was go forward.

"That's fine, Lilly," he said, almost certain that he would now be criticized by someone, somewhere, for dismissing her. "It really is."

"I . . ."

"What happened is not bad for me. You know that. Liv knows that. I'm almost—maybe not quite, but almost—grateful. Not that I enjoyed the way it was done."

"I just wanted to say good-bye."

"Me too. We're even, as you said to me six weeks ago. Now I know what you meant. But really, you earned this chance. And," he said, not caring if she understood, "so did I."

EIGHT

How many years had it been since he awakened so late and feeling so clean? How many years had he wasted?

At last Eric dragged himself from the comfort of this bed, and by the time he had dressed, he had to hurry to get to the restaurant to meet Poppy and Alice for lunch. The doormen had offered to get him a cab, even after he explained he was only going a few blocks down Montrose. The offer had struck him as an emblem of sedentary America, but now he knew why they'd regarded him with such puzzled looks; by the time he got to the small bistro, he was dripping with sweat.

Eric was mopping his brow for the fifth time when Alice came in. She looked fine in this stylish, wealthy crowd; she had dressed up—no longer the farm look—but, more important, she was radiant, which anyone would have noticed: she had so much to organize, was so essential to the proceedings. Everything was clear to her; what baffled her was that others did not see this. Eric wondered, not for the first time, what life would have been like if their parents hadn't divorced, and whether Alice and their mother would have waged a lifelong battle for the role of Mother Hen in the family. She took one look at his soaked polo shirt and craned her neck over to accept the least possible touch from him, a kiss on her cheek.

"You look fabulous," he said.

She pretended to be shocked, as if Eric never said nice things to her. "Why, thank you, Eric."

"I mean it. You look happy. Is Dad being nice to you?"

"He is, actually. He gave me a nice hug when I got here. I know it wasn't your idea. I know you didn't think of it."

"You know I don't do 'thoughtful.' But still, I love you."

She looked at him suspiciously. "Things go well in New York?"

"Maybe. My partner staged a coup in public. Is that good?"

"Oh dear."

"I had some adjustments to make before I left, but it's not something to worry about. I feel strangely great. I'm not looking too deeply at it just now. So how's things with you?"

"We're all here," she said happily.

"Sorry I couldn't make it last night. Maybe it was better to leave you all to it. And I was beat. But tell me about it."

Dad was good, she said. "Happy. Content. His job is getting done, I guess. And Poppy and Ricki had really done a wonderful thing for him. A lovely dinner."

"Adam said Dad wasn't having much luck with the words," said Eric. On the way out the hotel door he'd run into Adam, who said Frank had not been able to get a single word out all evening.

Alice allowed herself to look annoyed. "Adam is wrong. Dad wasn't trying to talk. He probably tried to say about six words. He was happy just to be in Poppy's house. He's got his objectives for this trip, and some of them may seem rather small to us."

"Like driving two thousand miles just to sit in her living room?"

"Right," said Alice.

"Saying good-bye," added Eric. "And how did Poppy take it?"

"You tell me. But I'll tell you one thing: Whatever Dad had in mind to say to her, I think it got said just by being here. I think even Poppy got the point."

Eric looked through the window and saw Poppy coming down the street, looking purposeful, her mouth tight. He could have spotted her a block earlier. Now and again Eric would see women with hair like hers, thick, curled in at the ends, black streaking into gray, and he'd think, *There's Poppy.* He'd think, *If I were a woman, that's how I'd wear my hair.* She had the sharpest, thinnest face of the three of them, most like their father's, and she had his thin lips, delicate and precise when she spoke, as if she were speaking French. She appeared to have walked over from the Rice campus, where she worked in the library, but seemed fresh and starched in her white shirt. She wore khaki pants—not something from the Gap, but tailored, with a nice high waist—with a silver-buckled cowboy belt, and she wore a big leather satchel, like someone who carries every single thing she needs everywhere she goes.

Before she sat, she kissed Eric, she touched cheeks with Alice, and it was odd to see them show sisterly intimacy, as unalike as they were. But that was siblings, a series of coincidences that endure for life, in some cases endure out of spite, traditional gatherings observed largely as forums for anger and resentment. But that was not the Alwin form of survival. Their family had celebrated no traditional gatherings; theirs was a family that created plenty of history, but little tradition, which was probably just as well, and in its place was simply a far-flung constancy. And here they were now, miraculously in Houston, Texas, the three of them, a good bit older than they had ever expected to be, but brother and sisters still, through the travails of childhood, through their lives, still joined. As they settled into their seats, flapped out the napkins in preparation for a meal, glanced at the menu through three pairs of reading glasses—first time he'd seen them on Poppy, happens to us all—Eric felt proud of them, survivors of the little indignities and bigger disappointments of mortality.

Poppy had caught up with Alice the night before. She turned right to Eric. "So how are you? How's Gail?"

"She's fine. She sends her love."

"Oh, cut the bullshit, Eric."

"Poppy!"

Poppy didn't respond to Alice's complaint, but kept her eyes on Eric. She had a right to do this. During a phone call a few years ago, he had blubbered out a particularly detailed confession of his affairs. He believed he was delivering a bombshell of sorts, a personal revelation of the kind contained in the letters and diaries of famous people under Poppy's care at the library, and he didn't notice until it was all over that Poppy knew about these women already—not by name, but by type: the woman on the plane; the slightly older marketing consultant sharing an account on the West Coast; the ice-cold Generation Xer, a one-night episode with all the spontaneousness of a tax audit. Poppy knew he was capable of being a not-nice guy. It was an involuntary cry of remorse during an unusually low moment but still, he had done it. One can't subject a sister—possibly a brother, thought Eric, though he had no experience to go on—to such an event and then pretend it never happened. But still, what he said was not bullshit. Gail was fine. She did send her love.

"How's Ricki? I'm looking forward to seeing her."

"She's fine. She sends her love."

"What does that mean?"

"The same thing it means when you say it."

"In other words, you're not sure."

"Yup."

After lunch, Eric paid the check. "Maybe we're all going to end up back in Maryland," he said to Alice as they were filing out. "Poppy and me in Dad's house, and you bringing over meals-on-wheels. Alden will outlive us all. He has absolutely the best equipment I know for withstanding the stresses of the modern age. I mean that as a compliment."

They walked out of the restaurant into the heat, a little less stifling now, with a faint breeze that might have blown in from the Gulf Coast. A few blocks ahead of them they could see the exuberant fountains of the traffic circle outside the Warwick, and behind it, the verdant stretch of Hermann Park. They walked past the hotel, where Frank was spending the day marshaling his strength. Alice had planned the evening ahead, her night, dinner in a private room at a country club somewhere in the posh environs of River Oaks, an invitation wangled through one of Alden's golfing buddies. It was going to be smoothly done: car and driver already ordered, menu chosen, all pesky details anticipated.

"Were you surprised that Dad came?" Eric asked Poppy. They'd made it to the park by now, were strolling comfortably down past a reflecting pool. Three small children—siblings, though closer in age than Eric and his sisters—were chasing ducks at the edge of the water.

"Of course I was," said Poppy. "I know it wasn't easy."

"He loves you the most," said Alice, a slight hurt in her voice.

"He ignored me for the first twenty-five years of my life; now he won't let go," Poppy answered, with a finality that made it clear she'd given all that she really wanted to give on this subject. They walked for a few minutes in silence.

"So what's the deal?" said Eric at last. They had stopped in front of the entrance to the zoo, and through the gate could see a few extremely hot-looking monkeys panting in the corner of their cage. "About you and Dad."

"You think it's all that hard to figure out?"

"No. But why do I think there's a missing piece that Alice and I don't know about?"

Poppy took a few steps back, out of the middle, as if heading for home. "A missing piece? A missing piece from what? I saw him *once* between the time I was ten and my freshman year in college," she said. "That was when he and Marjorie were getting married and she was playing the stepmother. I'm sure inviting me to visit them was her idea, but you know what, I still cared then. I still wrote to him, for Christ's sake. What the hell was I thinking? You can't imagine what little fantasies I had, getting on the plane that time. Girls love their fathers, even when they're shits. It makes me cry to think of a child hurt like that. He probably said three words to me that whole weekend. He picked me up at the airport and you know what he did? He stopped in Annapolis and let me sit on those goddamn statehouse steps for an hour while he went to vote, or to fuck Myra Podesta in the broom closet. I hadn't seen him in four years. I didn't see him again until Mom forced me to pay a call the spring of my senior year. That was when—" She stopped herself abruptly.

They waited for her to continue. "When what?" asked Eric.

She reddened: she blushed easily, an ironic flaw for someone who played her cards so close to her chest. "Well, things changed, right?"

Things had changed: that was sure. Eric did the math on the year that would have been, the situation at the time. He could see

Alice was doing the same calculation. Poppy's senior year: spring of 1983. Wasn't it the fall of 1983 when the rumors started, when everything had started to tumble down? The news stories, the expulsion.

"What?" Alice asked. "What had changed?"

"I don't know, Alice. Wasn't that when he was getting kicked out, or something?"

"No. That wasn't what you were saying. You'd graduated before that all started anyway. What did you mean, 'That was when'?"

There was a bench in the shade a few paces away. Poppy went over to it and sat down, and she reached into her satchel for a hairbrush, and began to assault her scalp. It was what she did when upset. Eric and Alice went over to sit at either side of her.

"By then," Poppy said, "it was even. Maybe even more than even."

"Even with Dad?" asked Eric.

She nodded. "What had changed was I had written a letter. I don't know why, but I wrote a letter. I had just come out, and I was going through that all-men-are-pricks stage. And our father was a first-class prick. My girlfriend said to do it. So I wrote a letter."

"To him?" Eric asked. What could she possibly have said to Frank, then or now, that would cause her so much drama?

"No. I wrote the attorney general's office."

"My God," Alice said. "You're the one who blew the whistle on him, Myra Podesta."

Poppy was crying now. "I didn't think anything would come of it. I just thought it would get him into trouble, make him squirm. I thought he deserved it."

Alice had stiffened into a board.

"I was just a kid. When it all blew up, I thought I was going to die. I thought I was going to be arrested. I couldn't tell anybody."

"How did you know about Dad and Myra Podesta?" asked Alice.

"I heard some things during that time I was in Maryland, and I didn't know if any of it was true. I just wanted him to be investigated. Because of what he had done to us, to Mom. I didn't want to hurt Marjorie. I didn't want any of what happened."

The three of them sat wordless on the bench as families headed toward the various happy destinations in the park, the zoo, the kiddie railroad.

"Alice?" said Poppy. "Eric? I'm sorry."

Alice turned to Poppy, gave her a little punch on the thigh, an odd gesture. Finally, she said, "Neither of you can imagine what it was like, day after day, reading the newspaper. After a while, Alden wouldn't let me see it. I'd go over and sit with Marjorie and we'd talk about our gardens, for hours, as if the whole world weren't falling apart. Neither of you had to live through that. You were gone; Eric had checked out."

Eric knew all this, but the truth was, he'd never really heard Alice describe it, describe the hundreds of ways that one can be beleaguered in such a situation. The whole thing, Myra Podesta on the payroll, had been going on for years before it blew up. No one knew why, not even Mike Billings, but at least they now knew who.

"So?" asked Poppy. "Alice."

"There may have been no other way for it to end. If you hadn't done it, he just would have kept spinning out of control."

Poppy blew her nose. "Thank you, Alice. That's nice of you. I don't think I deserve it."

"You do," said Eric, taking her hand.

"But here's one thing you are going to have to face," said Alice. "I bet he knew it was you. I bet he knew all along. That was the thing about your letter, there was something in it that suggested it was someone very close to us. That was what the attorney general said. Dad isn't stupid. He would have known it wasn't me, or even Eric. Or Mother."

"Should I say something to him? Do you think I have to?"

"No," said Eric. "Don't even think about it. You've told us. It's over. I love you. Now we all move on."

"Do you think he knows it was me?"

Eric tried not to be too visibly pondering that question. He found it difficult to imagine that his father would not figure out something like that: that was how he had stayed in power all those years. But the person he often dispatched to collect dirt and pry out indiscretions was Mike Billings, and Mike Billings didn't know. "No," said Eric at last. "He doesn't know. He'd lost heart for the whole career by then. Besides, if he was compiling a list of suspects, it would be a mile long. Let it go, Poppy. Let it go for both of you now."

When Eric got back to his room, he sat for a few moments and let it all sink in, the stunning unpredictability of life, of human beings, of the people he loved. He said these words to himself, out loud—"the stunning unpredictability of life"—and waited for further words, but none came. A twist had just occurred in his life, an answer provided to a question he'd never even thought to ask. What other questions, he wondered, had he never thought to ask? About his father, about himself? About his firm? About Gail? He'd asked himself a thousand times whether Gail might fall in love with someone else, might have an affair, might leave him. What other questions about his marriage could really matter?

He reached for the phone and called her. She was pleased. She said, "How are you, you know, about things?"

He said he didn't care about things, he just wanted her back. He reminded her of that dinner at the Thai, or was it Korean, place in the mall in Summit, now so far in the past, when she asked him to tell her what she could do to make him happy, to give him pleasure, and he said that he had decided on the first thing on the list, and it was not a small thing. "Just decide if I have a chance with you."

"Of course you do. Eric. My God. Yes."

"Well, maybe I'm stupid, but will you just think about that for a day or two. Really consider whether you think we have a real chance?"

After they rang off he spent the rest of the afternoon on the telephone to his office, a long talk with Paul, a strategy session, a plan to rebuild the firm, checking in with clients, getting new lines out. This felt good, this being in business, and he liked being in charge. He liked making suggestions and knowing that they were received as directions. What a relief it was to be collaborating with someone younger and less self-absorbed than Liv.

And then, because he was, after all, still in Houston, he went to visit his father in his room, and told him that whatever he might think about Alice's upcoming dinner in the country club, he had to give it his best. A hundred percent. The lecture wasn't necessary. Hanging over the door of the closet was Frank's cream-colored linen suit, elegant if slightly dated in cut, carefully pressed, a red tie slung over the hanger.

"You're going to wear that?" said Eric, delighted.

"A hundred percent."

And it was a hundred percent, from the moment Frank appeared in this getup, complete with his silver-tipped cane, at the top of the steps leading down to the stretch limousine that had come for them even though Alice had specifically asked for something more subtle. "I just wanted a car that would be easy to get in and out of."

"Oh, Alice, it's fine," said Eric. "In Houston they think these cars are swell."

They pulled up to the country club, down a long lane shaded with live oaks past various fairways and greens, and were shown to their private room, down hallways as cool as a cellar, the rugs and drapes rich in the colors of Central America. Theirs was the Sam Houston Room—next door to the Mirabeau Lamar Room—a snapshot of the days of the Republic, with the heavy, hand-hewn furniture, the booty of Indian artifacts and Mexican religious treasures, that one would expect in the private quarters of the elder statesman. Only the lighting fixtures gave the place away: crystal chandeliers, French sconces. Eric had always believed that shoes and lighting fixtures were the two foolproof ways of spotting a fake. But no one was in a mood to quibble. Not Poppy, who looked gorgeous and happy to be with Ricki, and not Alice or Eric, and not Adam, who had dressed in a red Hawaiian shirt that seemed to match Frank's tie, and not, finally, Frank, who—it seemed at the time, anyway—had gotten everything he could ever want, and could die tomorrow a saved man. The courses came and went.

Eric looked across the table at Frank and Poppy, turned in toward each other. What he saw struck him as nearly miraculous; words seemed to be pouring out of them both, the two wordless members of the family. It was a big enough table that he couldn't hear anything, with Alice and Adam deep into a spirited gossip session about the folks back home, and with himself and Ricki loosed by the wines, the place, the freedom from care. But Eric could see the words, the color of them, blues and greens, the hues of renewal and growth. He could see Poppy's occasional embarrassed averting of the eyes, what she might do when she was about to clam up or bolt, but Frank had his hand over hers, and again she would turn back to him. How Eric loved her; how desperately, in this moment, he wanted her back, and Frank was trying to make it happen. He was doing it; not changing everything, not making anything better, perhaps, but merely saying the unsaid, which was perhaps a higher deed when the subject spans decades.

Adam let out a monstrous guffaw and a high-pitched "Well, Miss Alice, I do declare!"

"Are we being too loud?" Eric asked Ricki, who was a lawyer and a person of extreme tact.

"They can handle it. It's why this place exists."

"We're not going to alienate any prospective clients?"

She gave him a puzzled and not very pleased look. "These are the people my clients sue," she said finally.

Yes, Eric should well have guessed that; he was clearly acting like a fool.

"I don't mean to be a wet blanket," said Ricki, noticing the pause. "This is good for all of you." She nodded over at Poppy and Frank. He was still holding her hand.

"Are you and Poppy all right?" he blurted out.

Ricki was one of those people who never begin speaking until they have composed a complete answer; the pauses used to unnerve Eric before he realized that this was just the way she was. The difference with Ricki was that she was composing the truth, and not an indirection; Poppy, on the other hand, spoke instantly and passionately, and almost never from the heart.

"We've given up trying to change each other," she answered. "It's the final stage of falling in love."

"Or falling out of love."

"Right," she answered.

"Do you think it can be done? To still fall in love after all these years together?"

"What's the alternative?"

At the end, Frank had a long line of raspberry ice down the once immaculate lapel of his suit, which Poppy had tried to mop away with cold water. The suit might be ruined, but that was no matter: he would probably never wear it again, anyway. When they filed back to the limousine, Eric gave the driver an opened but almost untouched bottle of wine and a fifty-dollar tip—Alice would give him a fiver, and worry that she had been extravagant and tasteless. They rode quietly as the car retraced its route, though Eric was now sitting sideways on the banquette, and the motion was making him carsick. After they arrived at the hotel, he staggered across the lobby behind Adam and Alice, each with one of Frank's arms, and when Eric finally made it to the blissful cool and silence of his room, there was peace in his world and he dropped gratefully onto his bed, regretting that he had drunk so much.

He heard a knocking at his door. He debated ignoring it, pretending the next morning that he had been in the bar, or had fallen instantly asleep, but the knocking came more insistently the next time, with a rap that seemed to say *I know you're in there,* and when he got up and opened the door he was not at all surprised that it was Alice.

"Hi, honey," he said, and beckoned her in.

"Was it okay?" she asked.

"You know it was. It was probably a last time of sorts, and I'll remember it all my life."

She remained in the midground of the passage into the room, pleased but still seeking compliments.

"Come in. Sit for a minute."

She did, and when Eric plopped down on his bed, she did the same, moving over beside him. They lay like that for a few minutes, their shoes pointing up at the ceiling, their hips brushing, enjoying the old intimacy. "I still think of us as kids," she said after this restful pause.

"So do I, sometimes."

"It seems hardly believable, that so many years have gone by, that we're so old."

Again, a short pause. "It's lucky," said Eric, "that none of us have gotten sick. We're all three in pretty decent shape, right?" he asked, because one really could never assume such a thing.

"Well," she said, changing the tone on this subject, "my allergies. And—"

"Oh, come off it, Alice. I meant cancer or something."

She was miffed by this correction, and sat up, twisted around with one knee in front of her to face him. "Dad's got his road atlas out. We have been talking. That's what I wanted to tell you. Actually, I wanted to be the one to tell you, and tell you that you have no choice but to go along. He wants to go to Colorado. To Tom. He's gathering us all in, whether we want it or not."

NINE

Into the desert now, out of the lush black earth and fecund air of the Gulf Coast, away from the milky South and into the bone-hard winds of the scrappy ranchlands; raw space, miraculous and deadly. A voyage for Eric. Did he do well, as a parent? Was he fair and kind even when he was wrong? How is one supposed to equip a child for life, when life is so perplexing? The same questions and purposes, but a different father, and a different son.

Eric observed the progressions of landscape through occasional moments of full consciousness. Thoughts of Tom had kept him awake, with a late call to Gail—it was even later for her, of course, but he needed to hear her voice—in which she counseled him to go easy, that the last thing Tom needed was a whole round of parental projections. Eric asked Gail to meet them in Colorado, and she said she would try. She'd love to, it would kill her to miss it, but a couple of her students were cramming for the TOEFL. "The what?" he had said.

"The Test of English as a Foreign Language. You should know that by now. How long have I been doing this?"

"Sorry. I did know. I guess I'm a little tense, talking to you."

There was a pause. "Sure," she said. "Tom will be okay about you coming, by the way. You're not thinking of just dropping in?"

"No," said Eric. "You can get away with that with a mother, but not a son."

Eric tried a few times before he got Tom on the phone. "Is it okay?" Eric asked, and Tom said, "Sure, why not?" Then Eric's telephone had rung again, and he thought it might be Gail saying that she was coming after all, but it was Poppy.

"You're going to Denver, I hear." Poppy sounded cheerful.

"Do you think it's a bad idea? An imposition on Tom or something? It's not that he's invited us. I get to veto it, if it's a bad idea. Besides, I don't have time for this. I've got a business to run."

"What's more important than a few days with Tom?"

"A son who doesn't think there's much to be gained hanging around family? You're the expert on that. Tell me. Is any of this worth anything?"

"Well, I'm coming with you. If that means anything."

He had hardly been able to keep from shouting with joy, but it did seem odd. "Why?" he asked.

"Because Dad asked. Because it's time for a vacation. Because this is never going to happen again."

"Did you tell him about the letter? Was that what you were talking about all through dinner?"

"No, it wasn't what we talked about all through dinner, but yes, I told him. I had to. It was so past time to do it that it really wasn't very difficult."

"Did he know already?"

"He wouldn't answer. It was the one part of the conversation that got sticky. And at this point, who cares?"

Eric celebrated all this by letting Alice drive and by dozing throughout the morning, his head rattling against the window; he woke when his elbow slipped off the armrest and into the inconveniently placed cup holder. This was a car replete with places to store drinks, a truly American addition to automotive art, a place for all those bottles of fluid Americans seem to need at their sides. Or during workouts at the gym.

The chatter from the seats ahead of him, from Alice at the wheel, from Frank, and from Adam, was full of cheer. They all had what they needed now, even Adam, who seemed to have come to some sort of rapprochement with his Miss Alice. It had taken on the flavor of a grand outing, an excursion and not, as it had seemed earlier, an expedition; not so much a voyage of discovery as a tour. It was the kind of thing that had never happened in their family before. They had never been a family that took trips like this; no suitcases strapped on the roof of the DeSoto. No time for any of that, a week in Disneyland, or even a weekend at Ocean City, even a day at Tolchester Beach, and Eric wouldn't have wanted it back then, anyway; he could not have imagined his parents passing the time in communal leisure while the children darted in and out of the waves. Eric was happy with his long boyhood summers on the farm. He recalled those years as spent mostly in solitude, as if he recognized that this was the safest bet, but he and Alice had spent much of their time together, sailing their Penguin with Alice taking the role of skipper, or trailing the men around the fields back when much of the heaving and hauling of farming was still done largely by hand. Alice was good company, a pal, a lifelong bond and rub formed in those early years.

They stopped for lunch at a Shoney's north of Dallas. No time for side trips now to find the local café or lunchroom; Frank complained about this stop, but it was convenient, and Adam was pushing hard now. From the moment they had packed the car under the porte cochere of the Warwick and had loaded themselves into their seats, Adam had taken a new kind of command. Perhaps he was emboldened by his truce with Alice, but in fact, they were working in concert, and he seemed to be working against the time when Frank would run out of steam. Let's get this done now, Adam was saying plainly, and then get the old guy back home where he belongs.

After lunch Eric took over the driving, and Poppy joined him in the move up front. The vistas were endless now, miles on the timeless road, and Eric could all but point the car toward a distant speck and switch to autopilot.

"So," said Poppy.

"Yeah. Here we are. I never would have imagined."

"Road trip."

"I guess. But I'm glad you're with us." He meant it, but it came out with a little more urgency than he intended, as if what he was saying was that he needed her.

"You seem a little tense about this part of the visit," she said. She pulled over into the middle of the broad bench seat.

"Tom's a good kid. But he doesn't like to be invaded. He parcels out the parts of his life he's willing to share with us. He was always like that, to be fair."

"He's not a kid anymore. The timing seems about right."

Eric concentrated on passing an ancient Ford pickup, the kind of relic that would long ago have been rotted out by the winters and road salt up north. With this minor obstruction out of the way, the road was once again endless.

"It's just that I know so little about him," said Eric. "He deflects me with his ironic humor. It used to charm me, but I know that he's evading me. Now I understand how little I really know of what goes on in his mind. He's like you," he added, for no particular reason.

"Well, some people want more privacy than others."

He glanced over and then faced back into the windshield, as if addressing the desert itself. "You just can't imagine how it eats at you, to feel so unconnected to your kid. It's this huge hole in your life, and you—or I—fill it with this constant low-grade anxiety. You feel you must have been missing the obvious for years, wasting your attention on things like his homework and keeping his room neat, when the real kid inside who needed you was left unloved. You blew your chance. That's the fear."

"This is ridiculous," said Poppy. "He's living his own life."

"I'm not talking about knowing what he had for breakfast, or who he slept with, or whether he keeps his feet dry. I'm talking about not feeling on the same wavelength. As little as you and I talk, I can always feel your presence as a complete person."

"If you say so," she said. "You're romanticizing me, as usual. The connection you're talking about is so much deeper than our sibling bullshit."

"Yes. And who, of anyone in the world, should you have that connection to more than your own son?"

"Or to whom, in the whole world, should you have it less?" She was exasperated by now, and Eric had to agree that he had carried this to an un-useful extreme. She moved to close the distance between them even more, and her knee brushed his thigh as she propped a leg up.

"You have always been this tense about him," she said. "Like you had to explain him or defend him or something. You've been like that since he was born. When he was in the room, your eyes never left him. Honestly, it used to drive me nuts."

He could remember that feeling, almost holding his breath, wanting everyone to love Tom as much as he did, ready to jump in instantly to translate a garbled word or to gain a roomful of praise for his boyhood triumphs. *Tom scored a goal in soccer last Saturday. His teacher says he's gifted in math.* It had a darker side, that was for sure, the panic he felt about any illness less diagnosable than an ear infection, or about the fact that there were too many ear infections. He knew all of this was more than parental devotion, far more desperate than true paternal love. "Maybe it was the extra pressure of an only child," he said finally, willing to go that far. "You've only got this one chance to give happiness. That's what you're trying to do, you know: give someone a happy life. Anything but joy breaks your heart." He glanced in the rearview mirror; a truck had closed on him without any notice and he realized he'd better keep a little more attention on the road.

"Maybe you were just making sure that Tom didn't grow up the way we did."

"I suppose I was. Each generation overcorrects. Isn't that what they say?"

"Then isn't that the answer? You were the most devoted father I ever saw. Ricki used to say you were like her dad"—she skipped a beat, a vague look of trouble at speaking Ricki's name, a pause she would not notice—"whom she loved ridiculously."

"Despite the fact that I drove you crazy."

"It's easy for people who don't have kids to make fun of what it takes to raise them. I wasn't criticizing you."

They rode for a few minutes without speaking, a silence restfully accompanied by the gentle drone of Alice's all-weather tires, and by the slight rasp of her delicate snoring from the seat behind them. "What I have been wondering is what Dad"—he turned around to make sure that they weren't being overheard too clearly—"means by this. Why does he want to see Tom?"

"I think it's his way of nudging you. Suggesting you not do what he did, not withdraw, but take a little more active role in your relationship with him. That's how he thinks he 'lost' "—Frank's word, all the way—"me. Don't let yourself get put on the sidelines." They both took a moment to reflect on this, Eric on the sidelines, with maybe Gail and Tom on the field. Not something Eric felt had happened, but it could. Not something mean or aggressive from them; just something they might do in a vacuum. Eric let it drop. There is a role waiting for you in the life of your children, and the only choice is whether you step into it or not. Frank did, and Eric discovered to his surprise that the role his father would play in his life was actually a rather big one: spiritual guide, professor of humanity, rabbi, and how unlikely was that? The difficulty, as Eric began to perceive it, was that he had tried to be some sort of teacher to Tom for years, which was not the role Tom had in mind, or heart, for his father. Virtually everything Eric knew or cared about had become, over the years, a forbidden subject: no discussions—or lectures, as they had been branded, perhaps correctly—concerning politics or poetry or Handel's operas; no—God, no—references to his own life, to the travails he had faced that struck him as similar to Tom's and thus as potential sources of encouragement; no talking about Tom's difficulties finding a good job or, more important, finding out what he thought a good job might be. Tom hated Dad's lectures more than he hated anything. There was some deep flaw in the way Eric presented himself to Tom, and all the wisdom in the world couldn't make up for it. But still, it was time to try again. Time to be a better father. Time, perhaps, not for the son to grow up, but for the father to grow up.

"Besides," added Poppy, when it was clear she'd hit a mark of sorts, "Dad's been a shitty grandfather." They both laughed; he had not been any kind of a grandfather at all. "One more person to make amends to."

Poppy turned back into her seat. They had made it to a slight high point in the terrain, a feature vaguely promised through miles of driving. Just as vaguely perceived, the land was less arid over this rise, and there were now small ranch yards dotting the plains, and ahead there was a small town laid out in a strip along the highway. Eric couldn't imagine this life; couldn't imagine the pull and hold a little community like this could have on its children, or even on newcomers, spouses brought in and deposited like settlers in a sod hut, enough blood for the town to survive, but out there on the flat there was a rancher bravely cultivating a crop, and when they slowed for the town, two little girls in overalls and with gap teeth gawked and waved happily at them.

The deceleration produced a stirring from the backseats, and then Adam moved forward to the middle seat and poked his head between them. Adam glanced at the gas gauge, asked the name of that last town, and pulled back for a moment to study the map. "Time for a pit stop," he said.

There was nothing on the horizon but ranchland. Eric kicked the cruise control up to eighty and then twisted slightly to speak to Adam. "So what's the deal?" he asked.

"I had thought we'd take two nights on the road to Denver, but we've made good time and it would be better if we could do it in one. Getting in and out of motels wears him out."

"How's he holding up? Is this crazy for him?"

"He's doing what he wants. It's his choice. Last night was good," said Adam finally. "But it cost a lot. This is against doctor's orders."

"Then let's at least put you and him on a plane for the last leg from Denver. Wouldn't that make sense?"

"I'm not sure," said Adam.

For the night they stopped at a Comfort Inn in Oklahoma, a state Eric had never been to before. A new one for his life list, with only a few of the lower forty-eight left to go: Nevada, West Virginia, Minnesota; once Eric got settled in his room, he reflected that he had never been in Colorado before either. He and Gail had talked about going to visit Tom in Denver once he'd gotten settled there, but that was the problem: the months had gone by and he still didn't seem to be set up. The other problem was that Tom didn't want them to come, which seemed fine, for a while. And now it seemed no longer fine, and Eric, anyway, was coming, and Tom had not refused him.

The group ate at the restaurant called Chuzzlewit's next to the motel, a little touch of Dickens in Oklahoma under an immense plastic sign that was supposed to look like the weathered oak of ancient England. There was nothing else around except for the smudge of a town, perhaps a mile across the scrublands, just this motel and theme eatery on a bank above the interstate. Eric had asked the man at the motel desk whether there was a restaurant nearby that was "locally owned," and the man had no idea what he was talking about. "I think the owner of Chuzwitt's lives in Dallas," he had said.

The décor of Chuzzlewit's seemed designed to encourage bawdiness, with pewter mugs and signs advising guests of the rules of the house, including the admonition to "touch not the Barmaid's bottom." The barmaid was a skinny girl, a nice kid. In a few minutes, her dad would be coming by in his truck to take her home, or a boyfriend would be waiting, a big hulk of a kid, who would almost squash her when they made love.

"What this place needs," said Poppy, "is better advertising."

Poppy had a point, Eric reflected. What was advertising about if it wasn't the process of replacing vernacular and indigenous cultures with something manufactured from afar. It was better, after all, to stick with the local accounts, products homegrown in the region, and leave the national stuff to the visionaries like Liv with FruitOut. And with Lilly.

In the morning, the plains continued for two hundred more miles, but they were going eighty-five, not a trooper in sight. Then—they were feeling it before they could see it—the flatness began to rise and fall, and soon they were in something that could almost be called hills. There was relief in this topographic change, and with it, the sensation of having accomplished something, perhaps a lift in spirits not unlike that experienced by the settlers in their wagons. Considering the danger and toil that awaited them in the passes ahead, they might have celebrated too early, but human beings are like that, happy to get whatever it is over and hopeful about what's coming up. He shared these musings with his father, who had once loved the history of the westward expansion; for a few years the family gave him books about it for Christmas, some of them coffee-table volumes with maps, portraits of Indians, and scenes by Bierstadt and Charles Russell. As they drove, Eric tried to get Frank to talk about these things, but of all the kinds of conversations one might try to have with him, this was one of the worst: a mind full of information and fact and no way to open it. His father dismissed the subject by patting him on the arm: *Thank you,* he was saying. *Thank you for remembering that I know about these things.*

"How are you holding up?" Eric asked. "We're worried about

you getting completely beaten up. I'm thinking that we should put you and Adam on a plane from Denver."

"No." The answer was clear and definitive. Eric glanced over at Frank. He was sitting up straight, solid; he seemed remarkably healthy, for all this wear and tear. His still-curious eyes were on this western landscape, the arid plains, so foreign to a man from the lush Eastern Shore.

They reached the hotel at seven after fighting through the smog and toil of Denver's rush hour, one experience, at least, that the settlers didn't have to face when they reached the mountains. Eric had to admit that, tired as he was of lodging on the road, the Brown Palace Hotel was a relief: four stars, a staff of bellmen and porters fanned out to greet them, and a front desk that knew their names before they gave them and acted as if they had done little all day except wait for the Alwin party to arrive. The captain worked through the names for the rooms, produced the magic key cards one by one, and then made a special, slightly odd celebratory gesture as he handed Eric his. "I'm sure you will be quite comfortable," he said. Eric wasn't sure why his comfort was more important than that of the others, but he was too tired and grimy with road sweat to respond.

Two porters wheeled a baggage cart onto the elevator—the luggage, Frank's ancient valise, Adam's gym bag, Poppy's knapsack, was perhaps not of the usual quality and character—and when they stopped at the fourth floor, Eric began to file out behind the others, when the second porter stopped him and said that his room was on the tenth floor. In fact, he had Eric's suitcase in his grasp.

"What is this room of mine?" he asked as they rode upward.

"The Roosevelt Suite."

"And?" he said, meaning what was he supposed to do in such a place.

"I believe Mrs. Alwin has already arrived."

Eric took the bag from the porter when they reached the floor— no need for an audience for this meeting—and walked down the long, hushed hall with his heart beating and his legs almost weak. He knocked—a warning, a request—and then slid his key card into the lock.

The living room he entered was a broad expanse of leather furniture and mission side pieces; the rugs were Persians, and several vases were stocked with lilies and other fragrant blossoms Eric could not identify. He was shocked by the tastefulness of this hotel room; none of those cheesy credenzas and Formica wood grain of the stops on the road. Across the room was a pair of French doors onto a balcony overlooking the city and offering the mountains in the distance. Gail was there, leaning against the railing. With the low rays of sun behind her, she was visible only as a luminescent silhouette. She was waiting for him to speak.

"Hi," he said.

"And hello to you, husband."

He put down his bag and walked over to her. She'd gotten her hair cut, short and youthful, and she was wearing slinky black pants and a white shirt. He took her in his arms, and they stood there for a few minutes, saying nothing. Her body was soft under the silk and she fitted herself to him, the top of her head just above his chin, her belly at his waist, the only body for him.

"Are you surprised to see me?" she asked.

"I knew something was up when we checked in. The porter said you were here. But am I surprised? Yes. Is this the answer to the question I asked you?"

"Yes."

"And?"

"I've ended it. It's what I wanted to do. And here we are, making a new start. Come. Look at this." She showed him to the bedroom, where there was an immense king-sized bed, more cut flowers. In the bathroom there was a Jacuzzi big enough for both of them.

"I think your father is trying to tell us something."

"Yes. He is. But it would have been the same if you were waiting in a Holiday Inn."

"I know. But we can enjoy this anyway."

There was a bottle of champagne on ice waiting for them in the living room, a final bit of luxury, with something to celebrate. Eric popped it: the full sound of celebration, and he poured them both a full glass. They settled gratefully on the couch. For a few moments they did what couples do, talked of airplanes and other details, and then she asked him about the trip, and he told her all, Poppy's revelation, the dinner at the country club, his conversation about Tom with Poppy in the car, last night's dinner at a restaurant called "Pickwick's, or something like that. You should have seen it: the Lost World."

"How's Frank?"

"I suspect he thinks that this has exceeded his wildest dreams, but we're all worried about his health. We've been having little powwows about it from time to time. This trip may kill him."

"Or save him."

"It already has," said Eric, taking her hand. "Gail?"

"What?"

"I love you. I love only you. I've been thinking about—"

She interrupted him. "No thinking. No more thinking. Doing. You're on a wave here. I can see it in your walk. So just ride it, okay? Freshen up, and then let's get naked."

When he came out of the bathroom in his towel, she was waiting for him in the satin sheets wearing an underwear set she might have picked out in a Victoria's Secret in the airport, or at Macy's before she left. They made love slowly, and then lay together for a good while before Eric picked up the phone to call room service. She had been dropping off a bit into the early morning of her eastern time, but she perked up immediately and said she wanted the brook trout, a salad, and a lime sorbet—she'd studied the menu earlier, and could easily have gone ahead and ordered what Eric wanted, the steak, the big steak, the potato, the crème brûlée, the Merlot. Was he that predictable, or was it just men?

They said very little during this feast. "Tom is glad we're coming," she said, about the phone call he'd known she would make, though he wasn't sure "glad" was what he had heard in Tom's voice. "Pleased," maybe, or "happy," with some kind of qualifier, like "wary."

"By the way, I knew about this plan before you did," she said. "Frank called me."

"He called you? You mean Adam did."

"No, Adam made the call and then put him on. He asked me to come to 'Gevner.' 'Tuesday,' he said. 'Brown Palace Hotel.' That was all I needed to know. And now I'm here."

The waiter removed the room service cart and they turned down the lights and retired to their rumpled bed. It was late now, and Gail was soon fast asleep, her body pressed against his in a tiny space in the expanse of sheet and pillow. Eric lay awake and listened to the hush of this night, but no demons came to him this time, no fear, no stirring of anxiety. There was nothing out there that could hurt him. There was nothing, at least at this moment, in here that could hurt him. He did want to sleep. He knew there was one person in this party who was awake now, and suddenly Eric wanted to see him. It was now quite late, but the hour meant little about sleep for his father. Eric dressed, called the front desk for the room number—which the woman who answered was willing to give him only after conferring with her boss—and walked out. A couple about his age was waiting for the elevator on his floor; they were in evening clothes, but the man was wearing bright red cowboy boots. Eric liked the way they looked, and liked them, their satisfactions about their clothes and wherever it was they were going, but Eric felt fine in his jeans. When he got off at the fourth floor they eyed him suspiciously, a lone man making interim stops on hotel floors: a thief, a lover?

He tapped on his father's door and then cupped his ear to the surface: the low hum of a television, a light but sure footstep coming his way. Adam opened the door. The lights were off and Frank's long covered form was visible only in the spooky blue of the television. Adam had pulled a chair right in front of the TV: a nurse's station, keeping watch. Yes, it would be quite like this at the end, dropping in and out, night and day, the breathing from the bed sometimes easy and sometimes labored. That moment was coming, coming sooner than Eric had realized.

"Hey," he said quietly to Adam. "Is he asleep?"

Adam looked over his shoulder. "Maybe. Go see."

Eric went over to the bed and took the good hand, which was resting, palm up, beside his face on the pillow. The skin was scaly, dry enough almost to seem as if there were no flesh left, the skin already hardening into bone, but the hand was warm. It pulsed once in Eric's hold. "Dad?" Eric said.

Frank stirred, but was not deep enough into sleep, or was at last sure enough of his fate, not to take his usual fright. He sampled the hand that had found its way into his palm. "Eric," he said.

Eric thanked him for the suite, the champagne and the flowers, the Jacuzzi. "A little over the top," he said, and Frank smiled, the look of someone who has done good. Eric told him Gail was safe and sound, that they were looking forward to seeing Tom. He told Frank how much he admired what he was doing, this crazy trip, and how brave Frank was, that he had shown a kind of courage in the face of so many years of mistakes, a kind of courage that Eric could not imagine in himself.

"This is my confession," Eric said.

And then Eric was saying that in the last few days he had seen just how far off his own good track he had fallen, with anger and bitterness about things he could hardly recall, and that he had almost made a mess of his marriage, rather as Frank had done. His marriage, his son, his business, his friends: he'd let them all slip through his hands somehow. He didn't know why, but he had become a half person, someone who stood at the side of things. People had begun not to like him—he realized this now. And now it seemed he was getting this chance to make it right. And he could not really account for it, except to say it was a blessing received in the form of his father's love, the same love that had shone through that frigid Maryland day so many years ago, when Frank had come out in the cold to say good-bye.

A kiss formed on Frank's lips, barely perceptible in the dark. Eric remained at his side even after this torrent of words had ceased. Adam seemed to have left at some point. Eric felt as if he were dropping off to sleep, but if he was, he could feel himself entering immediately into dream without the usual toss and turn. Eric could feel words coming out of his mouth as if his lips were not moving. He put his hand back in Frank's and found himself asking his father for his blessing, that Old Testament gift that fathers could bestow on one, and only one, of their children. Eric said that if he got it, he would use it well, to make increase where there was little, to make fullness where there was absence. Eric did not know where these biblical phrases were coming from; they flowed through him, an unproven river.

Father, sit up and eat of my game, so that you may bless me.
Come near and kiss me, my son.

Eric let go of the hand and leaned over his father, put his lips to his cheek. Was this a trick, his father nearly blind without his glasses, half asleep? Eric had no brother to supplant, but still it felt like thievery.

Ah, the smell of my son is like the field that the Lord has blessed.

May God give you of the dew of heaven, and of the fatness of the earth, and plenty of grain and wine.

Let peoples serve you, and nations bow down to you. Be lord over your brothers, and may your mother's sons bow down to you.

Cursed be everyone who curses you, and blessed be everyone who blesses you!

TEN

"Are you guys getting a divorce?" Tom had stopped dead when he rounded the end of his block and then drew up slowly to his parents, side by side, sitting on his stoop.

His house was in a neighborhood of almost identical small, wood-frame houses, packed window to window, with brown trodden patches of lawn in front of each, with bicycles on the porches, and here and there, bits of play equipment, faded or rusted. Most of the houses needed paint, but it was a tidy neighborhood, a place of families and students living in reasonable harmony. The cars parked on the street were mostly old Toyotas and Hondas; Alice's Ford Expedition looked like a spaceship. A yellow cat had been stalking Gail and Eric since they arrived almost an hour earlier; it seemed as if it really was going to pounce on one of them when the time was right.

They had spotted Tom the second he turned onto the street, recognized this distant, loved figure by his gait; he was a good athlete, but even now, he seemed all bones. Eric and Gail were getting to their feet, brushing the concrete grit off their bottoms, when he spoke again.

"I mean, what's up?"

Eric left Gail's side and walked down to him, his arms outstretched to give him a hug. Tom took a slight step back, but Eric kept coming, took a bead on Tom's body in a way that told Tom it was useless to run, that he'd have to submit to his father's embrace now, or be pursued all over Denver. Eric took him in his arms, rotated him slightly so he could no longer appeal to his mother, and told him that this was not about work, but about having some fun, that they missed him, missed, above all, being with him. He hoped that was okay. Tom grunted; it was his way of saying it was okay, with reservations. Eric finally dropped his arms, but barred the way toward Gail for another second or two: an assertion of privilege.

"So when do Aunt Alice and Poppy jump out of the bushes?" Tom asked.

"That's tomorrow. You'll have to pretend to be surprised."

Tom smiled, but then glanced uncertainly at his house, as if trying to discern what his parents might have seen if they peeked in the windows. "I cleaned the place up, but it's still kind of a dump."

"We don't care. I'm glad to see you. You look great." He did look great, if a little unwashed. He was wearing a white shirt and a slightly greasy-looking tie, the uniform of the temp worker. He wore no earrings; there appeared to be no tattoos. Perhaps he had put on some weight, though he would never be bulky. How he and Gail had fretted over that one, both going to his earliest checkups to peer worriedly as the nurse recorded his weight to the ounce, watched her find his dot just slightly off the growth chart. In not too many more years he'd start to feel grateful for his constitution, decades of payback for the few times in his childhood that he might have been called skinny, or Ninety-eight-pound Weakling. Eric wasn't sure this generation knew about that taunt, as Eric did, reading the Charles Atlas ads in his comic books and wondering whether the regimen might work for him.

"So what's the deal?" Tom said, fishing around in his backpack for his keys.

"There's no deal. We were hoping you could come out to dinner with us, if you have no other plans."

"Sure. I'll need a shower." He pulled back the combination storm door, and then entered. Gail and Eric traded hopeful looks as they followed.

The inside was exactly what they would have expected: a collection of worn furniture, a couch covered in stained yellow corduroy that might have been salvaged from the sidewalk. There were magazines on the floor, *Wired, People*—no sign of *The New Yorker,* to which Gail's mother had been sending him a subscription since his freshman year at Wesleyan. There was a tangled piece of piping in one corner, a roof rack uniquely engineered for some sort of sporting gear.

"I'm going to get ready. If one of my roommates comes in, just deal with it."

In a few minutes they heard the shower come on. Gail was still wandering around the room, and then into the kitchen, which Eric saw from the door. The white stove was chipped and blackened here and there and the room smelled like a combination of burned toast and unwashed laundry, but on one of the counters was a neat line of glass canisters: grains, dried fruit, brewer's yeast. At least one of the men was into a diet transported directly from Eric and Gail's sojourn in New Hampshire, but it wasn't Tom.

Gail was now back in the living room. She had begun to prowl increasingly intently, and when Eric met her eye he realized that she was stricken.

"What is it?" he whispered.

"It's like he doesn't live here. There's so little of his stuff here."

Eric had been noticing this, too, without realizing it, but he tried to put a face on it. The messy ordinariness of this graduate-student place was reassuring in its own way. "He's been saying all along that he wasn't settled here."

Gail looked as if she were going to cry. "I'm not looking for 'settled,' " she protested. "I'm looking for evidence that he's *living* here. This food"—she pointed to the kitchen—"not his; these CDs, they're all classical; this thing"—she was pointing to the roof rack—"not his. Nothing of our son here."

Eric made one more quick survey of the room, hoping to prove her wrong, but he couldn't. He sat down on the couch. A spring, a lump struck him between the buttocks. "Well, this is the sort of thing we're here to find out, isn't it?" She was still pacing. "Sit down, will you?"

She sat, at the edge of the cushion.

"It doesn't mean anything," he said. "If I lived here I think I'd keep to my room too. You remember what he was like." Growing up, Tom had spent a lot of time in his room, playing with his Legos and G.I. Joes. Sometimes, in the evenings or on weekends, Gail or Eric used to ask if he wanted to come down, set up a base in the living room with them, and he would consider it for a moment, and then say "No, thank you," in a small but firm voice. Once in a while, in the evening, they took their drinks and crackers upstairs to be with him.

"You can't say anything about it."

"I know," she said, calmer now. "I'm sorry. This is just what he was afraid of, that we would come here and find fault."

For dinner Tom wanted to go to a Mexican place a short walk from his house. It was a cheerful neighborhood spot that served sangría in small galvanized buckets and had masks on the walls from Día de los Muertos pageants. The place was filled mostly with young people, groups of three men or three women, and couples, pretty girls. Eric assumed Tom felt awkward being here with people so obviously his parents, but they were having a good time now, Gail recovered from her moment of despair. She sparkled around Tom, and what man of any age wouldn't be proud to show off a mother as beautiful as she. Eric could sit back for a moment and enjoy this scene. Someday soon they might be here with Tom and one of those pretty girls, someone who would spend the meal saying very little but giving Tom little high signs, and saying later, when they got back to her place, that she didn't think his father was so bad. Well, not now, but a lover would come. Tom was such a wonderful young man; his reticences could only, one day, be touching, even if perhaps frustrating; he would be, someday, a gift, to someone.

"So tell me about the trip," said Tom. He and Gail had finished catching up on home, what his friends were doing.

Eric told him of a few high points. "The new Merry Pranksters," Tom said. In college he had taken a course on the sixties. "Granddad as Ken Kesey. Or as Dean Moriarty. You as, what was his name?" Neither he nor Eric could recall the name Kerouac had given to himself. "Offers a new perspective," said Tom.

"I'd thought of it as the Magical Mystery Tour."

"No. What you're doing is more dangerous than the Beatles."

Eric sat up in his chair. "Well, thank you, Tom, that's one of the nicest things anyone has said to me in quite a while."

They walked back to his house at a leisurely stroll. The neighborhood was now alive, music from the windows, a couple of Latino men fixing a car, children in T-shirts having a water fight. The night was fine, soft and fragrant, unseasonably mild. It was a happy and companionable scene. This was not a lonely place, not like those villages of young professionals coming home and shutting themselves in their houses with NPR and *Sex and the City*. It was not, indeed, Summit, New Jersey, where the accomplishments of its residents resulted in houses that were not so much dwellings as territories. This was a safe place for Tom, for now; he felt comfortable in it, and as they walked, another man his age and a young black couple greeted him, clipped "Hey"s, a "What's up." At the curb Eric wrested a commitment from Tom to take the day off and show them the sights, a trip up to Boulder maybe, or out to Rocky Mountain National Park, which didn't seem so far on the map. Poppy would be there, Eric offered, "and Aunt Alice," he added.

"That was fun," said Gail as they drove away.

"I thought so, too. He's so great when he feels he can unwind."

"He's our son. If we listed all his characteristics, there isn't one we wouldn't love. So there, damn it. He's just what you and I would hope to create. That's all there is to it."

Eric laughed. "You know, someday I'd love to find out what he really thinks of me."

Gail slid over and put her hand on his neck. "It wouldn't hurt your feelings. It would be filled with love, and perplexity."

"And anger?"

"Of course. What else?" She left out the last unnecessary phrase: "You're his father."

In the morning, they gathered for breakfast: Alice, Poppy, Eric, and Gail. Frank stayed in his room. A trip was on to Rocky Mountain National Park, a picnic, though it would be cold, and Alice was fretting.

"The concierge said there would still be snow up there."

"Great. A chance to put that rig of yours in four-wheel drive," said Eric.

"Dad can't handle it."

"Dad's not coming anyway," said Poppy. "He says he wants to go to church." *That's right,* thought Eric: *it is Sunday.*

"What about Adam?" asked Gail.

"Well . . ." Alice started to say that he was simply doing his job, and would be well paid for it.

"Doesn't the guy deserve a day off?" asked Gail again. "I'll stay with Frank. I haven't seen him yet. I'll take him to church."

They packed the car and swung by to pick up Tom, who was sitting on the concrete stoop talking with a woman overseeing two toddlers in the yard. Alice and Eric sat in the front, and from the back came such mirth, howls of laughter, stories of Tom's most bizarre temp jobs, Poppy's scabrous appraisals of virtually everyone, and Adam's continued tales of road trips with his mother, June, and her two sisters, April and May. Alice and Eric rode contentedly in front, like parents letting the young people have their fun, and that was right, because Poppy always had seemed enough younger to be in a different generation, and her choices in adulthood had kept the divide intact, at least at times like this. Eric could imagine how much the Rice students loved her.

They stopped at a convenience store along the way and assembled what they could of a picnic: shrink-wrapped luncheon meats, Cracker Barrel cheese, a can of black olives, a loaf of bread, water bottles, soda, and a bottle of wine. A feast.

By noon they were in the mountains, amid the violent massive slabs of the earth's plates, thrust upward so recently that Eric could almost hear the crush and squeal of the event. Alice was driving and had the pleasure of powering through the remaining drifts at the roadside scenic overlooks. "I know you think this car is stupid," she said, "but I like it."

"Alice, none of this trip would have been possible without it. We seem to be filling it up."

For their picnic, they hiked up a rocky trail to a low peak. The vista at the top left them speechless, this massive act of creation: mountains, with all their drama, were part of the plan. And why were humans part of it, with all their petty hurts and profane deeds? Tom spotted the white dots of mountain goats grazing on the sheer cliffside below them. Eric wished he had brought a pair of binoculars, though what those goats were doing was terrifying enough at this distance. It seemed a life of folly, but even from here, their mere white dots seemed content with their lot, safe from predators, admired by the landlocked souls. A beast could survive anywhere. You can make a good life on a ledge, or anywhere else, if you're willing to try.

They ate their picnic in the lee of the summit. Of all of them, Tom had come best prepared for the temperature, with a sweater, a parka, a pair of gloves. Who but a parent could take such a thing as a sign of maturity? He had soon enough surrendered his parka to Alice, whose teeth still chattered. Poppy, the Southern girl among them, seemed perfectly comfortable in her blue-jean jacket.

"So, Tom," said Poppy. "How's your love life?"

"Oh, it stinks."

"Nobody just now?"

"No."

"That's no fun. Believe me, I've been there. Someone will come along."

"Yeh."

"Isn't anybody else cold?" asked Alice. She was so frozen that she had not jumped up and busied herself rewrapping the leftovers as soon as everyone seemed vaguely finished, designating a litter bag, clearing the small pieces of plastic wrapping off the grass.

"I better find a phone and check in," said Adam, a slight turning of the moment, a call from reality. Adam noticed the shift in the group and said that nothing was really up, just a precaution. "I really appreciate it that you included me in this."

Eric said that he better get back, too, and he almost added that Gail would be mad if it sounded as if they'd all had too much fun, but he stopped himself. He would have meant it as a joke, but it wouldn't have sounded much like one to Tom, so hyperalert for strain in his parents' marriage, and wouldn't have been appreciated by anyone else. The clarity of the moment settled upon him, the charity of these moments when, helped by others who care for us, we can see ourselves clearly, and the responsibility conferred by them, not to say more, but to do better. "I hope Gail and Dad had a good time," he said.

But in the car, with Tom now beside him in front, Tom seemed to have read his mind. He asked, "Why are you always so negative about Mom?"

"What did I say that was negative?" Eric protested.

" 'I *hope*,' " he mimicked. "In other words, she didn't."

"Really, if I sounded dubious, it was because of my father, not your mom."

This defense didn't register; Tom didn't seem interested in what Eric said, anyway. "You guys," he said. "What's with you guys?"

Eric glanced away from the winding road for a quick appraisal of Tom's expression.

"There's nothing with us. Marriage has its stresses and strains." Eric could feel the rest of the car listening. "I love your mother. I've been in love with her since I was nineteen. Doesn't that mean anything?"

No, it didn't. Eric glanced at him, and he was nodding his head as if continuing the conversation to himself.

"What's up?" asked Eric.

"What I'm saying is, why don't you guys just call it quits?"

"Who said anything about calling it quits? This really isn't the sort of thing a married couple, even your parents, has to explain."

"Oh bullshit. You fucking around all those years, and her doing God knows what. I mean, God knows what. It makes me sick. You want to know why I moved here—it's so I didn't have to hang around and wait for you to tell me you were splitting up." Tom paused, with nothing more to say on that topic, but then moved on to what was really on his mind. "All I'm trying to do out here is live my life my own way, and what do I get? Everyone comes out here like a jury on wheels. Whose idea was that? This is my place, damn it, and I don't need my family checking up on me." Then he came to the heart, the broken heart of it. "Is it me? Am I the problem you're here to solve? Why don't you just care for me? All you care about is yourself. Jesus, what about me?" He finished with a stifled sob, and tears were running down his face, and they were running down Eric's, too.

"I've got to pull over," Eric said, and as soon as he had guided the car just barely far enough onto the shoulder, Tom leaped from the door. Eric followed, caught up to him a few paces ahead of the car. "Care for you. Oh my God, Tom, I love you. You're everything to us. Nothing else even comes close. You're in my mind and Mom's mind every hour of the day. You think that's bullshit, but it's not. I'm going to love you forever. I can't ever get away from that, and neither can you." He reached in his pocket and found a napkin left over from the picnic, and tore it in half.

Tom rubbed his eyes with the small bit of paper. An RV lumbered by. Tom wadded up his bit of napkin and threw it into the bushes. He took a few deep breaths. "I'm not trying to get away from it," he said finally.

Eric had also finished wiping his eyes, but put his sodden remnant in his pocket. "Maybe you should. How could you not be stifled by our need, just you to bear so much weight. The day you were born—"

"No!" Tom shouted, and then, more calmly, "No. I don't want to hear about the day I was born. I wasn't there. I was just a blob. Don't tell me about tiptoeing into my room at night. So what? Don't ever make me hear, ever again in my life, the story of the time I tried out for the hockey team. Okay? None of this proves anything."

Tom took away what Eric had been going to say. If he hadn't, Eric might well have mentioned that hockey tryout when Tom was eight, Tom's earnest bravery in a sport that could not possibly have been more inappropriate for the boy he was then, and a thousand other remembrances, evidences of endless love, the kinds of snapshots that were with Eric every day, the kind of album of memories one flips through now and again to remind oneself of a meaningful past. Did none of this prove anything? No. Apparently not to the only one who mattered. Apparently this past life had nothing to do with who Tom was now.

"Okay, no more family stories. You're right. I promise."

"I don't care about family stories. I just don't see why they always have to reflect on you. It doesn't matter what the topic is, the subject is always yourself."

"Jesus," said Eric. But there it was again: another of those moments in life when something, something big, becomes clear. A door swinging open: a revelation. It was a clarity that Tom must have grasped for many years but had never before spoken aloud, as if he assumed it was as obvious to everyone else as it was to him. But it hadn't been, not to Eric. Suddenly Eric was imagining a field, a high meadow bathed in air and light, a vista of astounding simplicity. Perhaps they had just seen this place, but it now seemed inserted into his brain to see again for some purpose. *Be of good cheer;* those were the words that came with it. Eric kicked the pebbles at his feet. He looked deep into his son's eyes. "You're right. But what other proof can I give you of my love?"

"I'm not looking for proof. No one has to *prove* anything here." Tom was calm now. Perhaps he, too, recognized that he had finally been willing to articulate an outrage that had plagued him all those years. Perhaps he was asking himself why he hadn't said that ten years ago, back when it might have helped.

"Do you really think we don't care for you?"

"Hell, I don't know. It wasn't that, really."

"Your mother and I are together on this trip. Our marriage isn't perfect, but we are seeing how to make it better." Eric would not try to tell his son just how much a few nights of real lovemaking can restore commitment, hope, kindness. That sex, which had such power to lay waste to ordinary lives, could also offer a way out of its own damage. He'd learn that, or already had learned it, for himself. "We're trying to become a family again. We're trying to figure out how to do it with you living far from home. It's not easy."

"Well, sometimes things aren't too bad," Tom allowed. "Last night was fun. I liked your stories about the trip. I'm sorry for everything."

"This visit out here is something that could be important for the three of us. It's important for your grandfather to see us together, happy, before he dies. Will you help us?"

"How?" This was a brand-new thought for Tom. So much of what Tom thought was revealed by his sharp but mobile face; in this he was like his grandfather. There was now a tiny brightness of discovery, mouth drawn with a hint of skepticism, but eyes wide with interest.

"I don't know. Keep us honest. Talk to me as you have just now. Tell me I'm an asshole."

Tom nodded, and then smiled. He figured he could do that. Eric glanced, for the first time, back into the car: the other three were huddled into a conversation deep in the backseat.

"Mom. She can be pretty tough," said Tom. He shook his head, a response to some thought. He seemed to be preparing to head back to the car.

"I've got to make a full disclosure here," said Eric. "I wanted to ask you to come home. You've said this is your place, and I respect that. I liked your neighborhood. I just wanted to tell you that you would be welcome at home, under any conditions. We wouldn't harass you. You could do anything you wanted, nothing even, just come home, be around friends and family. Take a trip or two. Just take some time to figure out what might be right for you. Home can be a right place to recharge, sometimes, at certain times. That's all. There it is."

Tom didn't say anything, but responded with a slight nod, and a movement of his head from side to side that meant he would, or might, at least consider it. At least he didn't reject it.

"Let's get back into the car," said Eric. "My toes are freezing."

They climbed back in, and Eric turned to address the three expectant faces in the back. "Tom and I were having a rather biblical moment, and we're fine now."

"What Bible story was that?" asked Alice, the church lady.

"I forget which one. One about a father slewed by his son."

"It's 'slain,' " said Tom. "And what about the one about the father sacrificing the son?"

"That was Abraham," said Alice. "But he didn't do it."

"No," said Tom, "but he would have, wouldn't he."

They got back to Denver at five, through another rush hour. Tom came up with Eric to the suite, and they found Gail dozing on the couch. She stirred, opened an unseeing eye, then sat up. "How was the day?" she asked.

"Great," said Eric. "Don't you think?"

"It was okay," said Tom. "How was yours?"

"Fine. Nice. We went to church." She was still groggy, but as soon as she spoke the last sentence, she was suddenly wide awake. "I mean no, it wasn't nice. It was scary. I couldn't believe my eyes. I almost didn't recognize him."

"Dad?"

"Of course. You haven't noticed? I'll tell you the truth: he looks a decade older to me; he's aged a decade since I saw him two weeks ago. This trip is killing him."

"I'm not sure I'd say that," said Eric, but he knew she was right. He trusted her eyes more than anyone's on this subject, and Adam's guarded reports: tired today; not eating enough.

"I don't think he's up to coming out tonight, either."

"What's wrong with him?" asked Tom.

"What isn't?" answered Eric, but in fact, he was reaching for the phone to call Alice. "He's old," Eric added, and when Alice answered he got right to the point: was this not time to send Dad back in a plane? Alice was in the suite in a second; Poppy followed a few minutes later. They traded bits of evidence: looked awful that day after the visit to their mother; looked at the top of his game at the country club in Houston; seemed perhaps to be sleeping more in the car; yes, just yesterday Adam had to help him up to the seat and this morning, said Poppy, he couldn't get a single word, not even her name.

"It is clear to me," said Alice. "We do as Eric says. Send him and Adam back in a plane. That was always my plan. We'll charter a jet, if he isn't up to it."

"What does *he* want to do?" asked Tom, and Eric expected Alice to snap at him, tell him that "my father's" desires had nothing to do with it "at this juncture." This was the sort of locution she used at times like this, giving orders, using words like "mandatory."

"We need Adam in on this," she said, when she realized that the others, finally acknowledging that they needed her leadership, were waiting for her to speak. While she called Adam, Eric helped the others to drinks from the minibar. The extravagance of this place was suddenly dreadful, a mistake, something stolen from an old man on his last legs.

It took Adam twenty minutes to get away, and when he finally came in, he understood immediately the mood and the plan.

"You and I talked about this the other day, didn't we?" Eric asked Adam.

"Yes."

"So what do you think? How's he doing?"

"Not that good," said Adam, after a pause.

"What isn't good?"

"He's okay now, but he's taking a beating. But that isn't the real problem." They all waited for Adam to say what the real problem was, but he was hesitating, considering each phrase with care and reluctance. "He's not eating enough. He's not taking in enough to sustain him. He's living off his body."

"What would we be doing," asked Poppy, speaking into a slightly horrified lull, "if we were back at home?"

"Maybe nothing different, but we'd be at home."

"Can we get someone to look at him?" asked Eric.

"Sure. I guess. It's a good idea. I doubt we'll hear anything we don't know." Adam was laying down sentences like cards. At the end of each sentence, he stopped to gauge the reactions. "But there's other things to consider."

"And what might those things be?" asked Alice.

"Well, we don't want to get into an endgame. I've seen it a hundred times. You hook someone up to an IV or something, and they take it as a sign that everyone thinks they should let go. He's not there. At least, not yet."

No one said anything. Eric got up to get Adam a Coke; Tom took this chance to get another beer. He hardly knew the man whose life they were debating, whose death they were discussing. How many times had Tom seen his grandfather over the years? Was it just ten times? Could it be as many as twenty times?

"So really. It's decided," Eric announced. "We send you guys home tomorrow and make those determinations at home when we see the effect of all this."

Poppy had been silent during most of this, the one, after all, who had less experience, who had, in some ways, less at stake. Eric was surprised to hear her speak. "But there's another thing, isn't there?"

"What?" Eric asked.

"Yes, there is," said Adam. "He wants to drive."

"That's what you keep saying, but what the hell?"

"It's this way. In some ways, we've done this trip in reverse. He has one more stop he wants to make."

Gail turned to Adam. "What's it about? Do you know? What is this stop?"

"I know, but it's not for me to say. Believe me, it is not. All I can do is what he asks."

"Can you tell us," said Gail, "at least where it is?"

"Ohio."

"Ohio?" they all repeated simultaneously. As far as anyone could remember, neither Frank, nor anyone else in the family, had ever had one single piece of commerce, personal or otherwise, with anyone in Ohio. Tom wasn't even entirely sure where Ohio was, which made Gail grimace. "I mean, Ohio, Indiana, Illinois. They all get mushed in there."

"They don't study geography in school anymore," said Gail. "Obviously."

"Poppy?" said Eric.

"What?"

"You know something here that we don't?"

"No. I don't. But I have a guess. I mean, a real good guess." She and Adam looked at each other hard, a passing of wisdom, a complicity. At this, Adam's body relaxed; for the first time since he came in, he leaned back in his chair. "But I'm not going to tell you, either. I've delivered my share of bombshells."

"What do you mean, you're not going to tell us?"

"I can't. Adam can't. I won't. I won't," she said; these "won't"s seemed directed at herself, to buttress her determination. "It's something he has to do. I don't like it, but at this point, I'm not going to stop it."

"Let's put it this way," offered Tom. "There's something in Ohio he's willing to die for."

"Is that it, Adam?" asked Eric. "Is that how you would put it?"

"Yes."

They broke up on that note, but with the agreement that a doctor would be called in tonight—surely as fine a hotel as this one had someone on call—and if they heard anything new, they'd reconvene. The others left, and Eric slumped back into the couch. Tom looked gratified to have been included in this discussion, aware that in many ways he had carried the day. But Eric could not imagine what Adam meant by "the trip in reverse." It had seemed quite otherwise: that Audrey was the portal through which this plan had to pass first, and if passage had been denied, the three of them would have returned to Maryland by the weekend, returned to live it out in Sunday visits and bulletins from Alice, to the end.

"Ohio," said Eric.

"I don't care about Ohio," said Gail. "It's Poppy who interests me. This is not like her."

"Why not?" asked Tom.

"My sister Poppy doesn't connive," Eric said. "She blurts. But this"—he shrugged—"is completely out of the blue."

"I'm proud of her," said Gail.

"So am I."

"I don't think there is to be any family meal tonight," said Gail.
"No, thank God."

"We can have room service." She spoke to Tom. "A nice last night with just us."

"You don't have to leave tomorrow," said Eric, surprised. "You can stay here a few more days, just as we planned. We'll get you a more reasonable room."

"Not a chance. I'm coming with you. Tom and I have already decided he'll come back for a visit over July Fourth. Besides," she added, "this hotel wouldn't be the same without you."

He left them to make a quick look-in at his father, but when he got to the door, the doctor, a young and rather disapproving woman, was coming out. So what's the word? he asked her, and she responded with much the same observations and choices that Adam had already given them. "No one," she said baldly, "is talking about him getting better, are they?"

"No. I don't suppose anyone is."

"He's still lucid," she said. "And he wants to make this trip. There's no real reason not to let him." All of this she was saying in an accusatory manner; first implying that they had behaved irresponsibly in letting him do this at all, and then, with this last phrase, scolding them for even considering denying a last wish to a man who was slipping quietly away.

He went into the room, but his father was worn out from the effort of the doctor's call; surely he'd found her as graceless as Eric did. Eric took his hand and leaned over him. "Okay, you old bastard," he said. "You'll get your trip to Ohio."

"Good. Good." It was faint, not much more than breath.

"I love you," said Eric.

"I love you, too."

ELEVEN

So. Back now, from the farthest reach west, a flight back across the plains, leaving a swirl of dust, a few tread marks, fragments of talk. What was that? a farmer on a tractor asks himself, catching only a whirlwind of blue on the horizon to his left. A family on the move, with appointments to keep.

At last, this immense vehicle was being asked to perform up to its capacity. "Pack it however you like, Eric," said Alice, who then proceeded to direct him on every piece. Eric hadn't known that Poppy was on board for this final leg, but she said, "Might as well get us all in one car wreck," depositing her knapsack on top of the pile. "No squabbling over the family silver that way," said Eric. Then Adam went up to get Frank, brought him with his good arm firmly in his grasp.

Frank did not look too bad; Eric had seen plenty of people on the subway who looked more frail, going to work. And then Tom rounded the corner at a lope, his backpack bouncing from side to side, a slightly worried I'm-late gait with a panting entrance. He looked as if he had just woken up, but he was wearing a full smile.

Eric looked over at his father, expecting him to show pleasure at this full complement of family members in the car, but there was a small blush of trouble on Frank's face. He peered intently into the car. He was counting places, Eric suddenly realized, seven people for a car that could carry nine; no sweat, and still plenty of room for Frank to stretch out in the front seat. Eric began to point this out to his father, but the concern, so swift in onset, had passed.

"Granddad," said Tom. "How are you doing?"

"Good. Good."

"Been having fun with the family?"

Frank made his ironic sneer at everybody: a show of denial, a joke. "Tratter," he said.

Tom appealed to Eric.

"Torture," Eric said. He turned to Frank. "The question is, are we torturing you, or are you torturing us?"

"Both. Family."

The three women filed into the third seat while Adam helped Frank up to the front. Perhaps they would pull this off; perhaps he would survive this trip. Frank settled into the seat and reached across his body with his good hand to pull the door shut by the frame, a procedure that always made Eric wince, the vision of that hand being crushed. This time, Frank couldn't do it. He tried a second time to dislodge the door, and then gave up. He slumped back, defeated. Three days ago he had still been able to do this.

"Comfy?" asked Eric lightly, when Adam had shut it for him.

"Weak," he answered, but he wasn't admitting that he felt weak; it was a word he used as an insult, as in "weakling," a character trait. He had some humor still: the old jokes and ironies were still pumping. As if to prove this further to Eric, he turned to look back at the three women. "Hen party," he said. "Squawk. Squawk."

"Don't be mean, Frank," Gail replied. "We know you want to be back here with us, anyway."

"He's just trying to calculate whether we have too much weight in the back. Maybe Alice and I should switch places, you know, to balance things better."

"Very funny, Eric," said Alice.

Adam and Tom climbed into the middle. The hotel doorman had gaped at the Maryland plates when Eric brought the car around, a great blue heron so far from its mate and its waterway. He closed the door with a dubious finality, as if he were sealing astronauts in a capsule. "Safe home, friends," he said through the open window to Frank and Eric.

"A sweet man," said Frank, as they pulled away. "Lovely man."

"Yes. The kindness of strangers. He really seemed to mean it."

"And Tom," said Frank.

"Yes, a surprise the two of them cooked up. It's okay, right, that he's here?"

"Good. Good."

Adam reached forward to pass a liter bottle of spring water to Frank. "I want that gone by lunch, Mr. Frank."

"Gak."

It was an easy start, the opposite way through the rush hour, and remarkably soon they were cutting through the wildness of the mountains on the wide expanse of Route 80. They'd ride this road practically all the way home, depending on where in Ohio the detour took them. Frank had fallen asleep quite soon, but within an hour he was restlessly turning in his seat, trying to find a comfortable position, a place to deposit the two limbs that could do him no service but remained attached, useless painful appendages. "Goddamn," he said loudly, mostly in his sleep. Adam leaned forward and slid a pillow between his head and the door, and that seemed to help a little. The conversation in the car had been stilled. Eric tried to keep his attention on the road; no one said this was going to be easy. No one said what they were doing wasn't wrong by every standard but one: his father's wishes. Eric tried for a few miles to take consolation from that sour doctor's analysis of the situation. Frank now seemed to be dropping fully into sleep, but in just a few minutes he was back at it. His glasses were falling down his nose. Adam leaned forward again to adjust the pillow, and this time Frank grabbed it out of his hand and flung it viciously toward Eric. "No. No," Frank bellowed, as Eric fended off the pillow, the car taking a swerve.

"Now, Mr. Frank. Settle down."

Frank turned to Adam, a perplexed raising of the brow; his discomfort, his outburst, was now completely gone. To Eric it seemed that things were darting at his father now, bits of discomfort, come and gone in a second; a concern lasting only a heartbeat or two. Time was slowing in places, speeding up drastically in others. He caught the eyes of his passengers in the rearview mirror one by one: everyone was breathing easier, but of course, nothing had happened. They were laboratory animals here: somewhere above them the behavioral scientists were peering at them, making notes on a clipboard.

"Intense," said Tom.

There were no more incidents that day, as they wound down from Denver, back toward the plains, ears popping, the car's power slowly reviving after the sluggishness in the thin air. The drill was as before, with frequent stops, changes of drivers, Alice poking along at an inattentive fifty-five, which drove Eric crazy, and then Gail, taking the wheel because she asked for it, making up the lost time doing almost ninety, which made Tom nervous— her driving had been scaring him out of his wits since he was two years old, and she'd never before had control of a vehicle that weighed over three tons.

They had settled into a motel in Iowa, one in this now endless supply of structures seemingly airlifted, complete with linen and bath supplies, to a likely spot along these interstate corridors of commerce. They ate a meal in a café just off the lobby, with every-one watching anxiously as Frank ate a few forkfuls of scrambled eggs. Eric and Gail settled in, and then Tom dropped by to watch television with them, and Eric went to get drinks. He ran into Adam at the Coke machine in a breezeway outside the laundry. It was a chilly night, with a purple sky. "Day one," said Eric. "Four hundred and sixty miles down. One thousand nine hundred and eight to go." Adam nodded.

"It's a hell of a long way."

"That it is."

"He's going to make it, right?"

"He'll make it."

"But what if something starts to happen? Will we know?"

"For people like Frank, death is a choice. I've seen it happen again and again at the nursing home."

"And he hasn't made that choice?"

"Of course not. He's got stuff to do."

The next two days were the same. They were on the plains now, but on the northern track, where the lands rolled, and were green and fertile. Eric did not take a turn at the wheel the second day, a relief in more ways than one. He'd noticed that they were all vying a bit for a spot in back, away from anxious watch in the front seat, away from Adam's post in the middle, safely out of the fray.

Eric had to kick Poppy out of the back in the afternoon, because she had yet to surrender the place willingly. Up ahead, they could see Frank's head lolling in sleep, or turning slowly into the sights, and Eric could hardly imagine what he was saying to himself during these long hours, the diminishing miles between himself and this last stop, and beyond. Eric wondered what he was thinking about his body, this durable but flawed companion during his years on this earth: what were the new sensations, the ones like the lump in the cancer scare, or worse, that seem to be the first entry of one's fate; what did his stomach feel like, so empty of food; did it all hurt, this business of winding down, or was there a gratefulness, like bidding old friends good-bye. Maybe Adam knew the answers to some of these questions, words in a textbook, or real life from nursing, but Eric didn't think a text was what he needed. He could ask his father directly, already had, but the brief answers were really nothing more than an acknowledgment of the question. He said, "Dunnow," but Eric believed he did know, but wasn't in a mood to share.

In the backseat they whispered for some miles about the stop ahead, but did not speculate very much on who or what it was. Eric recalled well enough—had been recalling it since they left Houston—his mother's warning that one of the stops might be difficult for him. This was it, and there was only one possible answer, but if anyone else but Eric suspected it, no one volunteered to put it into words. Instead, they fixed on Ohio. The stop was in Columbus, "the capital of Ohio, as Tom undoubtedly knows," growled Eric, and Adam had detailed directions. A convenient jump off the highway. If their forward progress held, they'd arrive there about midday, on the third day after leaving Denver. Eric tried to picture Ohio, flat, industrial, populous, one of the Great Lakes to the north.

"Aren't there a lot of Polish people in Ohio?" asked Alice. "Don't they make a lot of sausages?"

"That's Wisconsin, and they're German," said Eric.

At night, Gail and Eric crawled into bed, tired, a little anxious. They did not make love during these nights; there was nothing erotic about these roadside motel rooms, small cubicles of homelessness. But they lay side by side and rehashed the day's events. Eric didn't want to be anywhere but here, anonymous almost to himself, broken from his own past and from the more recent events in their marriage. Free: the right place to start over by one's own free will. A vacation to a sunny spot is supposed to do that, children farmed out to friends or grandparents while the couple sits on the beach, makes love in the afternoons, and lounges in their bathrobes on their balconies, scenes from the travel section. Gail and Eric had never taken such a vacation, and maybe they should have done so on an annual basis, but it did not seem that anything would be as complete as this trip, perhaps a father's last gift, or sacrifice to his children. It seemed easy on these sterile pillows, with a man paying out the last lines of his life just a room or two away, to be true, and kind. The beginning, the beginning of a second chance, or fifth, or tenth, but there was nothing so wrong here, not, at least, in this motel room, and not even outside, in the world. Eric plumped his pillow, and settled gratefully back into the hum of air conditioners and traffic noise.

Up and down this low shed of rooms were all the people who were dear to him. He could picture Tom stretched out, sleeping as he always had with his head back and his mouth wide open. Alice was there, matronly yet unsure of the prospects for her soul. Why would she be fearful, with all her promises made and kept? Eric did not want to think of any of his family as lonely, and none of them were, at this moment anyway. It's time, is it not occasionally, to take stock of one's blessings, simply to note how it feels. Feels to be *here*. Isn't that all it takes to be redeemed?

In the morning, Adam pounded on their door and announced it was D-day. Gail and Eric woke up in each other's arms. When Eric emerged, Adam was already sitting in the car with the road atlas open on his lap, and was comparing a long list of directions in his steno pad with the large-scale insert of Columbus. Poppy was sitting beside him, and Eric could see her trying to peer past his elbow for hints, but the lines seemed to be just directions, the nearly illegible kind scribbled as one cradles a telephone receiver in a shoulder.

Columbus is one of those spread-out Midwestern cities, flat and unforgiving, featureless to strangers. In the three hours it took to enter the environs, Frank had not spoken the words everyone was straining to hear; he had not spoken at all. He seemed frozen in his seat. Poppy was at the wheel, prolonging the pressure with her excruciatingly precise and safe driving. It was the tensest hours Eric had ever spent—nothing in business could compare; more comparable, perhaps, would be a wait for medical test results for yourself or someone you loved.

"South on Twenty-seven," Adam said. A long pause, six pairs of eyes—all except for Frank's—straining to catch a road sign. "It must be up here somewhere. Look for a florist shop with a Santa Claus on the roof."

"A Santa Claus?"

"That's what he said."

So it was a man; at least, it had been a man giving Adam the directions. Eric glanced back at Gail; so much for her theory that it was an old lover; so much for a deathbed wedding.

Eric put his hands on the seat back ahead of him and pulled forward to Frank's ear. "Are you okay?" he asked. Frank took a hand with desperate pressure. "It'll be okay," answered Eric.

"My son," said Frank.

"Yes. I'm here. We're all here."

"My son."

"Yes," Eric continued, because he didn't know what else to do. "It's good to have a son, even if it's me."

"Eric," said Poppy: a warning. A warning of what?

"Turn right up here, Poppy. Oak Street." They were in a neighborhood of small houses, capes and bungalows on tiny lots, many with chain-link fences around the yards, with a 7-Eleven or some local market on nearly every corner.

"Listen to what he said." Poppy swiveled around quickly to make sure he had.

My son, thought Eric. And then he knew, for certain, what he had been suspecting for the past few days. A son: his father's fourth child. There was no sudden jolt of recognition, just the first stage of settling into knowledge. It was a unique kind of discovery: something that at once had nothing whatsoever to do with him, and involved his whole being right down to his genes. It was a missing link in a chain that still seemed unbroken. Jesus *fucking* Christ. His eyes darted around the car, looking for similar recognition on the faces of the others, but they hadn't figured it out yet. But still the big Ford proceeded, and like a drumbeat, Adam's directions continued.

"This is the hard part," said Adam. "We have to look for a light purple house with red shutters. On the corner. The street isn't marked."

"Light purple and red. How Midwestern," said Alice.

"The fifth house after the sharp right," said Adam.

"What is it?" asked Gail.

Eric turned, and now he knew there was the beginning of an involuntary smile on his face, a line of wonder and the release provided by a peculiarly baffling confirmation. A 2-plus-2 that any fool could have figured out. Even poor old Mike Billings had probably figured it out: *What did she have on him?* Eric knew who the mother was. A certainty, really, if anyone had ever stopped to consider it, and why had they never?

Eric turned completely around to look at the faces in the backseat, Gail, Tom, and Alice. "Did you hear what he said?" Eric asked.

Alice shook her head.

"It's his son," said Gail.

Alice's face went blank, and then, as Eric watched, it screwed into a soundless howl, her eyes black. Finally, under her breath not because she had any interest in sparing her father's feelings, but because it was all she could accomplish: "Why, that bastard." Gail took her hand, and Alice ripped it back from her.

"This is it," said Adam. "The green one. Number fourteen."

"How could you do this?" Alice yelled as loud as she could. "How could you do this to us, when we tried so hard?" It echoed in this tin enclosure. Frank still stared straight ahead, the accused not meeting the jury's eyes.

"Alice. Not now, for God's sake."

"What do you mean, 'Not now.' Not now? When, then? When?"

Poppy pulled the car to the curb and turned off the engine. No one moved, except for Alice, who was pounding her fists against her thighs. The little green house looked sealed tight, its curtains drawn, as if no one could possibly be home, as if those inside wanted it to seem that way. Parked in front of the freestanding garage was an old Datsun, a 240Z, a man's project, a folly, and just visible around the back was a swing set, a new one, with gay yellow and red spirals on the poles. A life was there, a family and a new brother, the eighth passenger. Eric waited for his father to move, but Frank seemed as frozen as the rest of them, as if he'd never suspected this child of his might live in such a modest working-class neighborhood. Or perhaps he was simply waiting for help.

"Eric," said Adam. "I think it's up to you. One last time." A small expression of sympathy and support. There seemed to have been no strategizing this time.

"Yeh," Eric said. "Dad?"

He answered in a high squeak. "Good. Good. Time."

In the house, a hand brushed the curtain aside, just as another hand—Audrey's—had done what seemed like months ago in Birmingham.

"Dad?" said Tom. "What now?"

"Yes," said Eric to Tom. "Come with me. I need you."

The two of them walked up the concrete pathway. A woman, a young woman in jeans with her shirttails out, opened the door as they approached. She was pretty, with a kind mouth, but her eyes were harried, suspicious, angry. She stood squarely at the edge of her little stoop to indicate that there was no reason and no way they were coming into her house. "He's getting ready," she said.

Eric wanted to say something, but the only thing that came to mind was to introduce Tom. "This is my son, Tom," he said.

"Huh," she said. She went back in the house, and from inside they could hear, though Eric wished they couldn't, the negotiations of his parting. "You don't have to do this," she said in anger. The response, in a tone of gratefulness: "I know. Thank you. I love you." Her parting "Call me," then the interruption of a small voice, maybe two or three: "What is it, Daddy?"

What to look at first, meeting a half brother for the first time? Eric had once told Gail that any time two men meet, the first thing they wonder is whether they can take this guy out, if necessary. He didn't think that. He noticed, instead, how completely different this brother looked from himself, Alice, and Poppy, and yet he had never before believed that the three of them shared much in the way of looks. But still, this man was different, with wavy brown hair, freckled skin, high cheekbones, and green eyes. He looked— this came to Eric at that moment—Slavic: his mother's child, perhaps all the more because he was uniquely hers, and hers alone, as if single unwed motherhood worked its way onto the child's body. His mouth was open, as if he might speak. He was carrying a small suitcase, not much more than a carry-on. Through the open collar of his white shirt Eric could see the dull shine of a silver chain, a Saint Christopher medal, patron saint of travelers.

The brother spoke first. "Are you Adam?" he asked Tom.

"I'm Tom."

"My son," said Eric. "I'm Eric."

The brother made it clear that he had figured that much out for himself, but still, he did not introduce himself. Why would he think it was necessary: these two had come to his door, come into his life; behind them was a car full of people who had driven thousands of miles to be here; among these people was his father. How could it be necessary to introduce oneself in such a situation? How could one not be known? On the doormat, at his feet, was written "Welcome to the Podestas'." His wife had been lurking behind, holding the storm door.

"I wish I knew what to say," said Eric.

The wife let out a derisive snort. "Then why don't you just leave?"

"Babes," said the brother, patiently, but Eric could tell that he was grateful for her fierce advocacy; this was maybe a good wife and a good marriage.

"I'm sorry," said Eric, to her.

"How is he?" said the man, the brother, making at last a reference to the person who was the father of them both. It was information he was after, not news; Adam must have warned him that Frank was not well.

"Holding up, I guess. We've been on the road for much too long." Another snort from the wife. "I've got to tell you, everyone is a little stunned." Even as he spoke it, this word "everyone" seemed freighted with meaning to Eric. Whose everyone was he referring to? Was it arrogance to assume this *everyone*? Because it wasn't everyone that was stunned, it was *the rest of us*. But who knew anything for certain here? Eric didn't even know if his brother knew anything at all about his shadow family. Eric couldn't be sure whether this man had ever before—before a few days ago—known his father's name.

The man nodded; his mind was on other things than the meaning and implication of words. For the first time, his face showed his fear. He didn't want to leave his wife's side, or the child behind her in the hallway, who had begun to fuss. This man needed help taking the next step, help that his young family could not give, and Eric at last could behold this younger man as a person coming face-to-face with the story of his birth, and Eric's heart began to flow out to him. "I want you to know that you are welcome. These are good people, my sisters, Adam. Our father, even though he has caused hurt and trouble to all of us over the years. He isn't going to live much longer. He can't really talk. Do you know that? This whole trip"—Eric was speaking without pause, almost as if he were engaged in one of his monologues with Frank—"has been about us, his children. That's all of us." Eric glanced at the wife, whose expression had begun to soften. "I can't imagine what this means to either of you, and I'm sorry for the pain we must be causing. I'll do anything, I swear, to make this easier for you, even fun, if that's possible. Whatever you want to happen, it can begin now."

These words helped, and at last there was motion, the man reaching for the sport coat his wife held in her hands, a kiss, and the first steps down the path. Five faces stared out at them from the car, but the only one that really mattered was Frank's, and there it was: joy. He had lived long enough for this to happen. He was beaming, and crying, fumbling with the door handle with his good hand, and as soon as the door popped, the name came out. "Anthony. Anthony."

Anthony walked up to him, shook his hand through the partly opened door. "Hello, Frank," he said. The greeting was wary, but familiar: this was not the first time they had seen each other.

Eric opened the back door and leaned in. "Okay," he said, looking at Alice but speaking to them all. "This is the way it goes." He had planned to give a pep talk, and seating instructions, but when he opened his mouth, no ideas came. It was Adam who spoke.

"Frank, Anthony, and Gail in the back. Me and Alice in the middle. Eric, Tom, and Poppy in front."

Alice said nothing and no one else complained. They extricated themselves from their seats, and found themselves standing around the car like tourists released from a bus. Anthony remained a few paces away. Gail and Poppy both went forward to introduce themselves, to give him their names, while Eric looked for Adam to help Frank get in the wayback. But Adam had broken off, had gone up to the house, and was talking to Anthony's wife. He was giving her a sheet from his pad, telephone numbers, where they might be stopping that night; whatever it was he was giving her, she was regarding him in a friendly manner with the little boy wound around her legs like a vine: Adam was along for the logistics, a hired hand and a neutral party; he wasn't part of this.

"You next, Anthony," said Eric, calling him over. He forced a cheery note into it: *Welcome to the nuthouse; time to join the screwy Alwins; what an expedition!*

"It's okay," said Anthony on the way in: *You don't have to perform for me.*

"I have to go to the bathroom."

It was Alice, the first words she had spoken. Eric had kept an eye on her the whole time as she paced off at the far end of the car, once spinning around completely as she wrestled with her private conversation. Now she headed for the house, toward Adam and Anthony's wife, paused only to ask permission. Her body seemed contorted. Poppy came to his side.

"Is she all right?"

"I don't know."

Frank and Anthony were now seated side by side in the back. They were trying to talk, and Eric heard his father's "Good, good," and he heard his own name, mangled as always. Frank was happy, but whether it was simply because he was in Anthony's presence, or because he was relieved to have this moment over, Eric could not guess. Both, surely. From the pauses and delays in their muffled conversation, he knew that Anthony was having trouble understanding the words, the perfect and incontrovertible measure of his, or anyone's, familiarity with Frank. If Eric had to guess, he would put Anthony's skill somewhat above Tom's, almost on a par with Gail's.

"Alice is taking a long time," said Poppy.

She was. In fact, both Adam and Anthony's wife had gone inside, and still there was no movement.

"You better go check," said Poppy. "I would, but she'll just yell at me."

He found Adam and the woman in the kitchen. It was a nice

house inside, better furnished than the exterior would suggest. They had made their home on the inside, within a privacy that did not concern itself much with what other people thought. As Eric passed by the small living room, he was struck by the traditional look, some dark mahogany pieces and a wingback chair, the look of the East and of old money. The kitchen was bright and new, with a refrigerator gaily dressed in the child's artwork. The boy was there with Adam and his mother, and though he had a slightly apprehensive look on his face when Eric came in, he seemed a sweet and industrious child, building a structure out of Duplos on the kitchen table. He seemed to have the trusting soul one would expect from a happy home. He was, Eric suddenly realized, a half-nephew, a half-cousin to Tom, but a full and complete grandchild of his father.

Adam and the woman were in front of the small door that must have led to the bathroom. "I'm sorry to have barged in again," said Eric, but she was not angry anymore. Her face had opened with concern for the stranger who had barricaded herself in her house.

"Have you knocked?" asked Eric. They had, and Alice hadn't answered. They both stepped back to let Eric try.

"Alice?" No answer. "Alice, please?"

"I can't," she said finally.

"Can't what?"

"Can't do it, Eric. I can't."

"Come here, Skippy," said the woman to the boy as she and Adam both backed out of the room. "We'll let them talk."

Eric watched them go. "I know it's hard," said Eric. "It's hard for everyone."

Again she didn't answer. Obviously, it was harder for her than for everyone.

"Please come out. It's crazy to hole up in a bathroom, for God's sake."

"That's what crazy people do. They spend lots of time in bathrooms."

"Oh, stop this bullshit. You're the sanest person in this group. Maybe that's why you're in there, and we aren't."

The wife came back in, holding up one finger to indicate she'd only be a minute. She went to her refrigerator and pulled out a few soft drinks and a carton of orange juice. She gathered the drinks on a tray with a few plastic cups, added a box of Oreos, and then, as a last precaution, shoveled a handful of the Duplos around the edges of the snacks.

"Maybe you just feel crazy because we're getting to the bottom of this. We're at the bottom now. The core of it."

"Who says?" He heard the rattle of the toilet paper holder as she pulled off a piece and blew her nose.

"Anthony's the missing piece. What is he, thirty, maybe? It must have been after Mom, and before Marjorie, whatever the hell that means. You can't fault Anthony for anything that happened to you."

"I don't fault him for anything. How could I?"

No, Alice's quarrel was not with him. Eric looked down the corridor and through the front door, and they were all having a snack, the tray perched high on the hood of the car. A wave of anger rose in Eric's chest. "Anthony, his wife—they're the people who should be freaking out now, not you."

The silence, this time, seemed to indicate some contrition.

"Come out, damn it, or I'll knock down the door. I'll fucking splinter it and wouldn't that be a nice little memento for us to leave behind for this nice little family?" He stood back, almost ready to charge, when he heard the lock click, and the knob turn, and she walked out.

She looked as he expected: red eyes, tangled hair, a stream of toilet paper flowing from her hand. She sat down at the table.

"What are they doing?" she asked.

"They're having juice and cookies. Look for yourself." She leaned far enough forward to see the scene outside.

"How could he do this?"

"Bad birth control, I guess."

"I don't care about that, but how could he keep it from me?"

"Just from you?"

"Yes, damn it, from me. I was there for him and with him and he lied right to my face."

"Well, he's trying to make amends now. We all are."

"How could he tell me like this?"

"I don't know. He just did. Maybe he didn't trust himself to do it at all, if it wasn't all the way, like this."

"Why do it at all?"

Eric took a breath. Anger would not do at this moment, but neither would selfishness. "Maybe for Anthony."

"I do everything for him. You don't know what I do for him. I'm just dumb, pathetic Alice: Wind her up and she'll run into another wall. How could he keep this from me?"

"Is that really the point?"

"I trusted him. I was the last person who trusted him. I was the last person on earth who believed him."

"Yes, and now that's over. That was false trust, something you persisted in because you love him. Because you were the last one to fall, you are the first one to build it anew."

"But it was a lie."

"No. It wasn't. It was as much as he let go at the time. Now he can go all the way."

She put both her hands to her face, pinching her nose. She ran her fingers through her hair, felt the tangles; no doubt she was wishing she carried her satchel everywhere, like Poppy. "I just was not ready for this."

"You should have been. We all should have been. It's the only thing that makes sense, and in the end, everything makes sense. Even Dad. You said Poppy's letter saved him, but you were only half right. This is the other half. This puts everything in his life together. One life. One man. One family, I guess. If that isn't being saved, I don't know what is."

She made another small effort to peer around the doorway. "What's he doing?"

"What he always does. He's trying to talk. Anthony seems to like him okay. Doesn't that mean anything?"

"I suppose."

"He's dying, damn it, and he was going to come here to see Anthony if it killed him. He's opening the door for us. All four of us. All we have to do is walk through it." He took her hand. "He obviously had confessions to make to everyone, each one of us with some kind of loose end. And, Alice, my dear beloved big sister Alice, with this second family of his he betrayed you. You especially, keeper of the family. This confession is to you. If there's any kind of forgiveness he's seeking, it has to come from you."

They were back up on the interstate in a few minutes. The juice-

and-cookie break had been a small miracle, a new start built upon a welcome nourishment of glucose and carbohydrates. Eric remembered how quickly Tom could revive from abject despair to cheerfulness with food; when he was little, it was as if he were the Visible Human at the science museum, and one could watch the enzymes run through his veins to his head. Anthony's wife's name was Debbie, and she had never met Frank, but whatever she might have dreamed of saying to him over the years, she could not be cruel to him now. Gail whispered all this to Eric as they boarded. Women could always like Frank, those eyes, and the special way they sparkled around the pretty ones, and that was because they were all pretty for him, all female, the smooth cheeks, the small hands, the hair: Frank heard the music of all these attributes; he gloried in women, his own daughters, his ex- and late wives, the wives of his sons, the girls in the street, and the ladies of the promenade. He had loved many people at the same time.

And he had loved all his children, all four of them, imperfectly, yet with his heart. Alice had not spoken to him when she returned, but she was here, with them, and no one, least of all Frank, could doubt her constancy. They were all together, Frank's progeny at last united. Eric kept glancing back at Frank through the rearview mirror, and Frank's face was radiant. He'd done it, pulled it off. He and Adam had obviously worked all this out in advance. *In some ways, we have done this trip in reverse.* Frank had his lost son, Anthony, at his side, thigh rubbing against thigh, the momentary certainty of his presence; and he had his lost daughter, Poppy, in the car, the one whose pain he could trust and whose forgiveness she seemed at last to be offering, because she had sought forgiveness for herself; and he had Alice—he would always have Alice—the one who would pick out his burial suit and castigate the funeral home for any second's delay in the proceedings, and then, if God was willing, get on with her own life; and he had Eric. Eric could not assign himself a particular dynamic of loss and love in his father's life. Only in his own. His own gratefulness for the truths that might have been revealed to him, and the plans he had to make honest and decent use of them. So maybe Eric's role was simply to do what he was now doing: driving. Just to be the driver. But if that's what it was, then Eric would do a good job of it, guiding this great beast of a car carefully toward home.

TWELVE

Frank died a month after they got home. Alice was there, and Adam. He had spent a week in bed since the return, but he was eating and drinking a little, conversing happily with Anthony and Poppy before they left. Life had seemed to resume its old rhythms, and he had not seemed to be even close to in extremis until the night nurse heard the change in his breathing during the early morning hours; she called Adam and Alice, and the breathing stopped peacefully with both of them beside him. No last tortured phrases, just—if Alice had perceived it right—a content farewell flicker in his eyes, a darting of the eyebrows that might even have seemed impish. They all knew he was pleased with the way things had turned out, and the end was what Adam had predicted, an infinite mercy from a body that had shown him few mercies in the last years of his life.

Frank had dictated, at an earlier time, detailed funeral instructions on one of Adam's steno pads—these were some of the pages Adam had excised before handing over the week's record for Eric's inspection—and most of them seemed predicated on what had been done and learned on the trip. Eric supposed that if any stop on his itinerary had failed miserably, or if going forward was deemed impossible for any reason, he would have come back and amended the plans. Or perhaps he had stipulated multiple plans, with Adam charged to bring out only the set that fit the circumstances.

As it was, Adam brought out instructions about cremation, and a memorial service, including the Navy Hymn, and a prayer of thanksgiving that Frank had dictated for being reunited at the end with the people he loved and whose forgiveness had made such a sweet death possible. But no eulogies, please, and the stated desire that neither Poppy nor Anthony need return for the memorial, since they had so recently visited with him when it counted most. Neither did return, and that made the funeral party small, since other instructions included a guest list, stripped of almost all busybodies and former associates, with the not surprising and finally deserved exception of Mike Billings and wife. Political if not personal loyalty, it seemed, counted right to the Gates of the Resurrection.

The service he requested included the saying of the Apostles' Creed, which surprised Eric, who had assumed that the Order of the Burial of the Dead in the Book of Common Prayer would specify the more government-inspected Nicene Creed. "Makes sense," whispered Gail back to him in the pew, though Eric did not grasp the theological nuances and historical controversies. Still, Eric had grown up saying the Apostles' Creed in Morning Prayer and as usual, usual at least for his spotty churchgoing as an adult, he grappled with the professions of faith at the conclusion. *I believe in the Holy Ghost:* Well, that could work, thought Eric, a transcendental presence of some sort that could reside at the edges and margins of waking reality. Weird things did happen in those old family houses of the Eastern Shore, hauntings and sightings of all sorts of residual beings: the old retriever still curled up in her favorite corner by the radiator, the child crying on the third floor. Eric had always liked the Holy Ghost, a controversial member of the Trinity, a nighttime visitor to maidens' beds, even after the new prayer book changed his name to the less-pungent "Holy Spirit." *The holy catholic church*. Yes, catholic—the lowercase "c"—was good; it was good to be universal at times like this, and not some remote enclave that could easily be overlooked. *The communion of saints*. A little more difficult now, but let's give that one the home-field advantage: if saints really existed, then they could commune, if they damn well wanted. *The forgiveness of sins.* No need to debate that; in fact, if there was a reason, holy or otherwise, for religion to exist, it was this promise. *The resurrection of the body.* Okay, okay: the bedraggled band needed a miracle at this darkest hour, and if there was some funny business in the cave—a tunnel out the back, a bribed guard or two—then who could allege that it had caused real harm?

And then there was the big one, *life everlasting.* Hour after hour, week after week, Christians all over the world profess to believe this, or at least to *look for it,* in the words of the other creed. Lacks the scientific illogicality of the resurrection of the body, but it is the largest claim of all. As Eric sat in his pew in Frank's tiny, beloved St. Luke's, he could only wonder whether his father would want such a thing, and why. He hadn't been run over by a truck, with only an instant of reflection; he'd seen his death coming for years. Frank had, in his own way, taken such relish in his endgame; it is, after all, the endings of things—stories, football games, college careers, lives—that give them meaning and sanction. Frank had *looked for* his end; had seemed, when the time came, to will it. He would want no continuation of what life had been for him since his strokes, possibly even since his political disgrace; he'd lived through enough of those years to reclaim the attentions of all four of his children, to win some sort of absolution from his first wife, to see—Eric thought back to the trip to recall any particularly memorable sights, but all he could think of was the aborted side trip to the French Quarter of New Orleans—well, to see enough of the world to know he had been there. No more of any of that was needed.

So life everlasting, whether any living person believed in it or not, was probably not necessary. Not, at least, to Senator Frank Alwin. But as Eric continued to think about these things in the days and weeks after the funeral—a busy time: Tom's relocation back east to an apartment in Brooklyn; a marriage to begin, if not anew, then at least afresh; a business to reconstruct; a house to put on the market; mercies and gifts to understand—he knew that there were always unfinished bits of living here and there, certain things his father would have liked to do if time or health had permitted, and Eric began to believe that if there were a merciful construct in the nature of being, it might include not life everlasting, but a final visit, twenty-four hours to put things to rights, a small dividend, a coda, a cadenza to be played exactly as the musician wanted. It seemed, as Eric recalled generally, that this sort of mopping up was what Jesus was up to when he himself enjoyed such a similar, documented reprieve.

One evening at home Eric looked through Gail's bookshelf for a Bible, came upon a version with the words of Christ in red, and he flipped through the Gospels and Acts. Yes it did seem that Jesus, as much as anything, was using his time to set things right: a visit of thanks to Mary Magdalene; a chance to scare the bejeezus out of Thomas—fun, no doubt; a last picnic at the Sea of Tiberias with old friends—"Please pass the meat," he said; and, of course, his final revelation to Paul on the road to Damascus. After that, two thousand years of silence.

"Got religion?" Gail had spied him through the open door of her study.

"Just checking on the evidence of extraterrestrial intelligence."

"The afterlife?" She was pleased with him. "But be careful. Most of the times that Jesus himself was asked about it, he dodged the question into metaphor."

"A typical Episcopalian," said Eric.

"And you," she asked, "since you're not anything at all?"

"Well. It's a pretty good metaphor, isn't it?"

And that was where he left it for the moment. He was busy with his more worldly matters. The morning after the three of them returned to Summit—Tom disappeared into his old room as if he had never left, but he seemed happy to be back, at least for a visit—Eric headed off to work. It was as if he had never left: the grimy must of the train, the clattering discomfort of the subway, three blocks of heedless Manhattan streets, the entrance to the building that, on her only visit, Alice had pronounced "most unprepossessing." He walked slowly up the two flights to their floor, hesitated at the door to reflect on what demons awaited him, wondering who of his reduced band would greet him. Liv and Lilly and the rest of the "Fruits"—as Paul Ramirez had taken to calling them—had been on track to move out a week earlier, relocating so that they might "focus all their energies" on persuading young actives to drink all-natural, electrolyte-replacing fruit juice after a strenuous session on the treadmill. It was for the better, if that was what they wanted. The firm would continue, with perhaps the old model as its guide: small-time, but fun, and principled, a disseminator of honest information, source of an occasional lightness for the readers and viewers.

When he opened the door of the office that day the sign still read "Alwin + Warren." He'd have to get that changed: they needed a new identity, something creative, with no more surnames, something more collaborative in spirit. The reception area, with its copies of *AdWeek, Fortune,* and *Graphis,* was still laid out for visitors, the desk with its telephones, bins of mail. No ragged edges, no wires dangling where pieces of electronics had once sat, no clean square absences on the walls where posters had hung, no pieces of built-in furniture excised as if Liv had wandered through the place with a Sawzall. It was as if his longtime business partner had simply decamped and left behind everything they shared, which left Eric a little sad and hurt. Sad for him and Liv both, the time they had shared, hurt that it mattered so little in the end.

He was early; the place seemed deserted, but someone had turned on the lights, and the coffee machine had been on long enough to emit the customary aroma. In years past, Lilly might have done this, but hers was the first office after the reception area, and it was empty, cleaned out. That much had happened. An end, an end to all that. From the men's room, he heard the sound of the shower running. Six years ago, when they were looking for new space, Liv's primary reason for selecting this building was that it had a shower, as if he expected to start jogging to work in the morning from the Upper West Side. When they had moved in, Liv promulgated a set of rules governing the use of this shower—NO TOILETRIES, SHAMPOOS, OR FLIP-FLOPS LEFT BEHIND—and he had devised a discreet signage system, rather like the old codes for telling your college roommate to get lost, so that women could use it without fear of being interrupted. As far as Eric could recall, the shower had been used about twice before becoming what it was now: a storage space for copier paper, a lost-and-found for garments left behind by clients.

He poked his head in the door. "Man or woman?" he yelled.

A snort came out, a male sound.

"Hi!" Eric yelled again. "It's Eric."

"Fuck that. It's Meriwether Lewis back from the Coast."

"Liv?"

The shower went off and a hairy arm reached out for a towel. There was shaving gear—travel-sized, disposable—on the counter above the sink, and draped over the trash can were a pair of jeans, a blazer, a worn white shirt. Tassel loafers on the floor; no socks.

"What are you doing here? You were supposed to be gone. Lilly's office is empty."

Liv pulled the curtain aside and stepped out, towel around his thick middle. He stared at Eric for a moment with a hostility that seemed less ironic than usual. "Lilly went back to Minnesota. Moved out. Went back home to be with the cows."

"She quit? What about FruitOut?"

"Oh, man. Where you been?"

"You know goddamn well where I've been. What's going on? What are you doing dressing here?"

"I slept here. Went out and got hammered last night. Couldn't find the key to the flat. This was the best I could do."

Eric could think of nothing more to say, but he stood there with the door propped against his foot until Liv asked if he could shave and dress in private.

Eric left him, checked in at the disarray in Liv's office, the unmistakably squalid look of a couch having been slept on alone, the old raincoat that had served as a blanket on the floor. He went into his own office. His desk was thick with work: two piles of pink phone messages, one pile—the thicker, messier one—marked "answered" in Paul Ramirez's hand. There was a stack of boards— art for new campaigns, storyboards, mechanicals—leaning against the wall. Proposals ready for his review and signature. Letters marked "personal." Something from the IRS. A file of résumés. An impossible and completely defeating sight, but a better sight than a clean desktop. He had just started the first tentative pokings when Liv came in.

"Welcome back," he said. He pushed aside the pile of newspapers on the couch and sat down heavily. "Jesus," he said. "I'd forgotten what it feels like to be really hung over."

Eric waited for him to speak.

"The deal's blown up," he said finally.

"FruitOut?"

"Yes, FruitOut. What other deal is there? A fucking horror show. See, the problem was the product."

"What's wrong with the product? It's just fruit juice, right? Isn't that the point?"

Out in the hall Eric could hear the sounds of others coming in, people darting by and no doubt tiptoeing back. He beckoned Liv to close the door.

"Lilly was the last one in on the deal, you should know that. Carlson made it a condition for the deal. Probably had a hard-on for her the whole time. It wasn't until you *harassed* her—as we say now—that she agreed."

"Fine. It's Wisconsin, anyway."

"Big deal."

"So what does she have to do with any of this?"

Liv seemed to prepare for another round of abuse and attack, something further to do with Lilly, no doubt. But instead, he slumped back on the couch, a miserable-looking, middle-aged preppy with a hangover.

"Oh Christ, she doesn't have anything to do with it. It's the product. It wasn't natural. Or good natural. Whatever 'natural' is supposed to be. See if you can get an answer on that from the FDA. But FruitOut wasn't natural. It was industrial waste. Some tiny squirt of something to preserve the color. I don't know and I don't give a shit. There was enough messing with the formula to make the venture capitalists think we'd lost our niche. MacRae was probably alerted to the problem when his piss came out ocher."

"So?"

"The venture capitalists pulled the plug. I'm out of a job."

"Sorry," said Eric.

This expression of sympathy, as limited as it was, seemed to remind Liv of how completely he had been taken in. "I was going to *invest* in it. I wanted all four of us to come in with some equity. I was pushing hard for it. I could have lost our refrigerators."

"But you didn't."

"No. There wasn't time enough for me to fuck up quite so comprehensively. You need time to do that."

"Yes. I guess you do. But, Liv, I've got to tell you. We've made some changes here, as you know—"

Liv interrupted; in fact, in the past two weeks, he'd had more chance to see what was happening than Eric. "Paul's doing a good job. You did the right thing."

"I don't think we can take you back, but let's see what happens."

And that was where it sat. Lilly gone, to a better job no doubt, as soon as she got around to looking for one. Liv in the next room closing out his involvement in his old accounts. New work seemed to be coming in fast, which might have seemed odd, but was actually typical: gossip had brought the firm's name to people's lips, and in advertising, any notice—within reason—was good notice. Alwin + Warren, whatever it would be called, could be a better place. Liv brought in a few new small accounts by behaving himself during presentations. After a week or two of complete ambiguity, chaos even, though productive, like those all-nighters before the big presentation, Eric called a meeting of the firm and announced to all that he and Liv believed it was better for the firm if they stayed united, and Eric saw no reason to change anything except to elevate Paul Ramirez to junior partner, and it was time for everybody to stop thinking about the firm and get back to doing great work. And since then that was what they had been doing.

Six weeks after the funeral, on a brilliant early beginning of what seemed certain to be a hot and breezy late-summer day, Eric was back on the New Jersey Turnpike, heading toward Maryland. It was a Saturday, a day to do business with Alice, decisions on the house, which Alice was preparing to move into. This meeting might have its difficult moments, because Alice would lay claim to all sorts of furniture and bric-a-brac that Eric, under normal circumstances, might like to have, but in the end, he thought she deserved pretty much what she wanted. He had written to Anthony and said that if there wasn't anything in particular he wanted, then Eric would assemble a share of the things their father loved most and send them to him, to do with as he wished. Debbie called him back and said, "Sure. You choose. Why not?"

But this was all to come later in the day, because Alice had said that she wouldn't be available until two, and Eric was grateful for that, a few hours to be in the house alone, to prowl through it one last time before this era of his life came to an end. The smells of box bush and honeysuckle greeted him, the perfume of this place, and the ratcheting buzz of locusts, its music. Certain of Marjorie's perennials and flowering bushes were blossoming, but already the weeds and creepers had reasserted themselves above the mulch, and the lawns were uncut. How quickly the grass does its work, especially in this humid, fecund climate. Raccoons had probably found a way into the house already. Nothing could resist them for long.

The windows were all shut and he went around the first floor opening a few. The kitchen still smelled of bacon, and on the table was a stack of maybe eighty steno books, every one of them with pages reinserted sloppily, a soft lace of once-private conversations. The musty, brocaded living room, with its tabletops crammed with pictures of grandchildren, Frank's and Marjorie's, felt even more unused than ever, if that were possible. He opened the French doors out onto the porch, stood for a few moments reflecting on his familiarity with the view, and then went upstairs to what he still thought of as his room, one of the four in this democratically sized Victorian arrangement. There had been nothing of his in this room for many years, and during Marjorie's life she had set it up as a storeroom for Frank's memorabilia. A wall of boxes—the same boxes that had landed in the hall those many years ago—sat undisturbed. What would they do with his papers? Do disgraced politicians get to donate papers, or do they get burned, lest people still living be exposed as crooks?

Eric ignored these considerations, and spent a few minutes sitting at a desk chair gazing out through the beech trees and into the fields, where agriculture was proceeding without an interval, sow and reap, live and die, the seasons continuing. He found a few of his childhood calling cards—a large dent in the maple flooring where he had dropped a cinder block by mistake, a small "E" carved into the windowsill, for which he had been punished—but other than that, he received no visions of himself in youth. He did remember the time when he was about ten that he had announced, purely to make mischief, that Alice had enjoyed the water view for all her life, and it was now his turn, and that she must trade rooms with him. For days she had come up with reasons why this was unfair, that everyone knew she needed a water breeze to sleep properly, that the pollen from the fields would make her sick, that Eric was a boy and was therefore incapable of appreciating a view, that no one loved her. Such a brat. Such a lovely lady. The things siblings know about each other should simply not be permitted.

He went back downstairs, hunted in the refrigerator for something to eat, and found some frozen bread and some cheese, a dry ghost of his father's and Adam's last days in the house. He broiled himself some toast and cheese, and took this and a cup of instant coffee out to the porch, sat in one of the wicker armchairs, and ate happily with the plate on his lap. The little sailboat was at its accustomed place off the dock. On the bay, the boats were heeling in the fine breeze, which always made him itchy to get out there, and also the occasional plume of water and high-frequency squeal of Jet Skis, and a parade of immense cabin cruisers frothing up and down the channel to God-knew-what destination.

Eric was avoiding the study. He knew that when he walked in, his father would be there, as certain as life. Eric just didn't know which father it would be: the man he had come to know so intimately, the father of his last years, immobilized and all but silenced by his strokes, the invalid making his deals with the devil and hatching his plans for absolution; or the other one, the one Eric had avoided for so many years but whom now, and only now, he believed he had come to understand better than he understood himself. His two fathers, who had seemed so divisible and irreconcilable, were now one. That was what they had witnessed, the redemption of a man finally becoming whole and himself, the one who caused pain and the one who caused joy.

As Eric sat in this wicker chair—it was an accoutrement of the younger Frank, his place of power, this chair and the old telephone in the office, and his closet upstairs filled with his suits and bow ties, his boats—all of the story seemed to be moving forward to claim him as a casualty, or as a survivor, and Eric did not resist. He surrendered with moist eyes and a posture rigid in his seat, and moved to the last chapter of the story of his father's life.

In this story, he finds his father sitting at his desk, busily scribbling on a legal pad. He is wearing seersucker suit trousers, a white shirt loose at his aged neck, and his signature red bow tie. As Eric opens the door Frank holds his left hand high, index finger pointed up: *Just a second; take a seat.* Eric does, in the wing-back; he watches the right elbow pump as Frank scrawls on the pad. He jots the last note, gives it a pencil-splintering period of conclusion, and then revolves in his seat.

"Ah, Eric. I was waiting for you to drop in." He seems delighted. His smile extends symmetrically; his eyes are ambiguous, clouded with his purposes.

"Dad?" says Eric.

"Did you have a good trip? That little car of yours make it all the way on one transmission?"

"Uh, yeh. Fine. No problem."

"Splendid weather," Frank says. "The kind of day that makes you glad to be alive. How's Gail? I wish she'd come."

"She's fine. If I'd known I was going to see you here she would have sent her love."

The sunlight washes the room; it seems to Eric that he is seeing things in here he hasn't seen in many years, the old floor-standing globe, the mounted bald eagle, the shelves of the *OED* and *Who's Who* going back thirty years. "So," says Eric, "what are you up to?"

Frank glances over his shoulder back at his desk. "Christ," he says. "It never lets up. The bastards want to build a marina on Wright's Neck. Someone's got a fix in on a commissioner."

Eric could recall this as a battle from the sixties. "You love that, don't you. You don't care about the marina, you care about the commissioner."

Frank laughs, full of mirth and eagerness for the fight. "But enough about that. Tell me about yourself. Tell everything."

What to do? This is one question, one invitation that Eric cannot recall his father ever offering with quite this much sincerity. "Well," he says, hesitatingly, "my office seems to be getting back to normal."

"Yes. I was wondering about that."

"My partner. Liv?" Frank nods. *Yes, yes, the one who tried to stick it to you.* "Well," says Eric again, and then he proceeds to tell the whole story, the evaporation of FruitOut, this strangely pleasant and productive status quo that had prevailed for a number of days, the exasperation of younger members of the firm who seemed to want either retribution or resolution. "But we decided," Eric concludes, "to keep him on. He does good work. Clients buy his act. I mean, what do you think?"

Frank pauses, a few scenarios apparently running through his mind, the kind of quick calculation of cause and effect he'd learned over the years. "I agree. You're creating some equity with that firm, and if you break it up, you won't have time to build it back before you get out. Besides," he says, an inevitable observation, "you'll be able to cudgel your old pal with this for years if he gets out of line. Sounds ideal to me, but I'm just an old schemer anyway."

"Yeh."

"And how about you and Gail and Tom? I was worried, not because anything seemed so wrong, but because you seemed to be making such trouble for yourself."

Eric answers that question fully, too, that Tom had moved back, and Eric and Gail, well, maybe they were growing up, at last; maybe they'd made it over the midlife hump. "We are grateful for what we have in each other. I know I am, and I hope she is."

"She is. I've never seen a girl so gaga as she was, that first time you came to visit. Remember?"

"Yes. I remember the visit, anyway. I thought you were trying to horn in."

Frank holds both arms wide, a powerful, physical response. "Guilty," he says. "But with a beautiful excuse."

Eric doesn't need to ask what the excuse was: youth, beauty, womanhood, all of them great excuses for momentary indiscretions we hope others do not notice. "We have a lot to thank you for, you know," says Eric. "I was getting pretty screwed up for a while. You taught me to look forward again, which is something I wasn't doing."

"Now *that* is a thank-you I will accept. But it was you who started the ball rolling. I couldn't have done a thing without your help."

"But even back when you said 'mistakes,' that first time, didn't you already have this all mapped out? You knew I'd do anything to make it possible."

"No comment, except to say this: I trusted that you would do the right thing."

"Well then, thank us both. You gave everything to it, didn't you? Your life, as it turned out."

"I gave almost nothing." He holds up his once-ruined hand and confidently pinches off a half inch of air. "That much of my life I gave." He raises both strong arms as far apart as he can. "This much I got."

"Yes."

Here his face begins to become more firm; the eyes come clearer, focused as if fixed on a dot on the horizon far over Eric's shoulder. "I had a few things I wanted to discuss with you," he says.

"Sure."

"You once said to me that if I apologized to you for the worst thing I'd ever done to you, and you could forgive it, then everything else was meaningless. A fine thought."

Eric can only dimly recall ever saying something like this to him. It seems reasonably likely that he never did.

"So there was one final apology that I always wanted to make to you. It really bothered me that it seemed I wasn't going to be able to do it. I—"

Eric interrupts. "Dad? Aren't we rather beyond that? God, I feel like a hypocritical little twit receiving any more apologies from anyone."

"No, we're never beyond it. We never are. It's never over. It's all that matters. It's what makes us human. Animals don't worry about how they have behaved."

"So?"

"So I've given a good deal of thought to it over the years, as you can imagine, and after a time I recognized that I was trying to answer the wrong question, which was, what was the worst thing *you* thought I did to you. It's an old debater's trick. You see the ploy there, giving the right answer to the wrong question. Once I got past that, the matter became much simpler, but a good deal less comfortable for me, because I really am a son of a bitch. No question there. But, see, it's the little things that matter. Someone told me that quite recently. One can lose perspective over many years, but then again, what endures and becomes larger is probably what mattered most in the first place, even if it seems trivial. Okay, when you were six I was trying to teach you how to ride a bicycle, which was ridiculous anyway, a useless skill for a farm kid. I thought I was being magnanimously parental. We were right out there." He waves toward the sandy lane, a miserable surface for bicycling. "You weren't very coordinated, and I didn't think you were trying very hard, although now I recognize that you were giving everything you had, that you would have done anything in your power to please me, but teaching a kid to ride a bike is a frustrating business, as you have now learned. Finally I just let go of the bike, let you topple over. I'll never forget the look on your face as you went over, when it suddenly occurred to you that I had done this, that I deliberately was doing what no person should do to a child, let alone a father to a son. You fell, and your little spindly leg was ground between the grit of the lane and all that sharp and unforgiving steel, the chain, the ratchet. Then I stood over you as you struggled to extricate yourself, and I said, 'Fine. Be the only kid in first grade who doesn't know how to ride a bike.' "

Eric has been listening intently, braced for true evil. When his father finishes his speech, he is sure it was all a joke, the old delusions, feints, half-truths, shattering cruel ironies, but he looks right into his father's eyes and there is no joke there, just the nakedness of mortal fear for his soul. Regret for all time.

"It's that? That's what I have to release you from?"

"Yes. As an emblem, maybe, but just that. Everything else is there, all the true fragments." His lips are quivering.

"It's a little sick, I'll grant you, but pretty easy to forgive you for it. I don't even remember it. Isn't it supposed to be harder for me, you know, test my love for you to the marrow?"

"It isn't a test for you. That's the mistake I was making. It's a test for me."

Eric cannot resist shrugging once. "Then sure. No problem. I forgive you."

His father seems to have been holding his breath for all this time, and when he hears these words, the air escapes from his lungs, his shoulders slump, and he raises his eyes in relief. They sit for a few minutes.

"Then if we're doing last things here," says Eric, "there's a question I've got to ask you."

"Shoot."

"Did you know it was Poppy who sent the letter to the attorney general?"

Frank's face brightens into a smile, the last good full smile Eric will ever see, or imagine seeing, from that man. It is the smile of someone who believes, at last, that he has behaved honorably, that he has done right even though it has cost him a great deal. "Of course I did. I deserved it. From the moment I heard about the letter, I knew Poppy had written it."

"Mike Billings didn't know. You never told him."

"Some information, even for a politician, is too precious to give away."

"I guess it depends on who you give it to."

"I was trying not to sound tactical," Frank answers, "but yes, of course. Still, I'd like not to go out on such a note."

"You didn't. You know that."

Frank nods. "A close run thing."

"But the ending alone, that may be nothing without the beginning and the middle. I've been thinking about the beginning and the middle, in light of the end."

"Uh-oh." Frank raises his elbow to his eyes. These old mannerisms; they endure.

"I've been wondering how to sum you up, and this is what I have decided. You were warm in friendship and uncomplaining in adversity. Through it all, that's what you were. It's why I loved you."

"Sounds like something for my tombstone."

"Well, maybe it is."

They remain for a few minutes in the old companionable silence. No one has been winding the clocks, so there is no sign of a heartbeat measuring the pause, no reassuring thump and ping from Adam in the kitchen, a sort of deadness out there in this abandoned house. The moment is broken only by the sound of the wind outside, a good blow, firm and full of possibility.

"You know," says his father, "we can't let this wind go to waste."

Eric doesn't hear him clearly; Frank says it with his face against the side window, trying to get a look at the bay. "Did you say what I thought you said?"

"Yes."

That's what he used to say, back in the best of times, back when he wasn't in Annapolis for the weekend, or huddled in his office with Mike, but was sitting at the kitchen table while Eric and his sisters were eating their cornflakes, and he would suddenly say, "Wait, wait," and would lick and raise a finger, gaze upon it as if gauging the direction and intensity, and say, "We can't let this wind go to waste. God didn't send this just to let it pass through."

The memory is there for Eric, bright and clear, and especially that wave of excitement as these most cherished words fall to his ears. He wants to weep, break down and sob right there, but he stifles it back and continues with the old script. "No. I suppose He didn't."

"I'll meet you at the dock in ten minutes."

Eric has paddled out to the mooring in the dinghy and brought the sailboat back to the old creosoted dock by the time his father joins him, a couple of slickers and a single life jacket in his hands.

"Shouldn't we have two jackets? Looks pretty rough."

"I don't need one. Besides, you're the only one who can't swim," he answers, which is true, one of Eric's athletic deficiencies. "Blame your mother," Frank had said over the years.

They rig the boat side by side, a practiced teamwork undiminished by the thirty-year pause. The sails are in surprisingly good repair, considering that they have spent a lifetime rolled in a bag, and when they are set, they flap cheerfully, like eager wings. They cast off, with Eric at the tiller, and soon they have tacked out of the small creek and are in the full force of the bay. The little boat feels like a racehorse under them, full of oats and vinegar, and it slices through the chop, all but flying over the troughs, the sail as firm as a belly, full of the spirit of the air. Frank sits forward in the full force of the blow and in the direct line of the pelting spray, and his arms are out to receive it all squarely on the chest. It is too loud for them to communicate, but Eric hears him bellowing with joy and screaming, as he had done years ago in similar conditions with his young son, "I'm free, I'm free," and then he is gone, become part of the wind, now just an element of the ages.

About the Author

CHRISTOPHER TILGHMAN's first novel, *Mason's Retreat,* was published in 1996 and was met with wide critical and popular acclaim both in the United States and abroad. His stories, collected in *In a Father's Place* and *The Way People Run,* have appeared in *The New Yorker* and many other publications, and have been selected often for *The Best American Short Stories.* He lives with his wife, the novelist Caroline Preston, and their three sons in Charlottesville, Virginia, where he is a professor of English at the University of Virginia.

About the Type

This book was set in Sabon, a typeface designed by the well-known German typographer Jan Tschichold (1902–74). Sabon's design is based upon the original letterforms of Claude Garamond and was created specifically to be used for three sources: foundry type for hand composition, Linotype, and Monotype. Tschichold named his typeface for the famous Frankfurt typefounder Jacques Sabon, who died in 1580.